Your Inescapable Love
(The Bennett Family, Book 4)

LAYLA HAGEN

Dear Reader,

If you want to receive news about my upcoming books and sales, you can sign up for my newsletter HERE: http://laylahagen.com/mailing-list-sign-up/

Copyright © 2016 Layla Hagen
All rights reserved.

Chapter One

Max

Nineteen years ago

Why is there a girl in our yard? She's just stepped through the gate and looks around, holding a backpack in her arms. Mom is in the kitchen with my brothers, and I probably should call her, but I won't. I can take care of this. I'm nine years old.

I run to the gate, and as I get closer, I recognize her. She's the new girl in my class at school, Emilia Campbell, who always looks like she's going to cry. I overheard one of the teachers say her mom died before she moved here. Probably why she's sad. No one should lose their mom.

"What are you doing here?" I ask her when I reach the gate.

"I live two houses away," she says quickly. "But I lost my key, and I can't get in the house. I live with Grams, who is working now, and she's usually not home until seven. I left the window to my room open, and I tried to climb in, but I couldn't. I fell, and now my knee hurts."

Wow. I don't know many girls who would climb through their window. My sister Alice does, but Alice is cool. I decide that Emilia Campbell is cool too.

"Grams says I'm not supposed to tell anyone that I'm home alone, but I can't get in, and I don't know what to do. There is a storm coming, and I hate storms. I'm afraid of thunder."

"You can wait inside our house," I say.

"But I don't know you." Emilia Campbell has long blonde hair. It's almost as blonde as my sister Pippa's, but shorter.

"Yes, you do. We have class together. I am Max Bennett."

"Emilia Campbell," she says.

"I know. I heard the teacher call your name. You're the new girl who doesn't play with anyone during recess."

She looks at her boots, and those are some butt-ugly boots. Pink with even pinker hearts on it. I open my mouth, and close it again, remembering my sister Alice saying people don't like it when I tell them their things are ugly. And Mom said I'm not supposed to say *butt*.

"I don't play with anyone because I don't have any friends."

She's weird. How are you supposed to make friends if you don't play with anyone? Maybe it's a girl thing. I'll never understand girls. A few drops of cold water fall on my face.

"It's raining. Let's go inside my house. Momma says it's bad to be out when it rains. We'll get a cold."

She looks at the house behind me and then back at me. "Are you sure your parents won't be upset?"

"No, they let me and my brothers and sisters bring friends all the time."

She looks down at her ugly-ass boots again. "But I'm not your friend."

A loud sound cracks above, and she jumps. She looks at the sky with wide eyes. Boy, she really is afraid of thunder.

"You are now. I want to be your friend, Emilia Campbell. And I will protect you from the thunder."

Chapter Two

Emilia

Present Day

"Please, please, please, let us have some hot rock star or actor on the list with new patients." My best friend Abby stands behind the reception desk, staring intently at her computer.

"Anyone interesting?" I ask her. This is one of the most sought-after physical therapy clinics in San Francisco. As such, we often work with high-profile athletes who must recover after an injury, and even the occasional celebrity. In the case of the latter, it's nice to get a scoop beforehand, because sometimes paparazzi show up. While Abby surveys the list on her computer, I make a mental note to stop at Target on the way home and buy a box of cheese crackers for my grandmother. No matter how bad a day she's having, they always make her happy. Because she has Alzheimer's, most of her days are bad lately. Watching the strong woman who raised me slowly fading away is excruciating.

"Nah." Abby shakes her head in

disappointment. "We've had a dry spell with celebrities lately. Just more businessmen."

I grin. Ah, yes, we also get the assorted businessmen who decide all of a sudden that their lifestyle is too sedentary and they have to incorporate training into their routine. They sometimes overdo it, which is a recipe for injury.

"Look at this one," she says with a laugh. "Went skydiving and screwed up the landing."

I cover my mouth with my hand. "That's not funny, Abby. He could have—"

"Been seriously injured, I know. But he wasn't. I mean, he needs therapy, but his ligament injury isn't too bad. I can't help laughing when a hothead decides to be adventurous and then screws it up."

"You're a bad person," I say, shaking my head. "Making fun of others' misfortune."

"I need to fill my free time with something. Judging and gossiping fit the bill."

"Have you tried reading or cooking?" I challenge her. "I've heard they can be fun."

"Nah, too much work."

"Who is he?"

"Forgot the name." She focuses her attention on the computer again. "Max Bennett. Hey, the name sounds familiar."

"Max B— Are you sure?" I ask, my heart suddenly doing a somersault. The name is not exactly uncommon, but still....

"Yeah."

"What's his date of birth?"

As Abby rattles off the date, I grin because it's *him*. Two different people sharing a name and a birthday would be too big of a coincidence.

"He's my Max. Come on, I told you about him," I admonish her when she raises an eyebrow. "My neighbor when I was a kid."

"Ohhhh, I remember now," Abby replies.

He was so much more than my neighbor. He was my best friend after Mom died, and I absolutely adored him. I haven't seen him in fifteen years, though, which is about fifteen years too long. "Can you assign him to me?"

"Your schedule is already full."

"Can you shift one of my other patients to someone else? You can do that for your best friend." I bat my eyelashes at her, certain I look absolutely ridiculous.

"Fine. I'll see how I can shift things and let you know."

"Thank you. See you tomorrow."

I leave the reception area with a pep in my step. Smiling, I remember the nine-year-old boy who used to walk next to me to school as if he was my own personal bodyguard. He made it his mission to make me smile when all I wanted to do was cry because I had lost my mama. Grams and I moved to Montana when I was thirteen, and Max and I didn't keep in touch. The boy I knew wasn't a hothead. Sure, he had his fun, and never backed away from a challenge, but I wouldn't have pegged him for one to skydive.

Ms. Henderson, the last patient I had today, exits the clinic at the same time I do. Her husband waits for her by his car and after kissing her cheek softly, opens the door for her. The look of awe and love in his eyes warms my heart. At the same time, it makes me aware of the unease that took residence in my chest months ago. Since I was a little girl, I wished for the kind of love the Hendersons share. But some people aren't meant to have happy endings. My parents didn't, and if the unused wedding dress in my closet is anything to go by, neither am I. My fiancé, Paul, canceled our wedding three weeks before D-day. That was six months ago, and part of me still can't believe it.

On my way home, I stop by the store and buy the cheese crackers for Grams. Suddenly, I have a burning desire to talk to Grams about Max, but I'm not sure if she remembers him. On some days, she doesn't even remember me. I resolve to test the waters when I get home and see how she feels first. Armed with crackers and a giddy happiness, I turn up the volume of the music in my car, pull my shoulder-length blonde hair up in a ponytail, and then wrap my jacket tighter around me, shuddering. My car's heater died a few weeks back, and I don't have the money to fix it yet. I earn a good paycheck as a physical therapist, but paying for rent and a caretaker for my grandmother eats up most of it. Grams's pension helps with her medical bills. Drumming my fingers on the wheel to the rhythm of the music, I drive away.

Thirty minutes later, I walk inside the house, and Ms. Adams, my grandma's caretaker, greets me.

"Thank God, you're home."

"What happened?"

"She's not been herself the entire afternoon, and I haven't managed to calm her down. You're in for a rough evening. I honestly think it would be easier for you if she were in a home."

The muscles in my back tense, and I roll my shoulders. I found a senior home a few hours away from San Francisco that would be cheaper than a full-time caretaker, but putting her in a home would just break my heart.

"No way. I'll manage. Where is she?"

"In the backyard."

"I'm going to her. I bought her favorite crackers. Thank you so much, Ms. Adams. Have a nice evening."

"See you tomorrow, Emilia."

After Ms. Adams leaves, I walk outside. Our backyard is small but full of flowers and plants. The back of the house also has a porch painted in dark green, with a couch and a swing. Grams is sitting on the couch, a vacant expression on her face. She snaps her head in my direction, leaping to her feet when she sees me. My grandmother is sixty-one, but her body is still sharp and quick. She always used to say, "Age is just a number. And it ain't catching up with me." Her silver hair frames her heart-shaped face.

"Violet, you're home," she exclaims.

I blink back tears. Violet was my mother's name, but I've learned it's best not to correct Grams; it just makes her confused and anxious. Grams loved my mama dearly, even though she was just her daughter-in-law. Mom got pregnant with me at sixteen. Her own parents kicked her out of the house so Grams, my dad's mother who was a widow, took her in, and the three of us lived with her. Then after mama's funeral, my asshole of a father decided parenthood wasn't for him and disappeared off the face of the earth. Never saw him again. It's just been Grams and me ever since.

Holding up the package, I say, "Brought you crackers."

She tsk-tsks, shaking her head. "Don't come home so late again tomorrow. You know what they say about girls who come home late, and I won't have anyone speak ill about my daughter-in-law."

I press my lips together, hating that my eyes are stinging with tears. I rack my brain, trying to come up with a way to bring Grams back to present day without upsetting her, when she surprises me.

"This house is beautiful, Emilia, darling. I'm so happy we found it."

"Me too. I like our yard the best. It's so peaceful."

Grams doesn't say anything for long, painful minutes, and when she speaks again, she shatters me anew. "I received a call from your principal today. He said you got into trouble again at school."

A knot forms in my throat. There she is, slipping away from me again. Sometimes she mixes up people, sometimes time periods. It's an emotional roller coaster.

"Let's have dinner, okay?" I ask in a strangled voice.

I finally coax her into eating dinner, and afterward she showers. Just before she gets in her bed, I comb her hair, the way she did for me while I was growing up. The worst thing about her illness is that it's episodic. Some days she's her old self, some days she's unrecognizable. After she goes to sleep, I pour myself a glass of wine and go out in the backyard, stretching on the bench. As I sip from my drink, my phone vibrates with an incoming message from Evelyn. She's my other best friend, and she also works at the clinic. She's not a physical therapist, but a psychotherapist. Some of our patients need that therapy in addition to the physical one, especially if they suffered grave injuries, or their careers have come to a halt—as is the case for professional sportsmen.

Evelyn: A friend of my sister's says she might be interested in buying your wedding dress. I gave her your number.

"Oh." Something painful twists in my chest at her words. *This is a good thing*, I tell myself. I need to get rid of it, and God knows I can use all the money in the world.

Emilia: Thanks.

Evelyn: You can celebrate getting rid of it by starting to date already. You know what they're saying about plenty of fish being in the sea.

This reminds me of joke I read recently. Chuckling, I type back.

Emilia: Yeah, and I live in the desert. I'm getting used to the idea of lifelong celibacy. I'll buy some cats.

I love my life. Some days it's hard, some days it's downright painful, but what the heck? I have two great friends, my Grams, and this piece of heaven I can call home. And I don't want to count my chickens before they hatch, but the childhood friend I've missed like crazy for years might just pop up in my life again. If that's not a sign of great luck, I don't know what is.

As I fiddle with my phone, I notice a message from Abby.

Abby: I shifted one of your patients to someone else. Max Bennett is all yours.

Giggling, I take a sip of my wine. I might be taking a lifelong break from dating men, but reuniting with my old best friend couldn't have happened at a better time.

Chapter Three

Emilia

My first appointment with Max is Monday of the following week. I pace up and down one of the training rooms, looking over his file for the hundredth time. He has a posterior cruciate ligament injury, a slight tear. He didn't need surgery or require crutches, but he needs a rigorous therapy to get that ligament back in shape. I'll make sure he'll be able to kick anyone's ass by the time our sessions are done.

The three other therapists in the room smile at me encouragingly, concentrating on their own patients. The clinic has ten such training rooms, and up to five patients and their individual therapists can be in one room at a time. I wish Max and I could be alone so we can catch up, but that will remain wishful thinking for today. My stomach is in knots as I glance up at the clock. Two minutes left.

I first met Max when I was nine years old. Mom had died, and Grams and I moved a few houses away from the Bennetts. I went to the same school as the Bennett kids and quickly became somewhat of an outcast, which was entirely my fault. I was shy, awkward, and grieving. Since I had buried my mother, I had retreated into a shell. Max pulled me out of it. When Grams and I moved to Montana four years later, I was devastated.

I glance at the clock again before returning to the file, sighing. One minute left. My palms are sweaty, and I wipe them on my pants, but the fabric of the spandex training gear isn't absorbing anything.

When I hear the door of the room open, I snap my head up from my file. Max and Kurt, the head of the clinic, are in the doorway. Kurt is talking, but Max isn't listening. His eyes are fixed on me, and his face breaks into a smile, instantly transporting me back to the day when he offered me his first smile.

With hurried footsteps, I walk toward them, inspecting Max from head to toe. The last time I saw him, he was thirteen years old, and a whole head taller than me. Now he towers over me. I've inherited Grams's petite frame, sure, but Max must be at least six feet and he's just... magnificent. Broad shoulders and strong arms. His dark brown hair is tousled and sticking out in every direction. His face is a mix of panty-dropping masculinity with a dash of that boyish charm I remember about him. Max Bennett is all man.

I stop less than a foot in front of him and Kurt. Max pins me with his gaze and his smile deepens. *Oh God*, I forgot about those dimples.

"As far as I understand, no introductions are

needed, since Abby said you already know each other," Kurt says. I open my mouth but find my throat too clogged with emotion to form words.

"We do," Max says, and his voice doesn't sound quite right. It's deep and strong, with just a slight hint of nervousness. "She used to be my best friend."

"Well, I'll leave the two of you," Kurt says. "Emilia will take good care of you."

"Of course, I will," I say, having found my voice again. Kurt nods at both of us before leaving.

The second the door closes, Max pulls me into a hug. I walk into his arms without hesitation, even though there are six other people in the training room. He hugs the same way I remember—wholeheartedly. But then again, there weren't many things Max the boy did halfheartedly, and I can't imagine Max the man to be any different.

"I can't believe this," he murmurs against my hair. "I always wondered about you. Where you were, what you were doing. I wanted to look for you, but I didn't know where to start." He rubs his hand up and down my back, sending sparks of warmth down my spine.

Pulling out of his arms, I say, "I, on the other hand, knew where you were all this time. I moved to San Francisco when I started college, but I didn't know how to reach out."

"Ah, it's a good thing I was a blithering idiot then and had the accident," he exclaims. "Otherwise, I wouldn't be here. Gives a whole new meaning to everything happens for a reason, right?"

I smile at him, surprised to learn that he kept his self-deprecating humor. Reading in magazines about his family's success always did make me wonder if he'd changed or if he'd become more arrogant. So far, it seems not. I wonder how his siblings turned out. There are nine in total. Sebastian, Logan, and Pippa were the older trio, and as far as I understood, they set up Bennett Enterprises—one of the biggest players in the jewelry market. Max and his identical twin brother, Christopher, also work at the company, but I don't know what the other siblings are up to: Alice, Blake, Daniel, and Summer. Can't wait for Max to fill me in.

"How did you manage to get yourself into that mess?"

"If I make up a heroic reason, will you believe me?"

I burst out laughing. He cemented his status as my hero one lousy, rainy day after school. We were walking home when we heard howling. After sloshing around in the mud for a few minutes, we located the dogs. They were on the edge of the road, next to a ditch. I counted four pups and what looked like their dead mother. The pups desperately tried to get a reaction from her, pushing their little heads against her belly, and one of them licking her nose. I felt such an instant kinship with the pups who'd lost their mother that I couldn't bear leaving them to fend for themselves. As Max and I bent to lift them, we noticed a fifth pup. He'd fallen into the ditch, which was very deep and narrow. Without hesitation, Max jumped inside it, pulling up the pup. It then took him nearly twenty minutes to get himself out. Grams and his mother, Jenna Bennett, nearly went into cardiac arrest when we returned home with five pups and covered in mud. I hero-worshiped him from that day on.

"I know you can be a hero, all right. But the skydiving accident is in your file."

He groans, then tugs with his teeth at his lower lip, and I can't help admiring his lush mouth. Had his lips always been this full? And why, in the name of all that is holy, am I having these thoughts? The training room suddenly feels too small, as does the distance between us.

"I never took you for the skydiving type," I continue.

"I'm not. Just made a bet with Blake. I was flying with a trainer and still managed to crash land."

At the mention of his younger brother, I can't help grinning.

"Damn, I have so many questions for you, I don't know how to get them out fast enough," he says.

"Pretty much describing my current dilemma." I hold up a finger. "But, we need to start with the session. Kurt warned me that I should keep the relationship *professional* during our sessions."

Max cocks an eyebrow. "What did he think I'd do? Jump your bones the moment I saw you?"

Heat rushes to my cheeks at his words, and I

lower my gaze, suddenly flustered. Thank heavens we're far enough from the others that they can't hear us.

"I see you still put your foot in your mouth every chance you get," I inform him.

"I do, but that came out wrong. I didn't mean there's anything wrong with jumping your bones. In fact, you filled out beautifully, Jonesie." He grins at the use of the nickname his brother Blake gave me years ago. He found Campbell to be quite a mouthful, and said I looked like someone who should be called Jones, which was completely random. Max turned that into Jonesie, and it became my nickname in the Bennett household. "As your oldest friend, I'm allowed to say that without sounding like a pervert, or like I'm hitting on you. You are beautiful." He utters those last few words in a lower tone and damn, it makes all my lady parts tingle.

"You haven't aged too bad either, Bennett. You wear a suit well," I volley back, though my skin is simmering. Teasing each other was one of the backbones of our friendship, but now it feels different. Max wears a gray suit, and he wears it as if he's been born into it, which couldn't be further from the truth. I saw him running around in jeans or shorts and simple shirts our entire childhood, but there is something about him in a suit that is absolutely irresistible.

"Now, go change into your workout gear so we can start training. The changing room is over there." I point to the door at the far back of the room.

"Be right back," he says. "Pity we can't get away with changing in front of each other like we used to, isn't it?"

I shouldn't blush at his words, I really shouldn't. But I do anyway.

"No, we can't."

I let out a slow breath when Max disappears into the locker room. As kids, Max and I often went swimming at a nearby pond. We discarded our clothes in front of each other and remained in our undies, and there was zero awkwardness. Except that memorable summer day when he hid my clothes while I was in the water, then he accidentally dropped said clothes in the water. I threw a fit and pushed him fully clothed into the pond. We made up as we walked home later, both looking like wet rats.

It was all so easy between us back then. Now... well, we aren't kids anymore. Seeing each other after all this time is bound to lead to some awkwardness... and apparently tingling in places I have no business tingling.

I'm so immersed in my thoughts that I don't realize Max is back until he calls, "Ready whenever you are, Jonesie."

Holy chocolate cake with whipped cream on top. Right. Max in a suit was irresistible, but Max in shorts and a formfitting shirt is sinful.

"We'll do a combination of mattress and machine exercises, and also aquatic ones. Obviously, no aquatic ones today, we'd have to be near a pool for that." Oh God, I'm rambling. I blame his impossibly dark eyes and tongue-in-cheek smile for it.

"For how long will the therapy last?"

"I'd say four weeks, twice a week."

He groans, dragging his palms down his face. "Lucky one of my oldest friends is my therapist. Will give us lots of time to catch up."

The words "oldest friends" snap my mind out of the gutter. Friends don't ogle each other.

"Serves me right, I suppose."

"How did Blake convince you?" I inquire. "The boy I knew didn't take such risks."

"I've become dumber with age." He does one full turn of the room. "So, with which of these torture instruments are we starting?"

"They're not so bad," I assure him. "They look like regular gym machines."

"Except creepier. Well, I'm all yours. Tell me what to do."

"Why, Max Bennett, I never thought the day would come when I get to boss you around. That was your role."

He shrugs, but the mischievous smile on his face tells me he hasn't given up his ways. "Your gym. Your rules."

The rest of the session passes quietly, as I do the exercises with Max, patiently explaining every move.

"Let's go out to an early dinner," Max

suggests at the end.

"No can do. I have two other sessions."

"I can pick you up later then?" he pushes.

"After work is generally a bad time for me." Taking a deep breath, I admit, "Grams has Alzheimer's, and it's come to the point where she needs a lot of supervision. She has a caregiver during the day, and sometimes a lovely neighbor helps out in the evening if I have seminars, but I like to spend the evenings with her."

"I'm sorry about Grams," he says gently. "Especially since she's so young."

"Yeah." Grams is sixty-one. She had dad at eighteen and became a grandmother at thirty-four.

"I always liked her. Except when she took you away to Montana."

"It's hard seeing her like this," I say in a small voice. "I'm used to her being this strong person, and now she's just…. Anyway, I spend evenings with her. Sometimes I read to her or just rattle on about my day."

Max raises his hand to my cheek in a soothing gesture, the way he did when we were kids. Only now his touch doesn't just bring me reassurance, but also a wave of heat.

"She does remember me, most of the time," I say softly.

"D'you think she'd remember me?"

"You're a hard man to forget. Even as a boy, you made an impression," I say with a grin, which fades when my next patient walks through the door.

"Oh crap, my next appointment is here. About your leg, you don't have much swelling, but just in case, put some ice on it when you're home."

"Will do, boss. See you on Thursday for our next appointment." He leans down to me, his lips brushing my cheek. The light touch sets my skin on fire. I take a deep breath, inhaling his masculine scent, and all my senses go hyperalert. This is ridiculous. We were once best friends, and I hope we can be that close again. Lusting after him is out of the question. I have an unused wedding dress and years of dates gone bad to remind me that my romantic relationships always take a turn for the worse. I want Max Bennett in my life, and I want him as my best friend.

Swallowing hard, I wave at him as he leaves the room. I was expecting our reunion to wreak havoc on my emotions, but not my hormones.

Chapter Four

Max

"Thank you so much for coming with me," Alice says as she climbs into my car. I parked in front of her restaurant, which is located high on the Twin Peaks. It's highly successful, and I'm damn proud of her. She's been scouting for a location to open a second restaurant and asked me to go see a place with her. She shoves a take-out bag in my lap as I gun the engine.

"You brought me a turkey sandwich?" I ask, unwrapping the sandwich in record time.

"Yep, can't let my little brother starve."

I scoff at the word little. "I'm only one year younger than you." Christopher and I are firmly convinced we were the accidental pair of twins. But then again I'd bet my ass a lot of us were accidental. On the drive to the new location, I tell Alice, "You're never going to believe who I ran into today. Emilia. She's my physical therapist."

Alice frowns, and then she exclaims, "Oh! Jonesie? Our neighbor way back when?"

"That's the one," I say.

"How is she?"

"Didn't get to talk to her much, we had to start our session. But her Grams is sick. She has Alzheimer's."

Alice sighs, sinking down the seat a little. "That's so sad. How's Jonesie holding up?"

"As I said, we didn't talk much, but I imagine it's hard." In fact, I think hard doesn't even cover it. Emilia all but shrunk before me, closing herself off when she mentioned her grandmother. I instantly recognized that look. As a kid, she withdrew in herself whenever she was hurting. It made all my protective instincts spring to life, and the same happened today. As a kid, I was loud, careless, and confident, and I couldn't understand why everyone around me wasn't the same way. Something about Emilia beckoned to me, and I made it my mission to replace her sadness with laughter as often as I could. I was successful, and she became my best friend.

When the clinic director mentioned her name, I was ecstatic. When I met her face-to-face, it was a shock to my system. She has the same warm, green eyes I remember, but Jonesie has grown into a beautiful, hot woman, and I turned into a horny moron the moment I saw her. Dick move on my part. She walked into my arms all trusting and open, and there's no way I'll take advantage of that. Emilia is the white-picket-fence type of girl, and she deserves someone who can give her that. Right now, that's not on my radar at all.

"Earth to Max!" Alice exclaims.

"Huh?"

"Did you hear anything I said?"

"Mmm," I say noncommittally.

"Never mind. Just bring Jonesie around to see Mom and Dad if she has time. They'll be happy to see her. Can I have a bite?" She points to my sandwich.

"You're always stealing my food," I accuse.

"I just want one bite." Out of the corner of my eye, I see her batting her eyelashes at me. "That's not stealing. And I brought it to you."

"Why didn't you bring one for yourself?"

"I didn't want one, but seeing you eat with so much gusto, I kind of want a bite."

I groan, concentrating on the road.

"You know I'll bug you until you give in, right?" Alice continues.

Unfortunately, I do know. "Fine, but just *one* bite. I mean it."

She ends up eating half the sandwich, of course.

"It's so good to have you back home from London, Max. I don't like it when any of us is away. Can't wait for Summer to get back." Our youngest sister, Summer, is a painter, and she's currently in Italy, working on a special project for a local museum. She'll be gone for another few months. "At least you're back. I missed fighting with you over food."

"You have seven other Bennetts you can pick

a fight with."

She shrugs. "Yeah, but none get as adorably annoyed as you do."

"Give that back. You're lucky I love you so much," I mutter, wolfing down the remaining part.

"Holy fuck," I exclaim ten minutes later when we arrive at the location.

"I think holy fuckity fuck with a side of shitty shit is more appropriate." Alice puts her hands on her hips, disbelief etched on her face.

"Are you sure this is the right address?"

"Yeah." Alice's enthusiasm is all but gone as she looks at the dump we came to look at. We climb out of the car, and then hover in front of it. Disappointment comes in waves from my sister. Kind of wish I hadn't eaten the entire sandwich, so she could have it. The women in my family are big on comfort food, and I hate seeing Alice like this.

"Now I know why they didn't upload any photos of the building itself, just the surrounding view," she says bitterly.

We are looking at what looks like a run-down barn. The surrounding area is magnificent, if a little remote. It's on a high hill with a fantastic view of the city.

"It did say it needed heavy renovations," Alice continues.

"I have a great plan for that. I'll bring the gasoline."

"I'll light up the match," my sister adds.

"You're essentially just buying the land." I do a full turn in slow motion, inspecting the area. There's a lot of green, and the property is large enough to build a generous parking lot next to the restaurant.

"Looks like it."

"Which means the asking price is far higher than it should be." One of the reasons my sister has asked me to join her here today was because I have a knack for negotiations.

"Let's go inside."

"No banter once the guy is in sight," I warn her. Nothing damages credibility more than bantering. Alice merely shakes her head, rolling her eyes.

"You play the bad cop," she tells me. "I'll play the good one."

The dump looks even worse inside. The pervasive smell of dirt and mildew turns my stomach.

"Mr. Emmerson?" Alice calls to no one in particular. No one answers, and my first thought is that the owner bailed on the meeting, but the door was open. Then again, it's not as if anyone's going to rob this shit hole even if the door was open and had a neon sign saying Rob Me on it. At last, a grunting man in his fifties comes stomping toward us, wiping sweat off his bald head. He gives Alice a blatant once-over, looking with hunger at her, which instantly gets him on my bad side.

I step forward. "We're here to see the property."

The man extends his hand to my sister, and Alice shakes it vigorously before stepping back. "Thank you for agreeing to meet us on such a short notice. I'm Alice, and this is my brother Max." She sighs dramatically as she scans the room. "Unfortunately, this isn't quite what I imagined."

"But this location is top notch," Sleazeball says.

Putting my hands in my pockets, I pace the dump. "I know the price per square foot in this area. Your asking price is at least forty percent too high."

Sleazeball jerks his head back. "I'm afraid you got the wrong information."

"I don't. The price you asked for would be fair if we were standing in a decent building. This is a barn."

"Max," Alice admonishes in a gentle voice, which is very unlike her but plays well for the good cop method. Turning to Sleazeball, she adds, "I'm afraid my brother does have a point. Revamping this place up would take a considerable investment. I'd say that investment makes up that forty percent you're overcharging."

"It's the only deal you'll get," I say calmly. "Take it or leave it."

The man wipes his forehead, clearly taken aback by our stance. "I need to think about this."

"Perfect," Alice says. "Let us know your decision within three days max."

"We're looking at two other options," I add, which makes him snap his head in my direction.

"We're making our decision this week."

That's a blatant lie, but I know these people. If you don't give them a deadline and put pressure on them, it doesn't work. Alice walks to the window at the far end of the barn/dump and looks out the window at the scenery with hopeful eyes, which means she really wants this place. I have to admit, the location is perfect. Turning on my heels, I catch Sleazeball looking at my sister as if he wants to eat her up. My blood boils instantly. If Alice ends up buying this place, she'll meet with him again, and I might not be with her. Sure, my sister knows how to kick ass, but she's vulnerable and a little oblivious to what's happening around her when she's passionate about something. Like now.

"If you ever look at my sister like that again, I will shove your balls so far up your ass, you'll spit them out," I tell him in a low voice so my sister can't overhear us.

Sleazeball flinches, because he didn't see me approach. Then he takes a step back as if wanting to put as much distance between us as possible.

My sister turns around, gesturing at me to head out. "It was nice meeting you, Mr. Emmerson. I'm looking forward to hearing from you."

"I'll e-mail," Sleazeball says, his eyes darting between my sister and me.

"We were badass," Alice says once we're in the car.

"Very," I agree. "I bet he'll write by tonight."

"Mmm, why did he look as if he was about to

shit his pants when we left?"

"No idea." I suddenly become very interested in a dirty spot on my windshield. As I drive into town, we talk about everything and nothing, and then the conversation veers to Emilia again.

"How long will your therapy last?" Alice asks.

"Four weeks."

"Wow, that sucks."

"Tell me about it."

"At least you get to spend time with Jonesie."

"Yeah," I say dryly. Just thinking about her sends my mind into a tailspin. Damn it. Being friends with Jonesie was one of the best parts of my childhood, but being friends with a grown-up Emilia might just be my most trying challenge yet.

Chapter Five

Emilia

My head is pounding as I arrive home after a long day. Ms. Adams tells me that Grams is already asleep, so I take a sweater and a book and hang out in the backyard for the rest of the evening. I settle on the outdoor couch, shoving my favorite pillow—dark blue with silver stars—under my head. Perfect reading position. But as I crank my book open, my mind flies to my encounter with Max yesterday. Now that twenty-four hours have passed, I can view the event critically.

Of course my hormones went haywire when I saw him. He's a drop-your-panties gorgeous guy. Not that I plan to drop my panties, or anything else. But I'm a woman after all, so seeing him in all of his gorgeousness confused me. This is all that it was though. Confusion. As I attempt to dive into my book again, my phone beeps with an incoming call. A fleeting look at the screen tells me I don't know the number, but I answer anyway.

"Hello?"

"Sword, or bow and arrow?" Max asks.

I grin, sitting up straight so abruptly that my book tumbles on the floor. "Bow and arrow. Always."

Playing pirates was one of our favorite games as kids. The first time we played it, he shoved a makeshift sword in my hand. I dropped it as if it were a snake, proudly claiming that the bow and arrow was my weapon of choice. We launched into a long debate about the benefits of each weapon before finally agreeing to disagree. In ten-year-old behavior, that meant a mud fight.

"Still making the wrong choices," Max says. "Swords will always win the fight."

"Suit yourself." I grin like an idiot. "How did you get my number?"

"I called the clinic."

"But they don't give out our personal numbers," I argue.

"I can be *very* persuasive, Jonesie."

His tone jolts every nerve ending in my body alive. "I bet," I murmur. "Well, I'm glad you asked for my number."

"I want us to catch up. We need to exchange fifteen years' worth of information."

"This will be one long phone call, then." My grin stretches even more as I lean back on the couch. It's been a while since merely talking to a man brought me to this state of excitement.

Not a man. You're talking to your childhood friend.

"We have plenty of experience with talking

for hours," he says.

"Yeah, but I have to say, spending said hours on the roof had more edge to it than talking over the phone."

Max had a habit of sneaking up to my house in the dead of the night. We'd go up to my roof so Grams couldn't hear us.

"You start," I tell him. "You and Bennett Enterprises have been in the papers a few times, but I want to hear everything from you."

"After you moved away, Sebastian asked my parents to sell the ranch because he needed capital to start Bennett Enterprises, and—"

"Oh, no... I loved your ranch." I'd spent so many afternoons there, it felt like a second home.

"Then you'll be glad to know Sebastian bought it back for them about two years ago as a gift for their wedding anniversary."

"Wow! Your brother is something."

"True. My parents turned it into a B&B. We could go see it sometime."

"I'd love that." That place holds many dear memories for me. "So I know quite a few of you work at the company, but what are the others doing?"

"Alice owns a restaurant and is about to open a second one, Summer is a painter, Blake opened a bar a few months ago, and Daniel is looking to open his own business."

"Holy crap, there's a lot of stuff going on."

"Never a dull moment in the clan. I was in

London for a few years, expanding the business."

"And now you're back in San Francisco for good?" For some reason, my heart constricts as I wait for his answer.

"Yeah. For now, at least. We're moving into new territories all the time, and opening offices. Until now we've always sent someone from the family to oversee new markets, but it doesn't mean we'll be doing it again. I'm overseeing our international development from here, and it's working out great. Your turn."

I shudder as a breeze sweeps over me. Digging my hand under the couch, I retrieve the thick blanket we keep there for chilly evenings and drape it over me. "As you know, I moved with Grams to Montana after I left California." I pause, because thinking about that time is bittersweet. We were financially better off because Grams had a better-paying job as an accountant, but I'd missed Max terribly. "It was actually nice there."

"Did you find another partner in crime?" Max asks, and I can practically *hear* his smile.

"Nah, you were pretty much *it* for me during my childhood. What about you? Found a replacement for me?"

"As a matter of fact, I did."

My heart sinks as an irrational jealousy grips me over that nameless and faceless playmate of his.

"Christopher," Max clarifies, referring to his twin brother. "We got over the fact that we looked the same. Actually, we started using it to our advantage."

I chuckle. During my time with them, the twins hated that they looked alike. That meant they made a point to have different haircuts and clothes, and they spent time apart as often as they could.

"You finished school in Montana?" Max asks.

"Yeah, then I moved here for college. Grams also got a job offer and moved here, which was just as good because I could take care of her after she got sick." I wrap the blanket tighter around me as another gust of wind sweeps over me.

"About Grams," Max says. "I know a very good neurologist. He's the father of a college friend. I called him today and asked him about the disease, without mentioning names or anything personal. If you want, I can set up a meeting with him. You wouldn't even have to bring Grams to him. I can drive him to your home."

For a long moment, I remain silent as a rush of emotions overwhelms me. This is what I missed most about having Max in my life. More than the banter and laughter we shared, I missed his warmth and the kindness that runs bone-deep in him. And right now, I miss him so much that the ache is almost physical.

"Thank you for doing that—calling your friend's dad. I'd love to take you up on it, but I have to convince Grams first. She already has a neurologist, but another opinion wouldn't hurt. But she hates doctors. Seeing one is always an emotionally draining experience."

"I'll be there with you this time."

And cue the fluttering in my stomach, which feels dangerously close to butterflies.

"Let me know when you want to go," he continues. "Let's move on to more cheerful things. Do you still like pancakes?"

"Absolutely. Once a pancake girl, always a pancake girl. Only now I almost always pair it with decadent toppings."

"Describe decadent, Emilia."

His voice has a husky undertone that sends ripples of heat down my arms. Also, I realize, it's the first time he used my first name, and it sounds so perfect coming out of his mouth. Almost… decadent.

Damn, I'm losing it.

"Let's see," I reply in an uneven voice. "Whipped cream and caramel. Sometimes chocolate topping on top of everything. Decadent enough for you?"

Is it my imagination, or did I just hear him swallow hard? Definitely my imagination, because when he speaks again, his voice is perfectly composed. "Absolutely. Just concerned you might overdose on sugar."

"There is no such thing."

"Do you still clip photos on notebooks with all the places you want to visit?"

My jaw drops. "I can't believe you remember that."

"You stole my car magazine. Of course, I

remember."

"I didn't steal it," I argue, recognizing our familiar bickering routine. I pull the blanket up to my chin and wiggle my butt on the couch. "I borrowed it when you weren't looking."

Max snickers. "And returned it with a hole."

"You didn't need the picture anyway." Vividly I remember that moment when he realized his pristine magazine collection wasn't so pristine anymore. There was an ad about London, promising cheap flights and accommodations, with Big Ben in the background. I couldn't help myself; I cut it out and clipped it in my notebook.

"It's a matter of principle," he volleys back. "Anyway, do you still do that?"

"Well, I don't glue pics on notebooks anymore, but I do collect pics on my laptop. Traveling is still on my to-do list. Haven't been out of the ol' US yet though, but I will eventually. So, why did you return from London?"

There is a long pause before he starts talking again. "I loved it there, but something was just missing. I worked sixteen hours a day, so building a life there was hard. And I wanted to be closer to my family."

I melt at his honest response, happy to learn the Bennetts are as tight-knit as I remember them. I loved being at their house. They were loud and fun, and they made me feel as though I was part of the family—an adopted Bennett, they used to call me. Feeling a yawn form at the back of my throat, I fight to stifle it and fail.

"Was that a yawn?" he asks.

"No," I answer too quickly. Max chuckles. "Fine, it was. This was a long day."

"Go to sleep, Jonesie. We'll have time to catch up. And this will go down in history as the world's shortest longest phone call."

After battling another yawn, I say, "I'm glad you're back. Grams used to say that some people show up in your life when you need them the most. I first met you after Mom died and Dad left, and now you're back in my life when I'm losing Grams more each day. I missed you, Max. I'm happy you botched your knee ligaments. Good night."

"Ah, your concern for my health is touching. I missed you too, beautiful. Good night."

As I hang up, my breath catches in my throat at the way his voice dipped as he said *beautiful* and heat singes me in my most intimate spot. *What the hell?* I'm reading way too much into this—well, my body is. Friendly banter, that's all this is, and it has to stay this way.

Yet as I hug the pillow in my bed a little while later, smiling as I recall the care in his words, the huskiness of his voice, every fiber of my being disagrees.

***

"Darling, you're staring at that clock as if you can make it go faster just by looking at it. Are you going on a date after we finish?"

"No," I tell Mrs. Devereaux. "I have four more patients today."

Mrs. Deveraux gives me a questioning look, clearly wanting to know more, but I keep my mouth shut. She loves gossiping, and once she senses a story, nothing stops her. Right now she is sitting on her exercise mat, her snow-white hair up in a bun. Even in workout clothes, Mrs. Deveraux never looks anything less than regal. She is in her late sixties, and as healthy as they come, aside from the odd joint or back pain due to age. She has no real need for physical therapy, but she insists on having regular sessions. I think it's because she feels lonely. She has five kids, but they don't visit her often.

"Is the next one the hot stud who left here the last time I came?"

I look at her in shock, and all I can do is nod. A glance around the room confirms that the other therapists are too busy with their patients to pay us any attention.

"Oh, that explains it." She winks at me, then takes a sip of her vitamin-powered drink. I sit cross-legged on the floor in front of her, unsure I want to know what she means. Still, common courtesy means I must ask anyway.

"What do you mean?"

"Well, if I had a date with him, I couldn't wait to get rid of this bag of bones either."

"You're not a bag of bones, Mrs. Devereaux. And I don't have a date with him. He's my patient.

And a childhood friend. I hadn't seen him in years before the other day."

"Let me guess, it was a big surprise to find out your childhood friend is now a sexy man? I might be sixty-eight, but that doesn't mean I don't look. If anything, I have more experience recognizing the good ones. For instance, I can tell your *childhood friend* is fantastic in bed."

Only Mrs. Deveraux can say that sentence with a straight face.

"How would you know that?"

"He has that way of walking and moving. A kind of self-confidence men only have if they know they're very good at what they consider important skills. And being a good lay ranks high on their list."

I blush, not wanting to give too much thought to Max's skills in the bed. "We should get back to your exercises."

"Sure. So tell me, what type of friends are you and hot stud? With benefits?"

"No, not at all."

"Well, good. I can tell you straight up that doesn't work. Tried it a few times."

Of course, she did. Mrs. Devereaux refers to herself as an adventurous woman, which I suppose is a fair way of summing up her life. She's lived in nineteen different countries and been married four times.

Despite myself, I ask, "So why didn't it work out?"

"Sex complicates friendships. You might tell

yourself in the beginning—no strings attached, but then one day you find yourself jealous when you see him with another woman. You can't go back to just being friends after having done the nasty with each other either. But then again, being friends with an attractive man is a difficult thing too. Someone who looks like him is bound to stir up your hormones."

You have no idea.

"Just know what you want from him, sweetheart. And stick to one thing. Friendship or romance."

"Friends. Romance can fall apart—it always does for me anyway, but friendships are for the long term."

She nods thoughtfully. "That's a very smart thing to know. I was quite a few years older when I reached that conclusion."

Mrs. Devereaux reminds me of my grandmother, even though they have nothing in common in terms of their upbringing or past. But they are both strong, opinionated women who don't take shit from anyone.

***

I pace around the gym after Mrs. Deveraux leaves, her words still ringing in my ears as I wait for Max, who arrives fifteen minutes after the scheduled start of our session. He walks in holding his hands up as if he knows I'm preparing myself to scold him.

"Sorry I'm late," he says. "I was in a meeting

that went on for too long." He undoes his tie as he speaks, clearly happy to get rid of it.

"No need to strip in front of me, Bennett. You know where the changing room is."

He winks at me before striding to the other end of the room. Five minutes later, he returns, wearing the same workout clothes as last time.

"So what kind of exercises are we going to do today?" he inquires as he paces the training room, eyeing the various machines. I can't help notice the way his lean muscles flex when he moves. Belatedly I realize Max is watching me too. Drawing in a sharp breath, I look away. Biting the inside of my cheek, I point to one of the treatment tables.

"Lie there."

He grimaces. "What are you going to do to me?"

"Max Bennett, are you afraid?" I ask while leading him to the treatment table. He walks a few steps behind me, yet knowing he is so near messes with my senses. Thank heavens there are four other people in the training room, though they are at a considerable distance from us.

He shrugs as he stands in front of the table. "I've seen videos of exercises done on these tables. They look like torture."

"You *are* afraid," I exclaim. "Well, well. I wouldn't have expected that from the boy who convinced me to jump with him in the pond from the top of the cliff."

Max grins at me, and I'm instantly reminded

of that particular day.

It was a warm Saturday morning, and Max showed up at my house like a boy with a plan. I was sitting on the porch, reading a book. He convinced me to go swimming with him at the pond we regularly went to. But when we arrived at the pond, it became clear he had more in mind than just swimming.

"Let's go jump off the cliff," he said.

"But that's dangerous," I countered immediately. The pond was surrounded by high cliffs—one of them particularly high and pointy.

"Nah, it's pretty high, but I've seen some tenth graders do it."

"That doesn't mean it's not dangerous." I folded my arms over my chest, shaking my head.

"Why are you so afraid, Jonesie?"

I shrugged. "I've never been brave."

"I think you are, but you just don't know it."

"But what if something happens to us?"

Max sighed dramatically. "Look, that group looks like they're about to jump. Let's watch them. If something happens to them, we don't do it."

I balanced my weight from one foot to the other, but didn't argue anymore. "Okay."

Max and I looked as everyone in the group jumped, some alone, some holding hands. Nothing happened to any of them. Of course.

"See? They're all fine," Max said.

I was afraid, but I also didn't want to seem like a coward. I was more afraid that if I didn't do it, he wouldn't want to be friends with me anymore, which sounds silly now, but to a ten-year-old, it made perfect sense.

"Okay," I said.

We both shed our clothes, remaining only in our undies. Then we climbed up on the cliff, and as I stood there, my heart in my throat, I looked up at Max and saw him all tall and sure of himself. There was not one sliver of fear in his eyes, whereas I had enough fear for both of us.

"Take my hand," he says. "I'll make sure nothing happens to you."

Remarkably, those few words calmed me like nothing else. The second his hand touched mine, the rhythm of my heart settled, and the water below didn't seem so threatening anymore. We jumped, and nothing happened. If anything, I became braver after that day.

"Can I confess something?" Max asks, snapping me back to the present.

"Sure."

"I almost peed myself when we were on the top of that cliff. I just wanted to impress you."

I jerk my head back in surprise. "But you were the one with the idea. Why even bring it up if you were afraid?"

"Christopher told me you'd like me more if I jumped. He challenged me, saying I wouldn't have the balls to jump."

"You never walk away from a challenge, do you?"

He points to his injured leg. "After this, I might."

"Right, I know when a patient is stalling, and

that's what you're doing right now." Pointing to the table, I instruct, "Lie on your back, so I can do you." Panic flares through me as I realize what I just said. I thank heavens again that the room is big enough that the other trainers and their patients can't hear me. "I mean so I can show you what you have to do."

Laughter rumbles out of Max in a deep, heartfelt sound. I desperately try to come up with something clever to say. A strand of my blonde hair falls from my ponytail, and Max tucks it behind my ear, the pad of his thumb lingering on my earlobe. Heat radiates from that small point of contact, spreading to my cheeks, my neck.

"Lie on the table, Max," I eventually say. He does as I instruct him, and once he's on his back, my fingers accidentally touch his chest and an electrifying zip makes every part of my body heat up. He exhales sharply.

I attempt to decipher the expression on his face. There is heat in his eyes—that much is clear, but the way his brows are arched indicates that he's as surprised by my reaction to him as I am by his reaction to me.

"Emilia," Max says in a low voice. "I think we have a problem."

"Mmm?" I urge, not wanting to say anything unless I'm certain we're on the same page. I wouldn't put it past my sex-deprived body to be messing with my mind.

"When I found out you'd be my therapist, I thought we'd pick up where we left off years ago. But then I saw you all grown up and sexy and… *well.*" He cocks an eyebrow, a devilish grin crossing his lips. "Just thought I'd put this out there. They say communication is the key to everything, right? And it used to work for us."

I chuckle, shaking my head. His breathing is labored, and so is mine. Stepping back, I put some much-needed distance between us.

He nods slowly, scratching the faint stubble on his jaw. "It's only a matter of time."

"What is a matter of time?" I ask, not following.

"Until we're comfortable with each other again."

Oh, I hadn't thought about it like that. "Maybe you're right."

Judging by the way my entire body seems to go hyperalert when he's around, that seems like wishful thinking.

"Let's start with your exercises."

He groans. "I hoped you'd forget about that."

"No chance." I explain the exercise in detail for the next few minutes, and Max's already nonexistent enthusiasm for the exercise turns to downright annoyance. To his credit, this particular exercise *is* a bitch. He follows through with my instructions and does a set of twenty reps.

"You're in great shape," I commend him. "Most people are out of breath by the time they reach twelve."

Max draws a deep breath. "I worked out a lot

before the accident, and I also play water polo on occasion."

The thought of Max in a pool, shirtless and playing polo is fodder for my brain, which turns everything into a dirty picture.

"You know, the faster you finish the physical therapy, the faster you can do your regular workout again and keep those hard abs of yours in place."

"You noticed?" he asks smugly.

"Couldn't help it," I admit. "It's all messing with my hormones big time. Like you said, just putting it out there."

"Maybe communication doesn't always help. It didn't really clear the air, did it?"

I chuckle nervously, pulling with my fingers at the hem of my shirt.

Seeing as how the air seems to consist of hormones and sexual tension, the question is almost rhetorical. When we were kids, we used to talk out loud about everything, and it helped us put some awkward incidents behind us fast. But openly admitting our attraction for each other just seems to be making everything worse.

Clearing my throat, I say, "Okay, new resolution. We'll just ignore the chemistry until it goes away."

Max curves his lip up in a smirk, and I can tell he has a witty reply in mind. He remains silent, though, and now I'm dying to know what he's thinking, of course.

"Are you seeing someone?" I ask, realizing I

have no idea what the status of his love life is. My stomach is in knots as I wait for his answer.

His smirk becomes more pronounced. "This coming from someone who wants to ignore the chemistry?"

"Just hoping to alleviate my conscience. As light as our flirting was, I'd feel like shit if there's a woman in your life."

"I'm not an ass, Emilia. I wouldn't have flirted back if I was seeing someone. What about you? I have to say right off the bat that if you are, and you're blushing like that when I'm just looking at you, dump him. He's clearly not good enough."

"You know, one thing did change about you, Max. You weren't so full of yourself before. Now you're bordering on being cocky."

"Bordering? Please. I'm far past that border, deep into Cockyland."

"Cockyland?" I giggle, then remember what Mrs. Devereaux said, that confident men are usually great in bed, and I can't help the heat rushing to my face.

"Something about you changed too, Jonesie. You laugh a lot more. It suits you. But you haven't answered my question."

"I'll tell you everything while you do another set of twenty."

He gives me the stink eye but doesn't argue.

"I'm not seeing anyone. But I almost got married six months ago."

"What happened?" Max asks in a soft voice,

pausing for a split second.

"He dumped me three weeks before the wedding."

"That son of a bitch."

I smile at his indignation. "How do you know it's not something I did?"

"I have a hunch. Tell me."

I instruct him to do a set of straight leg raises, then tell him what happened.

"We'd been together since college, and we got along well until Grams got sick. Things became more difficult, I was stressed.... Three weeks before the wedding, he said it was all too much responsibility for him, and he hadn't signed up for this."

"He was a jerk. You got off easy."

"Maybe, but it still hurt. Like I wasn't worth fighting for, you know." It also twisted the knife into an age-old wound, hitting too close to home. My father took off right after Mama's funeral, claiming that raising a kid was too difficult and he was meant for other things. "I suppose it's better that it happened so early in the game before we signed the papers, but it hurt. I've put my romantic life on hold since, but I could use a friend, Max."

My fingers are on the edge of the treatment table, and Max feathers the back of his hand over them, a devilish smile on his face. "I volunteer for that spot, Jonesie. Now, if I accidentally make an inappropriate comment or look at you the wrong way, please chalk it up to the fact that I'm a weak man."

I point a menacing finger at him. "No messing around with me. I mean it."

"Or what? Will you spank me?" He wiggles his eyebrows. "You already have me lying down."

"You're a pest, you know that?" I say under my breath, but can't hold back a smile.

"I've been called that before. Nuisance, plague."

"You say that with pride, as if it's a badge of honor."

"It is. It means I'm determined." Max resumes a serious expression. "And I'm determined to be a good friend to you, Emilia. I promise. Now, what's the next torture you have in store for me?"

As I explain the next exercise, his eyes zero in on my mouth. Nervously, I lick my lower lip, and Max's gaze smolders me, like that of a man ready to break his promise. Damn it. How is this ever going to work?

Chapter Six

Max

"You're not getting ten percent. You're not even getting one percent more." I'm in one of the meeting rooms at Bennett Enterprises, negotiating a contract with a new distributor, and the moron is trying to rip us off. It's late in the evening, and I have an early morning tomorrow, but I'm not letting him off the hook. I promised Summer we'd talk on the phone in the morning. Since she's in Italy, we have to coordinate every call around the time zone difference. My baby sister puts up a brave face, but I know what it's like to be in a different country on your own. It's exciting and fun, but also lonely—which is why I make time to talk to her whenever she wants to.

"That's the price I ask of all of my suppliers." He sits back in his chair, smiling lazily.

"That's not true now, is it? You ask for a seven percent discount from Deli's, and a seven-point-five from Flawless," I say, referring to our competitors. His face falls. "I've done my homework."

Yeah, competitor discounts are hard to find out but not impossible. The two keys in negotiations are knowledge and patience. Sebastian and Logan used to handle most of the negotiations way back. One time they couldn't make it, and they sent me instead. I spent the day prior to it researching and calling in favors to find out more information. The meeting lasted two hours longer than if Sebastian or Logan had been in it, but I ended up getting a better deal than my brothers would have, which somehow made me the official negotiator. As Director of International Developments, negotiating with local distributors isn't something I'm supposed to do personally, but I don't mind. In fact, I like it. It's my family's money. Anyone trying to rip us off is in for a nasty surprise.

"Bennett Enterprises is much bigger than Deli's and Flawless," he says. "You can afford to pay more."

"Bigger doesn't mean we're stupid. You're offering me the same in-store placement as you offer them. Same price. In fact, because you tried to fool us, I want a better price."

The guy turns livid and I know I'll wear him down. That's right, moron. No one messes with my family's money and gets away with it.

***

The next morning I arrive at the clinic about

twenty minutes before my session with Emilia is scheduled to begin. I talked to Summer for an hour and then left my home without checking the time. The weather isn't too chilly, so I just sit on a bench in the small park in front of the clinic, going through the e-mails on my phone. I'm about to make a phone call when I raise my head and see Emilia a few feet away. She has a baby on her hip. What the hell? She coos at the baby, making silly faces until the kid laughs. Damn, she's sweet.

"You're full of surprises, Jonesie," I say, walking up to her and the baby.

"What are you doing here so early?" she asks.

I shrug. "Miscalculated the distance and traffic. Whose baby is this?"

"The owner of the clinic. She comes over three times a week before we open for an hour, talks with Kurt—the director—and I babysit this champion here while she's inside."

"You do this often?"

"I have a few babysitting and even dog-sitting gigs. I need the money. My salary at the clinic is great, but after paying the rent and Grams's caretaker, not much is left." With a grin, she adds, "But I'd babysit this adorable little thing for free anytime."

A number of people would show frustration or at least annoyance at having to work themselves to the bone, but Emilia takes it all in stride, and with a smile. She's grown into one hell of a woman.

"You're a baby person," I say when she

covers the baby's bald head with kisses.

"You say that like it's a bad thing."

"Not at all. Just an observation."

"I'd love to have some of my own, but I think that's not in the cards for me."

"Why?"

"If being left three weeks before your wedding isn't a sign you're meant to be an old cat lady, I don't know what is." She looks so vulnerable in this moment that I want to take her in my arms and not let go. The urge hits me to go after that moron and give him a piece of my mind—or fist. No one can hurt her and get away with it.

"What about you? When will the world be blessed with little Max Bennetts?"

"Kids aren't on my radar. No father material here." That right here is a solid reason why I shouldn't have anything else other than friendship on my mind when it comes to Emilia. She's in a different place than I am.

When Christopher and I turned eighteen, Logan lectured us about treating women right. He rambled on for about an hour, and I zoned out ten minutes in, but one thing did stick into my thick skull: treat every woman the way you'd want men to treat your sisters. That sounded like good advice, and it worked for Logan, but not for me. I was up-front with the women I dated, telling them I wasn't looking for anything for the long term, just fun and company, and I treated them right. They always seemed on board with me, but then ended up wanting more than I could give them, turning bitter and unhappy. I hurt them without wanting to, but the truth was I couldn't see myself having a future with any of them.

Emilia wants kids and a relationship and deserves someone who can give her that. But damn, the thought of my Jonesie with someone else makes me want to punch something. And knowing she shoulders the responsibility of caring for her grandmother alone makes me want to swoop in and solve everything, but that would be a surefire way to piss her off. Jonesie doesn't take handouts. I learned that when we were nine, and I'm sure that hasn't changed. She's grown into an independent, hardworking woman, and I respect her for that.

"Yeah, Mommy's coming out in a few minutes," she tells the baby, kissing its little bald head some more. I'd seen this nurturing side of her as kids, but now it's different in a way I can't describe. She's delicate and strong at the same time, and I could watch her carry this baby around for hours. *What the actual hell?*

"I'm done for the day!" A woman in her late thirties walks out the front door and takes the baby from Emilia. "Thank you for watching him." The woman nods curtly at me before leaving.

"Let's go inside," Emilia tells me. I gesture for her to walk in front of me, which ends up being a bad idea, because I have a perfect view of her ass in that sinful pencil skirt of hers. Two vaguely familiar faces press against a nearby window, watching Emilia and me. I think one of them is the receptionist.

"What the hell?" I motion to Emilia, who turns red when she sees them.

"Those are Abby, our receptionist, and Evelyn, our psychologist. They are also very good friends of mine, and they are—"

"Checking me out?"

"They've done this since the first time you came. Now they're... assessing your potential."

"For what?" I ask, dumbfounded. When she turns a deeper shade of red, I have my answer. "Emilia!" My voice is brisker than I intended, startling her. We stop a few feet in front of the entrance.

"What?"

"You're right to want us to be nothing more than friends. I have a bad record with women."

"I can't imagine you hurting women on purpose."

"I wasn't. Still ended up doing it. So yeah... can't promise I won't flirt with you. But if I do—"

"I'll shoot you down." She grins, clearly enjoying my mortification.

"You do that."

"I'll do more, keep you all the way in the friend zone." Her grin widens. "I'll tell you all about my dates and sexcapades."

"Sexcapades." Every muscle in my body contorts. "You have those?"

"Oh, yeah. All the time. The stories I can tell you—"

"Don't. You're supposed to keep me in the friend zone, not hell." Groaning, I'm beginning to wonder if they aren't the same thing.

"I was messing with you, Max." She doubles over with laughter as tension bleeds away from every corner of my body. "I'll do my best to keep you in a non-hellish friend zone. Glad we cleared the air. Worked better than the last time."

Really? Because it's about as clear as mud to me. We enter the clinic and my eyes fall on her delicious hips again.

Friend zone feels like hell already.

Chapter Seven

Emilia

On Thursday, I arrive late at the clinic in the morning. Grams was very agitated, and it took some time to calm her down. Thankfully, Max is my first appointment for the day, but that doesn't mean it's okay to be late. I've built my reputation in the clinic by having an impeccable work ethic. As I drive my car into the parking lot behind the clinic, I see Max emerging from a sleek black car. He gives me a thumbs-up when he notices me and leans against his car, obviously waiting for me. Today he doesn't wear one of his suits, instead sporting jeans and a simple white shirt. After stepping out of my car, I smooth down my skirt and beam at him.

We walk into the clinic together, heading to the elevator. Max's assigned training room is on the second floor. I press the button once we're in the elevator, and as the doors close, we head upward with a jolt. I focus on the buttons, acutely aware of Max's presence behind me. The space is tiny, almost claustrophobic, and even though my back is turned to Max, I can smell his cologne. The scent is a danger to my senses, instantly sending my thoughts into

Dirtyland. The faster we get out of here, the better. But when the elevator finally comes to a stop, I know something is wrong. My fears are confirmed when the doors don't open.

"Hell, no," I exclaim, pushing the button that should open the doors. Nothing happens.

"Are we stuck?" Max asks.

"I think so, yeah." With a tsk, I push the emergency button.

"How may I help you?" A female voice resounds through the speaker above the emergency button.

"We're stuck in the elevator," I inform her, adding the address of the clinic.

"All right," the woman says. "A repair team is on their way."

"How long will they need?" I ask.

"At the very least forty minutes."

Max swears from behind me. I elbow him gently just as the woman says, "Did you say something, miss?"

"No. It's fine. I'll wait. We'll wait. There is a patient with me inside the elevator. Are you sure there's nothing you can do so the team gets here quicker?"

"Afraid not."

"Okay."

The line goes static, and unable to put it off much longer, I turn around to face Max. He leans against the wall opposite the elevator doors, his arms crossed over his chest, an uncharacteristic sour expression on his face.

"Max?" I ask tentatively.

"I hate small spaces," he murmurs.

"Oh my God, that's right. You do."

Drops of sweat dot his temples and his gaze darts to the doors every few seconds. His hands are curled into tight fists at his sides. I know what I have to do—take his mind off it, make him focus on something that isn't our location.

"How's work?" I inquire.

Max doesn't reply. His eyes travel up and down the doors before he finally slides down the elevator wall, assuming a sitting position on the floor. The instinct to hug him—comfort him in any way—is overwhelming. Briefly, I wonder if I can use the need to calm him down as an excuse to kiss him. But that would be a bad, bad idea. I join him on the floor wordlessly.

"Stressful at the moment. We're preparing for a show. We do those regularly to present the new collections."

"I know, I've read about it in magazines. Pippa is the designer. How is she?" I ask, melancholy hitting me mercilessly as I think about the eldest Bennett sister. She was always a warm presence in the Bennett household, even when she was being a spitfire because someone crossed her. I adored her.

"Happily married and pregnant with twin girls."

"No way. Wow. How far along is she?"

"Around seven months. Yesterday the girls

kicked her constantly while she was listening to music in her office. Now she's convinced they will be musicians."

"I'm banking on soccer players," I say thoughtfully. "All of you loved playing soccer."

"That's what I told her, too." He winks at me, and I'm sure women worldwide would drop their panties at that wink. Not me, though. My panties are firmly in place.

"Can't wait for them to be born," he continues. "I'll make it my mission to teach them how to prank everyone."

If I thought his wink was heat inducing, his words are atomic, albeit in a different way—pulling at my heartstrings. Max might think he's not father material, but I disagree. I think he is, just doesn't know it yet.

"Do they already have names?" I inquire.

"Mia and Elena."

"Those are beautiful names."

Max nods, and I'm pleased to observe that he seems more at ease than before. His breathing pattern is calmer, even though his hands are still curled into fists. He also eyes the floor right next to me from time to time, which is a telltale sign he's not completely at ease. Almost driven by a will of its own, my hand inches closer to his, reaching for him. I touch the back of his hand with my fingers. At first, nothing happens, but then he opens his fist, letting me in. Having my hand in his feels familiar and new at the same time, which I suppose is the perfect way to sum up our renewed friendship. Trying to ignore the way my body hums at his nearness, I scoot even closer to him, until my left hip touches his right hip. Max moves our intertwined hands on his lap.

"I think it's every man's fantasy to be stuck with a woman in an elevator," Max says. "And when it happens to me, I'm nearly having a damn panic attack."

"I'd say you're doing fine, Bennett. You scared me a little in the beginning, but now you're looking good. I knew I had to get you to talk in order to distract you."

"You're a distraction all by yourself. Especially since your skirt slid up when you sat."

"Oh crap." I inspect my skirt, and sure enough, it slid up my thighs. Damn me and my habit of wearing skirts on the way to work and only changing into training gear at the clinic. My ass is not hanging out, but there's enough to see if you look closely. And Max definitely is looking closely. That's why he was peering down regularly. It wasn't a sign of nervousness. It was a sign of him being a pervert. I've been so focused on him, I didn't even notice my panties are almost on display. Hastily I cover myself, pulling at my skirt and wishing it were longer. "Why didn't you say something?"

"And ruin all my fun? I'm not stupid."

"I, on the other hand, am an idiot. A complete and utter idiot."

"No, you're not." He opens his mouth as if he would like to add more, but then closes it again.

I remain silent, watching the vein pulsing at the base of his neck. Up close, I can smell *his* scent beneath the cologne, and it's intoxicating, awakening every single cell in my body. Unexpectedly, he turns my palm up, tracing the almost invisible white line at the base.

"The scar almost faded," he murmurs. "Did you tell anyone how you really got it?" he inquires.

"No, I kept our secret. Did you?" On the night before Grams and I moved to Montana, I snuck out of my house to meet Max for a farewell walk around the places we used to hang around. I cut my palm badly in the process.

"I don't kiss and tell, Emilia." I don't know if it's the fact that he used kiss and Emilia in the same sentence, or that his tone is low and husky, but a delicious shiver slithers down my spine.

"You call me Emilia a lot lately."

"Jonesie doesn't fit you anymore, does it?" With his thumb, he draws little circles at the base of my palm, driving me crazy. How can a gesture so innocent stir so many sinful sensations inside of me? My breath hitches as I hear Max swallowing hard. Risking a glance at him, I notice his jaw is clenched, as if he is exerting the utmost self-control. Raising my hand, he places a kiss on my scar. The contact sends a jolt directly to my center.

I let out a sound somewhere between a moan and a groan, energy strumming through me. Max turns his head toward me, focusing on my mouth. He is *so* close. I'd barely have to tip my head, and....

Almost involuntarily, I lick my lower lip.

A groan reverberates from deep inside Max. "Are you trying to kill me?"

Shaking my head, I become acutely aware that our hands are still intertwined. Worse still, we're both shaking. To someone watching us, it wouldn't be noticeable. But I can feel it in my bones. Our last vestiges of control are about to give in. I pry my hand out of his and push myself further away in an attempt to put some distance between us, but as soon as I move my ass, my damn skirt slides upward again.

"Fucking hell," Max exclaims, his gaze following the hem of my skirt as if he wants to set it on fire. Cursing, I cover myself again. He snaps his gaze away, staring at the door instead. "Earthquake, flood, waxing."

"What?" I ask, wondering if he's lost his mind.

"I'm trying to focus on evil things to distract myself."

I snort. "How are earthquake, flood, and waxing in the same category? Wait! What would you know about waxing?"

"I pissed off Alice badly once. Her revenge was cruel."

Before I have a chance to ask more, voices from the other side of the doors startle us both.

"We're going to force the doors open," a deep, manly voice informs us.

"Okay. What does that mean?" I ask. Max and

I pry ourselves up off the floor in unison.

"You're in between floors now, so we'll have to pull you up."

Max curses and my stomach dips. I might not be claustrophobic, but the thought of exiting an elevator that is between floors makes me uneasy.

"Can't you fix it first, and let us out when it's on one of the floors?" I inquire.

"It can last hours, I'm afraid," the man answers. Well, between being stuck with Max in here and being pulled out, the latter feels safer. I'm pretty sure that in a few hours, he and I will both run out of *evil* things to distract ourselves with.

Max seems to be thinking along the same lines, because even though he's pale, he says loudly, "Go ahead."

We both wait in silence for the man to open the doors, and I breathe out in relief when I see that our position is not too bad. The upper floor is at roughly the same level with my navel, so I'll only have to push myself up a little to crawl out.

"Do you need any help, ma'am?" the mechanic asks.

"Thank you, I've got this," I say confidently, placing my palms firmly on the floor. Just as I'm about to push myself up, I notice Max is holding the lower hem of my skirt between his fingers.

"What are you doing?" I hiss.

Max motions with his head toward the mechanic, who's a few feet away. Then he whispers, "Making sure that guy over there doesn't take a peek at your ass. Trust me, by the time you get out, your skirt will be up and around your waist."

I'd argue with him if I didn't just experience how undependable my skirt is.

"Thanks."

"No problem."

Several minutes later, both Max and I are safely outside on the second floor.

"Oh shoot." I glance at the clock hanging over the elevator. "My next appointment will be here in ten minutes. We—"

"Can reschedule," Max says.

Something shifted between us while we were stuck in there. I can't quite point out what, but I feel it in my bones. Looking up at Max, I'm certain he does too.

"Thanks for being a distraction inside there," he says.

"Thanks for having my back when we got out. Or more accurately, my ass."

Max grins widely. "I'll always have your ass, Emilia. Always."

As he leaves, he gives me a wink—one of *those* winks—and I'm fairly sure my panties just shifted a few inches lower on my hips.

Chapter Eight

Emilia

Over the next week, the tension between us grows so thick it's almost palpable. Remarkably, we keep things light during the training sessions, focusing on his exercises and reminiscing about childhood memories. But in between sessions, we frequently send text messages to each other, and that's when the blips in our control show.

I could stop texting him, of course, but I can't help myself. Whenever something funny occurs, he's the first person I want to share it with.

Right now I fiddle with my phone, wondering if it would be inappropriate to snap a picture of what is happening in front of me and send it to Max. I'm attending a seminar on rehabilitation, hosted by a highly reputable name in the field. He's constantly doing research on techniques, and I've learned a lot from his seminars in the past.

I make a point to keep up-to-date with the latest research even though the clinic isn't paying for all of the seminars I attend. Still, I consider this an investment in my future and the well-being of my patients.

Unfortunately, this particular seminar is one mishap away from earning the title *epic failure*. The host started off by apologizing for having a sore throat, and thus being unable to present his findings himself. He left that task up to his assistant, who is clearly unfit for this. He mumbled and stumbled through his presentation, spending more time apologizing for said mishaps than actually talking about the subject. When he nervously knocks a glass of water over his notes, I almost give up. He insists on a five-minute break while he prints out a fresh set of notes. As soon as he dismisses us, I leap from my seat, taking advantage of this to stretch my legs.

"Well, this is a waste of time," Florence says, following me out of the room. She is a therapist too, working at a clinic outside of San Francisco, and we regularly meet at seminars. I like her. "I might as well leave now."

"I'll give him another chance," I say. "Let's grab something to drink."

While we help ourselves to drinks from the small buffet outside, Florence says, "You look different. More radiant. Is your grandmother better?"

My stomach plummets. "No, not at all. She's hanging in there."

"Sorry to hear that."

We nurse our drinks, standing near a floor-to-ceiling window.

"Hmm... care to share the secret to your

newfound glow?" she asks. "Is it a man?"

I laugh nervously, tapping my fingers on my glass of orange juice. "No, it's not."

Florence gives me a look full of meaning. "If you say so." She looks at me expectantly, but I simply continue to nurse my drink. Thankfully, before the silence becomes too awkward, the break ends and we're ushered back into the seminar room.

As the assistant starts mumbling through the presentation again, my phone vibrates with an incoming message from Max.

Max: I just had someone spill an entire glass of wine and the contents of their plate on my shirt. Please tell me you're having a better evening. How's the seminar going?

The corners of my lips lift in a smile, butterflies roaming around in my stomach. He remembered about my seminar!

Emilia: Dreadful. I'm watching the guy's assistant make a fool of himself. Your evening MUST be more interesting. You're at the rehearsal for the show after all. I pause, unsure whether I really want to know the answer to my next question. **Do you have your eyes on a model?**

Max: It actually was a model who spilled her dinner on me. On the plus side, she eats. I think she's the only one from the gang who does. I swear these girls are a mystery to me. How do they survive? They must be aliens.

Emilia: Don't be an ass. Looking runway-ready requires sacrifices.

Max: I'm still going with aliens.

He still hasn't answered my original question though. My throat is dry as I hover with my fingers over the screen. Should I ask again? What if he was deliberately avoiding giving me a straight answer? Shaking my head, I chastise myself. Max can do whatever he wants, and it shouldn't bother me. I shove my phone away, only to immediately grab it again.

Emilia: Do you have your eyes set on any alien? Taking one home with you tonight?

I swear I'm holding my breath waiting for his answer.

Max: Nah, just came here for work. Who do you take me for?

Instead of replying to him, I place my phone on the table and direct my attention to the front. The guy finally got to an important part, and I'm taking notes like crazy. I knew it would be worthwhile to stick around. After several minutes, an incoming message pops on the screen of my phone.

Max: Jonesie, you can't leave me hanging like this after almost insulting me.

Emilia: No offense

I press Send by mistake before finishing my sentence. Max writes back immediately.

Max: I have a feeling I'm about to be offended.

Emilia: I have three weeks of sessions as proof that you suffer from acute wandering eyes syndrome.

Max: You're not so innocent yourself. Don't think I haven't noticed your eyes doing some wandering too.

Emilia: Hey, eye muscles must be trained too from time to time.

Max: Me ogling you is classified as acute eye-wandering syndrome, while you ogling me falls in the category of eye training. That's a double standard right there.

I grin like an idiot as I hover my fingers over my phone, unsure what to write back. I saw him two days ago, and I'll see him again on Saturday, albeit outside of the clinic. We're going to have a long, lazy breakfast together. Ridiculous as it sounds, I wish I'd seen him today too. It's like a switch went on inside of me, and I yearn to make up in a few weeks for the years we've been apart. A screeching sound behind me jolts me from my thoughts. When I look up from my phone, I realize that the room is far emptier than when I last looked around. The screeching sound came from two chairs being pushed back as their occupants rose from their seats.

Emilia: Officially more than half of the attendees have left the room. I'll stick until the end, though.

Max: Of course you will. You and I have that in common. Determination.

Trying to ignore the flip my stomach gives as I reread the words *You and I*, I type back quickly.

Emilia: How do you know I'm determined? And DON'T mention that time I

walked home from the fair in high heels just to prove I could. That wasn't determination, it was stupidity.

I had just turned twelve, which meant that heels and lipstick were the height of sophistication in my mind. I had giant feet for my small frame (still do), and Grams's shoes fit me perfectly. So one day I snuck out of the house wearing her favorite pair. In retrospect, I looked like an absolute idiot walking in them, but I was ridiculously proud. Until the balls of my feet started burning. I had gone with some of the Bennett siblings, Max included, to a junkyard sale nearby. I insisted on wearing the stupid shoes until I got home. My feet were burning, and I broke a heel. Grandma didn't speak to me for three days, and I walked in flats for a week.

Max: No, I was referring to that summer you spent hours a day trying to shoot hoops.

Emilia: How do you know about that? I didn't tell anyone.

Max: Who do you think happened to leave a basketball hoop for you to find?

I gasp, which earns me some ugly looks from the remaining seminar participants. I quickly mask it with a look of fake interest at the presenter. I count the seconds until everyone returns their gaze to the front before typing again.

Emilia: It was you?

The response comes right away.

Max: I knew you wouldn't take a handout, so I just bought a hoop and broke it a bit, so you

could fix it quickly. Then I made it look as if someone got rid of it and a makeshift backboard by throwing them away at the edge of the road.

I read the message a few times, allowing his words to sink in. The idea that a twelve-year-old Max planned and carried that out is... wow. I sucked at scoring in basketball, hence why I was the last one picked every time we played in teams. I vowed I'd get better. I saved my pocket money to buy a ball, but I still needed a hoop when I saw the discarded one and the wood plank next to my gate. I mounted them both on the branch of a tall tree in my yard and practiced for hours each day. Grams and I moved to Montana by the end of the summer, but I kicked ass in basketball on my new school's team.

Sighing, I type back.

Emilia: I just melted a bit.

Max: Does that mean I get a free pass at eye training on Saturday during breakfast? It seems I can't help myself anyway.

Shaking my head, I prepare to write back something witty when I notice that the battery sign in the right upper corner is red and blinking.

Emilia: My phone is going to die soon.

Max: I'll take this as a yes.

Soon becomes *right now*, becomes a few seconds after hitting Send, the screen goes dark. I drop my phone in my bag and dedicate my full attention to the seminar. One hour later, it's a wrap. I'm about to leave the building when someone calls my name from behind.

"Emilia!"

I spin around and find myself face-to-face with John. We've attended a few seminars together and grabbed dinner afterward twice. I realized too late he'd considered those dates. I'd just considered them having dinner with someone who is in the same line of work.

"Hi, John!"

"You still owe me that third date. It's very late, but would you like to go to dinner with me? I know a great burger place just a few blocks away. Or we could just grab a drink."

I shift my weight from one foot to the other, rubbing the back of my neck with my palm. I don't like his pushy tone, but I don't want to argue with him. It would make future seminars awkward. As I look into John's expectant expression, my mind conjures up quite a different image. One of a six-foot-tall man with chocolate brown eyes and a smile that seems to permanently say *I am up to no good*.

"Sorry, John, I can't."

His friendly expression wavers for a split second. "Of course, you probably have plans already. Next time, maybe."

He walks away before I have time to say anything back, but I already know I won't take him up on any future invitations. Securing the strap of my bag over my shoulder, I head out of the building, musing over my short interaction with John. Once I climb into my car, I sigh loudly. *Max*. Why is he always on my mind? This wouldn't be problematic if my thoughts would roam in the friend zone, but more often than not, they cross to Dirtytown. My dreams have taken up permanent residence in Smutland.

The ridiculous thing is that since my engagement went balls up, I haven't had one dirty thought about any man, and I routinely work with great looking men. But maybe because I never could separate matters of the heart from matters of my lady parts, I consciously decided not to lust after men. It worked great until Max walked into that training room and every fiber of my body was acutely aware of him.

As I gun the engine, a realization dawns on me. If I can't even entertain the idea of going out with a man for drinks without Max's image popping into my head, I'm in bigger trouble than I thought. And I have a hunch I'll be in even more trouble after Saturday.

Chapter Nine

Max

"Why the hell did you bring food for ten people?" I ask Alice. My sister stands in the doorway of my apartment, carrying one enormous food bag in each hand. It's Friday night and we're watching a soccer game on TV. Christopher will join us too.

"Hello to you too, ungrateful bastard." She kisses my cheek, walking past me into my apartment. "I brought you pecan pie, but I'm reconsidering if I should give it to you. Maybe I'll eat it myself to punish you."

"I'm deeply sorry," I instantly say, giving her a mocking bow. That's my favorite kind of pie, and I'd do anything for a slice, including being on my very best behavior. I relieve Alice of the food bags and we both head to the kitchen.

"I signed the papers for the new restaurant today, by the way," she informs me.

"Congratulations. Did Sleazeball give you a hard time?"

"No, he actually looked like he was scared out

of his wits. Kept asking me if my brother will join us. He wasn't even making eye contact most of the time. Do you happen to have anything to do with it?"

"Not at all," I say with a straight face. "Why didn't you say something about signing the papers? I would've bought champagne to celebrate. I only have beer."

"I like beer."

"Yeah, but it's not for celebrations. Let's go out somewhere. You deserve a treat. I'm inviting you."

She tilts her head, pursing her lips. "I spend my days in a restaurant. I like celebrating at home. I'm going to watch soccer, and I have two brothers to annoy. That sounds like the perfect way to celebrate to me."

"Okay." I chuckle as I steal a bite from the pie she brought. "Wait a minute, your restaurant doesn't have pecan pie."

"No, I asked the cook to make it especially for you," Alice explains as we arrange everything on plates. "And I brought some extra so you can eat leftovers tomorrow. Can't let my little brother starve." She opens the door to my refrigerator, pointing to the emptiness inside and smirking.

We carry the plates to the living room, placing them on the coffee table in front of the enormous couch. I live in a condo in downtown San Francisco, on the tenth floor. My favorite part is by far the large balcony, on which I hung a hammock. The biggest downside is that being downtown, there's permanent traffic noise I can hear even from up here. I could have chosen to live in a quieter neighborhood, but from here, I only need ten minutes to get to the office. In London, I lived in a quiet, residential area, but I wasted a big chunk of each day in traffic.

"You do know that I survived living in London all by myself for years, right?"

Alice shrugs one shoulder, slumping on the couch. "But you came back because you missed us."

I hold up a finger. "I never said that was the reason."

"You didn't admit it, but I know it. Say it." She gives me a smug look, and her eyes flash with amusement. "Say. It."

For a moment I debate holding my ground and teasing her some more, but I know Alice. She'll pester me until I give in, and the secret to outsmarting Alice is knowing when to choose my battles.

"Fine, I admit it. I missed all of you."

Alice fist bumps into the air before digging into my pie. "Switch on the TV. The game will begin in two minutes. When is Christopher arriving?"

"No idea." I click the remote, switching on the TV. At the same time, the doorbell rings. "It's open," I say loudly, and Christopher comes in.

"Food," he exclaims when he reaches the couch, immediately digging into the pie, his eyes glued to the TV. I exchange a look with Alice.

"Your already appalling manners seem to further disappear by the day, Christopher," Alice admonishes him.

"Hi, Max. Hi, Alice," he greets. We concentrate on the game for the next forty-five minutes.

"Anyone want to join me in furniture hunting for the new restaurant tomorrow morning? Pippa is coming too."

"Pippa shouldn't go anywhere. She's doing too much stuff as it is," I reply. Her belly is round and huge even though she has a few months until she's due, and it can't be comfortable to carry around.

Alice smirks. "You know, I'm getting tired of you guys acting like clueless alphas, and so is Pippa."

"What's that supposed to mean?" Christopher asks.

"That you have no clue about pregnancies, but you like to talk a lot. *Oh, she shouldn't do this, she shouldn't do that.*" Alice glares at both of us. "Pippa has plenty of books about pregnancies. You can always do some reading on the subject before opening your big mouths."

Christopher and I grimace at the same time. No way.

"You think your balls will fall off if you read a pregnancy book?" Her glare becomes more pronounced. "Men."

"Sisters...," Christopher mutters. "You worry about them, and all they do is give you shit."

I'm smart and keep my mouth shut, but I'm in complete agreement with him. We return to watching the game, and during the break, Alice asks, "You didn't answer. Can either of you join me tomorrow? I'm not actually going to buy anything, but I need inspiration and would love your opinion too. Blake is coming too, but the more the merrier."

"I'll go," Christopher says, at the same time I reply, "Can't."

They both look at me.

"Care to share your plans?" Alice asks.

"I'm having breakfast with Jonesie." I try to sound casual. Alice nods, taking her phone out of her bag and typing on it.

"How is she holding up with her grandmother's illness?" she asks.

"She doesn't speak about it much, but I know it's hard."

"You're dating Jonesie?" Christopher asks abruptly. Alice is focusing on her phone again, but she has that expression on that says, *I'm not eavesdropping, but in fact, I totally am.*

"No, it's not like that," I answer quickly. "We're just going out to catch up."

Christopher snorts. "That friendship thing isn't working out, is it?"

When I told him about Emilia weeks ago, he insisted there's no such thing as friendship between a man and a woman. I countered by insisting that we'd been friends as kids.

"Oh my God," Alice exclaims, dropping all pretense of typing on her phone. "I can't believe this hasn't even crossed my mind."

"Spill it out," Christopher says with a shit-eating grin on his face.

I eye the two of them with suspicion. They have the habit of ganging up on me, but I don't see how I can avoid it now.

"I thought we could just pick up our friendship where we left off years ago...." I shrug, leaving my sentence hanging.

"And let me guess. She grew a pair of breasts, and you're suddenly thinking with your penis instead of your brain?" Christopher asks. Ah yes, I can always count on him to deliver a punch straight to the gut.

I groan in response. "It's not just that."

Alice cocks an eyebrow.

"All right, that's a big part. I'm attracted to her. *Very* attracted to her. But she also means more to me."

"Define more," Alice presses.

"I want her to be safe and happy, and every time I imagine her going out with someone, I feel the need to kick something. So...." My voice trails off, because I'm not sure how to put everything into words.

"Holy shit!" My sister sits cross-legged on the couch, resting her head in her hands. "I can't believe I was so oblivious. Pippa would have picked up on it immediately. I should tell her."

"Please don't," I say.

"You're right. Her twins are almost here, so she has enough on her plate already. You're stuck with me, then. The family's second-rate matchmaker. I can't believe it. You were inseparable when she lived on our street. It would be so romantic if the two of you ended up together."

Christopher and I both take a good look at her to make sure she's not pulling my leg. Nope, she's serious.

"You sound like Summer now," Christopher says cautiously.

Alice gives us both the stink eye. "I *do* have a romantic side, but if the secret gets out of this room, I will kick both your asses."

"Alice, the game's started again," I tell her.

"But this is so much more interesting." She grins at me, rubbing her palms together in excitement.

"So what's keeping you from moving from friendship to something else?" Christopher asks.

When I don't say anything, Alice says, "Let me guess. You're afraid that if whatever *something else* entails goes south, you'll lose her friendship too?"

"Yeah, that. Exactly." I'm somewhat stupefied at my sister's ability to put my struggle into a coherent sentence.

"When's the last time you got laid?" my brother asks.

"What's that got to do with anything?" I retort.

"A long time then," he concludes.

"Almost one month," I say.

Alice frowns, counting on her fingers, then

smiles triumphantly. "Since you started your therapy sessions with Emilia."

I nod, scratching my jaw. "It's ridiculous, but just thinking about going out with other women makes me feel guilty."

Christopher stands up on his feet. "Let me get this straight. You don't want to sleep with her because she's your friend, and you don't want to ruin your friendship, but you also don't want to sleep with other women because you feel guilty?"

"That sums it up," I say.

"You're screwed," my brother concludes.

"Tell me something I don't know."

"Your logic is screwed," Christopher insists, sitting again. "If you want her, go after her."

"It's not that simple."

Christopher shrugs. "What's the worse that can happen? If it doesn't work out, you move on, and she moves on."

That's exactly the problem. If things don't work out, we won't stay friends. Moving on will mean she won't be in my life at all, and I'd rather have her in my life, no matter how.

"How about this," Christopher says. "I can be her friend instead. I look the same as you. Then you can get in her bed. Or I can do what you don't have the balls to do, and you can be the friend."

"I'm not in the mood for jokes."

"The world is officially coming to an end then," Alice says dramatically.

"What can I do to get the two of you off my

back?" I ask, regretting my decision more and more with each passing second. Celebratory sounds come from the TV screen, a sure sign that one of the teams scored, but no one is paying any attention to the game.

"Err, not invite us in the first place?" Alice suggests.

"Great idea. I'm revoking the invitation."

"Too late," my sister says. "Besides, if you invited us, it's because deep down, you know that you need to be talked into doing—"

"Emilia," Christopher finishes the sentence for her. Now I'm just pissed at both of them.

"I don't need to be talked into anything. I'm this close"—I hold my thumb and forefinger close to each other in demonstration—"to jumping her bones in that training room. If anything, I need the two of you to hold me back."

"Oooookay," Alice says. "Clearly, someone's bottled up too much sexual tension." Looking at Christopher, she tells him, "I bet he lasts two more sessions before he lashes out at poor Emilia."

Christopher taps his finger on his bottle. "One session. Actually, I bet he won't make it through breakfast tomorrow."

Alice frowns as if considering her words. "No bet."

Fucking fantastic.

Chapter Ten

Emilia

On Saturday morning Grams is in a good mood, and remarkably present. I'm leaving in one hour to meet Max for breakfast, and I'm nowhere near ready. Right now I'm sitting with Grams on the couch on the back porch. I'm braiding her hair in an elegant bun. She's always happier when her hair looks beautiful.

"I've been thinking about your father," she says out of the blue when I'm halfway done. My fingers freeze in her silver hair. Good thing we're sitting, because my knees have turned to Jell-O. Grams hasn't mentioned my father by name or referred to him at all since he left. Exactly one year after, she rounded up all the pictures she had of him and burned them.

"You have?" I ask quietly. "Why?"

"I was wondering what became of him."

Pressing my lips together, I continue to work on her hair, which proves to be a challenge because my hands turned sweaty all of a sudden. I am one hundred percent sure *nothing* became of him.

"I'd like to see him again," she continues, her words shocking me to the bone, even more so because at this moment Grams is herself, not in the clutches of her disease. An age-old pain washes over me, reminding me that some wounds don't heal with time.

"He left us, Grams." My voice is strong, and I'm proud. "I don't—"

"I know, child. But you and I both know I'm not going to be myself much longer. You think I don't know I lose my mind at least once a day?"

"You're not losing your mind," I say with a shaky voice. Damn it. She needs reassurance right now, not for me to break down. At least she sits with her back to me, so she can't see my eyes, which are burning.

"I'd like to see him once before it's too late. Call me soft, but he's my son. Blood is blood. Promise you'll think about it?"

"Promise." You don't say no to the woman who worked herself to exhaustion to raise you. With trembling fingers, I finish her hairdo, then go about preparing for my outing.

I spend a long time in front of my closet, trying to decide what to wear, which is ridiculous. This is not a date; it's just two friends going out. *We did this hundreds of times when we were kids*, I tell myself. Yeah, but that was before we both developed a flirting muscle. I end up choosing a knee-length, blue dress with a rather deep V-neckline, but what the hell. I also straighten my wild mane until not one hair sticks in the wrong direction.

Mrs. Wilson, the elderly neighbor who agreed to watch Grams while I'm out, arrives just in time. She's a lovely woman, and she's Grams's best friend. My grandmother doesn't have any living relatives with the exception of my father and me, but Mrs. Wilson is as close as family. Since Ms. Adams, Grams's caretaker, only watches Grams on weekdays, Mrs. Wilson kindly offered to help me out in the evenings or weekends when I need a break. I don't often take her up on her offer, but today I did.

Before I leave the house, I grab a jacket. It's mid-March, but it's not too warm. Grinning at the sky, I take a deep breath, climbing in my car.

When I'm a few blocks away from my destination, my engine begins coughing, and I know I'm in for trouble. I pull over, cursing, and call the tow service, and then I text Max.

Emilia: My car just broke down. I'll head to the restaurant as soon as the tow service is here.

Max: I'll pick you up.

Emilia: No need. I'll walk. It's just a few blocks.

After the tow service takes away my car I head to the restaurant, and by the time I reach the gate, I'm feeling blisters in the making on the balls of my feet. I have a love-hate relationship with high heels, and right now, it leans pretty heavily on the hate side.

"Well you look amazing," Max's voice resounds from behind me. I swirl around, facing him. He takes a step back, whistling loudly, scrutinizing me from head to toe, his eyes revealing that he's entertaining dangerous thoughts. Just as I am. He's quite the looker, wearing simple jeans and a black polo shirt, which showcases his upper body. Those strong arms and shoulders are my kryptonite.

"I'll have to work hard to fend off any suitors today, Emilia. You look absolutely stunning." Leaning in to me, he adds, "I'll have to work even harder to keep myself from doing any *eye training*."

"I have full confidence in you. And I'll return the favor and protect you from women. I'm sure you're a magnet."

"You have no idea."

I roll my eyes, even though my breath catches a tad as he invades my personal space. "You're too cocky for your own good, Bennett." Then I turn around, scanning the restaurant. It's an eclectic mix of new and old, shabby chic and sleek elegance. "So, what is this place?"

"You didn't look it up when I texted you the address?"

"Nah, didn't occur to me," I admit.

"They have the most famous pancakes in San Francisco. They even have strawberry jam. Not sure if it'll be as good as the one Grams used to make, but we can try it."

I try to croak out "thank you," but the words

catch in my throat. When we were kids, Grams used to make the most delicious strawberry jam on the planet, and pancakes with jam was our secret, rebel midnight snack.

"I can't believe you remember that," I say softly. In response, he winks at me, then asks the waiter to give us a table. We're led to the center of the room to a table for two. I take my seat, wondering how this can feel so easy and so weird at the same time.

"I told you I remember everything about you. Including that your hair was all wild, and I miss it. It suited you."

Holy crap. This man gives the best compliments, and I'm not even sure he knows it. "Well, I like it tame these days. It's shiny and glossy."

He tilts his head to the side, scorching me with his eyes. "Wild always trumps tame, Emilia."

"Depends on the... situation." And cue my thoughts veering to Smutland again. Time for a change in topic. "How about those pancakes?" I'm hungry now as I open the menu in front of me. "Wow. They have thirty-three types of pancakes."

"Hey, this isn't some run-of-the-mill pancake stand. I did thorough research. Only the best for my girl."

My cheeks heat up at the words *my girl*, and we exchange a furtive glance.

"There was another one downtown that had great reviews, but there is a beach near this one. Thought we could take a walk afterward. You always loved the water."

"I did. I still do."

We each order coffee and pancakes—one of mine with strawberry jam. As I wonder if it'll be as good as Grams's, my mind slides to the conversation I had with her this morning.

"Emilia, everything okay?" Max asks.

"Mmm... yeah...." Usually, I'd make up a reason for my momentary blip, but this is Max, *my Max*. Being open with him comes to me naturally in a way it never did with anyone else. "I had an interesting conversation with Grams this morning. She'd like to see my father again."

Max's features instantly harden. "The asshole who took off after your mom's funeral?"

"That's the only father I have, unfortunately."

"But she hated his guts. She made a bonfire to burn his stuff."

I smile despite myself. Max would know all about the fire. We were lurking around in the shadows, waiting for Grams to leave so I could salvage at least some pictures before they burned to a crisp. When Grams finally went back to the house, Max claimed it was a man's job (he was ten), tried his luck—and failed. Then I tried. We ended up with no pictures, and four hands full of blisters. Fun times.

"I know, and she's never mentioned him before...."

"What do you want?"

"To stab him with a butter knife repeatedly."

"That's my girl." He leans his hand over the

table, rubbing the pad of his thumb on the back of my hand in small circles. I think the gesture was meant to calm me, but instead it sets me on edge.

"But I should at least try to find him, for her. I owe her so much. And I want her to be happy. I don't even know how to go about it, though. No idea how much a private investigator would cost."

Max remains silent, the pad of his thumb still on the back of my hand, wreaking havoc on my senses.

"Bennett Enterprises works with professionals who run background research on potential business partners. I can ask them to locate your father. It wouldn't cost you anything, and before you protest, we're already paying them a shitload of money anyway."

It takes a few seconds for his words to sink in. "You'd do that?"

"I'd do anything you ask me, Emilia. I want you to be happy."

My shoulders feel suddenly lighter, as if a weight was lifted off them, but I'm not sure I can say thank you without tearing up. This conversation went too serious just a few minutes into our breakfast. Time to lighten it up.

"Anything is a big word, Bennett. You sure you can make good on that?"

"I don't make promises I don't intend to keep. Especially big ones."

Heat spears me at his last two words. My mind has two directions today. Sad or smutty.

"Let me know what you decide," he says, pulling back as the waiter arrives with our pancakes.

"Thank you."

"Oh my God, this is pancake heaven," I say through my full mouth about one hour later, while finishing my third pancake. "You've spoiled me for other pancakes. None will measure up to this."

"We can come back here anytime you want."

He smiles at me, and I swear the sight sends me into a tailspin; then he glances at my empty plate. "Another pancake?"

"Nah, I'm full," I declare, but then I eye the half pancake lying abandoned on his plate.

He chuckles. "Take it, I know you want it. Just so you know, this is very special treatment. I usually give shit to anyone who tries to steal my food."

"Why, thank you. And it's not called stealing if you're giving it to me." I take it without hesitation and dig in to it right away.

"If you're done, we can take off to the beach."

I nearly squeal. Through a mouthful, I try to explain that it's a great idea, but Max holds up a hand, stopping me.

"No words needed. I got the idea."

No words needed. That could sum up our friendship. He could anticipate what I wanted even before I said it, that much was true in the past, and it hasn't changed. When the waiter brings us the bill, I nearly choke. I noticed the high prices on the menu, but somehow I wasn't adding numbers up while I stuffed my face.

"How can they charge so much for pancakes?" I ask, already hyperventilating.

"I've got it covered," Max says, "don't worry."

"No. I don't want you to pay for me."

He clenches his jaw. "I asked you to come here."

"It's not a date."

Silence stretches for a few seconds. "No, it's two friends going out and catching up. And since I was the friend who suggested coming to an expensive restaurant, it's only fair I cover the bill. Anything against that?"

"No," I mumble.

"When did you get so stubborn?" he asks, but now his voice is gentle again.

"Grams says I always had the gene, but I was a late bloomer."

Max laughs, and I love the sound.

The beach is a few minutes away on foot, and it's swarming with people walking up and down its length when we descend on it. Max and I both take off our shoes, holding them in our hands as we walk on the sand.

"Brave enough to soak your feet in the water?" I ask, half joking.

"It'll be freezing," he warns.

"Afraid your balls will fall off, Bennett?" I elbow him playfully.

"You're bad for my no-challenge resolution, Jonesie."

He stalks toward the water, and I trail behind him.

"Men are so predictable," I inform him. "Whenever someone challenges you, you can't help yourself."

Max spins around, tilting his head to one side. "You think you have me all figured out, don't you?"

I shrug. "I don't want to brag, but...." I point to his feet in the water, as if that would explain it all. Without any warning, Max lifts me, one arm under my knees, the other one around my back. We both drop the shoes on the sand before he walks into the water up to his knees, with no signs of stopping.

I shriek, then laugh, and he laughs with me, and it's the most perfect moment.

"What are you doing?" I ask between fits of laughter. "You're crazy. The water is freezing."

"You make me crazy," he says, and he's up to his waist in the water. "I was the bad influence when we were kids, but I think the roles are reversed now."

"You make me proud, Bennett."

We both stop laughing for a moment, long enough to look straight at each other. I can practically see my question mirrored in his eyes. What the hell are we doing? Is this friendship? Is it more?

He's up to his waist in freezing water—but holding my ass carefully over the water so I don't get wet—and even though this isn't a date, it feels better than any date I've had.

And maybe if we weren't so lost in each other, we would have noticed the wave about to hit us, but we don't until it's too late and we're both drenched. The universe's way of saying, stop eye fucking your best friend.

"Holy shit." I shriek, tightening my arms around his neck. "This is c-c-c-cold."

Max doesn't say one word, and when I look up at him, I realize it's because his teeth are chattering.

"Let's get out," I say, and I'm not sure if my words are intelligible, because my teeth are chattering too. But Max gets the gist of it and starts moving back to the shore.

"You can put me down, I'm wet anyway," I tell him. "You'll move faster if you're not carrying me."

Max merely shakes his head and pulls me to him protectively, which I find incredibly sweet.

"So cold," is all I can say once we're on the beach. Max puts me down and then runs his hands up and down my arms in an attempt to warm me, but that's not doing much good.

"Let's go to my car," he says, "I have a towel."

"Why do you have a towel?"

"I have the bag for the training session on Monday inside, and I always shower after the session."

We pick up our shoes, which we left on the sand, and a tourist group is staring at us like we're crazy, which I suppose we are. So why am I grinning from ear to ear even though I'm about to go into hypothermia? Because I'm with Max, that's why.

He leads the way to his car, taking my hand in his. I relish the warmth radiating from the point of contact. When we reach the car, Max opens the trunk, fishes the towel out of his gym bag, and wraps it around me.

"I can do it," I murmur.

"Let me," he says, and I don't object anymore, because it feels too good.

"Go change into your training clothes," I tell him. With a nod, he slings the bag on his shoulder and heads inside the restaurant where we had our pancakes, returning a few minutes later. "I'm still cold."

"Short of taking off your clothes, I don't know how you'll stop being cold," he says.

"Oh shucks, I always thought that you asking me to take off my clothes would sound sexier than this."

He groans, and that's when I realize what I just said.

"You thought about me telling you to take off your clothes? You're killing me, Emilia."

Well, the cat's out of the bag now. Still, I try to turn the tide around. "No, I'm just blabbering, I—"

"Well, I have."

"Of course you did."

"Yeah. Since I saw you the first time again. I'm a man, and you're beautiful. But you're Emilia. My Jonesie."

"Max…."

He is inches away from me, and our lips are so close I would only have to lean in a little to touch them.

"I need to take you home. If you get sick, it'll just give Grams another reason to hate me."

"She doesn't hate you. Just thinks you were a bad influence. She caught us smoking on the roof. We were eleven."

"*Attempting* to smoke," Max corrects. "And she chased me out of your house with a broomstick. She hates me."

Once we're both inside the car, Max guns the engine and turns on the heat, and things feel infinitely better within seconds. I have his towel covering my shoulders and chest, but since it's wet too, I pry it away, tossing it in the back. Max tightens his hands on the wheel, suddenly very focused on the road.

"Max?"

"You're not wearing a bra," he says in a gruff voice.

Oh shit. The towel was covering me before, but now…. My nipples usually behave themselves, but obviously the combination of cold water and Max is too powerful a cocktail for them. I cross my arms over my chest, embarrassed.

"Things are more complicated when you have a dirty mind," he says, more to himself than to me.

"You're the complication," I inform him.

"Just so you know, you're the only one who can call me a complication and get away with it."

"Get over yourself, Max." Turning my head to look out the window, I can't help giggling.

Chapter Eleven

Emilia

"This is a beautiful house," Max says as we arrive.

"Thank you. Grams loves it too." As we step inside, I ask, "Mrs. Wilson?"

"Emilia," she exclaims when she sees me. "What happened to you?"

Max answers for me. "Got in the ocean, didn't see the wave coming. Afraid it's all my fault. I'm Max." He holds out the hand, and Mrs. Wilson shakes it, eyeing him shamelessly.

"Since you returned, I'll be going," she says. "Grams is in the backyard."

After she leaves, I turn to Max. "I'll go take a hot shower and change quickly. Make yourself at home."

After taking a hot shower, I put on a dress made out of wool—and I'm still cold. I think it seeped into my bones.

I find Max inspecting my mini library—four shelves the size of my arm—as if searching for something.

"Let's go in the backyard. But she's not the way you remember her. I can't promise she'll know who you are," I warn him and then lead him outside.

"Grams?" I ask tentatively, sitting on the couch next to her. "Look who's here."

She snaps her head up to me, and then to Max, and then to my relief, she says, "Max, my dear boy. You've grown into quite a man."

She quickly gets to her feet and pulls Max in for a tight hug.

"You don't look a day older then when I last saw you, ma'am," Max says, and that is almost true. On the outside, my Grams looks almost exactly as she did fifteen years ago.

"Ah, you're such a charmer." She looks him up and down. "You grew up to be such a fine man. Are you a smoker?"

"No, ma'am. Learned my lesson. Whenever someone asks me if I smoke, I still remember you chasing me with that broomstick."

"As you should." Grams looks around confused as she sits back on the couch. Max sits on a small stool we keep near the couch.

"Violet dear, did you ask him if he wants something to drink?"

My stomach constricts and Max blinks. After having been so lucid this morning, I hoped I would have my old Grams back for a while longer.

"Vi—" he begins, but I interrupt him with a headshake.

"Don't correct her," I whisper to him.

"I'm good, ma'am." His voice wavers on the last word.

Grams inspects Max from head to toe, her eyes darting to me and then back to him. She's becoming increasingly more agitated.

"So, what are your intentions with Violet? She and her little Emilia are precious and deserve to be loved."

Stunned, I fiddle with my hands in my lap, biting down on my lip.

"Then you have nothing to worry about," Max says, sounding like his usual, relaxed self again. He turns his head to me, his gaze lingering briefly on my face before dropping to my hands, which are trembling. Without hesitation, he reaches out, placing a strong, reassuring hand above mine.

"I promise to take care of both your precious girls, make them happy for as long as I can."

It's a good thing that neither Grams nor Max addresses me, because I couldn't bring up any words. I focus on blinking back my tears and keeping my smile in place.

"You have a wonderful boy, here, Violet," she says. "Take good care of him. I'll keep an eye on you, young boy."

"As you should," Max replies.

Standing up, Grams says, "Now, I'll leave you two lovebirds here."

"I'll help—"

"No need," she cuts me off. "I might be an

old woman, but I don't need to be babysat. I'm going to watch some TV in my bedroom."

She enters the house, and I let out a long, shaky breath.

***

Max

"That was rough," I say, moving next to her on the couch.

"Yeah." Her voice is small—damn it, she seems to have shrunk in the span of a few minutes. It kills me to know she's hurting.

"If it was hard for me, I can't imagine what it must be like for you."

She purses her lips, as if trying to swallow her words, hide her feelings.

"Talk to me, Emilia. You don't have to hide from me, or pretend."

"I—" She takes a deep breath before finally opening up. "It's an emotional roller coaster every day. I never know when she's going to have a good moment or a bad one. Even though she's been sick for a while, I can't get used to it. I can't accept it."

I pull her into my arms, and she tucks her feet under her, molding the side of her upper body against my chest, not even attempting to move away. I kiss the top of her head, inhaling her floral scent, brainstorming for a way to calm her down. Cracking a joke doesn't seem right, and I'm at a loss for what to say. How can I be so clueless? Maybe I should listen more to Sebastian and Logan when they talk about their women. I've never been in this position before, because I never got close enough to a woman for her to show me her vulnerable side.

Hand me any situation at the office, I can handle it. Emilia hurting in my arms? Zero solutions come to my mind, and that better change fast. My girl is a mess, trembling in my arms. Her pain is so raw I can almost feel it.

"Thank you for telling her that you'll take care of…." Her words fade as small sobs take over. "It calmed her down."

One of her hands is on my chest, and I clasp my fingers around her wrist.

"Now I need you to calm down, Emilia. You're so brave."

"Doing what you have to do isn't brave."

I pull her even closer to me, running my hand up and down her back, but it's not helping. Her next words tumble out unintelligibly. "I'm so afraid of losing her, and—"

"Emilia!" With my thumb, I tip her chin up until she has no choice but to look at me. She inhales sharply, and I slide my thumb over her lower lip, tracing the contour of her mouth from one end to the other.

Feeling her soft, plump lip under the pad of my thumb sends a jolt right through my groin. She opens her mouth infinitesimally. For a split second, both of us stay stock-still. And then I kiss her. *Jesus.*

Her mouth is exquisite. Her lips are full and sweet, and she opens them up for me without reservation. She lets out a low, delicious moan when I slip my tongue inside, claiming her warm, sweet mouth, exploring it. Our tongues intertwine, and I take control, commanding the kiss. In this moment, nothing else exists except this woman. I need more of her. I want more—everything. I move my hand, which was on her waist, up to her chest and groan when I discover she's not wearing a bra. I cup one breast over the fabric, and her nipple turns to a pebble in my hand. She rewards me with the most delicious moan. I instantly turn rock-hard for her, and pull her closer to me, needing to touch every part of her. She shifts around, hiking one leg over me, straddling me, and putting both her breasts right where I can touch them. Like a man possessed, I lightly twist one of her nipples through the material of her dress. A crazy thought takes shape into my mind. *This woman is mine, and I won't let her go.*

She moans against my mouth, fisting my shirt, pressing her center against my erection. We groan in each other's mouths. It takes every fiber in my body not to push the dress up her waist and rip away her panties. I pull away from her just before losing my last shreds of decency. Emilia buries her head in my neck, and feeling her hot breath on my skin isn't helping. At all. She fists my shirt with both her hands. I thread my fingers in her hair, not ready to let her go, to let the moment end.

"Tell me one thing," I say in her ear, enjoying

the way goose bumps form on her arms. "Just one."

"What?"

"Are you wet for me?"

"Oh." She tightens her fists, pulling at my shirt. "Yes. I am, Max. I really am."

My control damn near snaps, but she smartly pulls away, moving to my left on the couch.

"This was the only thing that occurred to me to calm you down," I say honestly.

She chuckles. "Funny, I thought the same in the elevator. Dirty minds think alike."

I can't take my eyes off her lips. They're swollen from the kiss, and all I can think about is kissing them again. As if sensing danger, she shifts further away from me.

"You think this space is enough to keep me from you?"

She sighs, her expression growing serious. Guilt gnaws at me.

"I'm sorry," I offer.

"I know you," she says lightly. "You're not sorry at all."

"Damn you, Jonesie, I was trying to say the right thing." After a brief but charged pause, I add, "Are you sorry?"

"I don't want to lose you as a friend, Max. I—"

"I crossed the line."

"I didn't exactly stop you." She smiles, but my insides constrict because I want this, and at the same time, I *don't* want to want this. I try to read her body language. Her shoulders are straight and tense, and desire glints in her eyes. A slight tremor still runs through her body. "I'm not good with romantic relationships."

"That makes two of us," I say. The thing is, I've never made an effort to make relationships work. I hadn't felt the need for more than a good time. But now, looking at this amazing woman in front of me, hell. I do want to make things work. Shit. I'm in deep shit, or shitty shit as Alice would say.

"Friendship is different. It runs deeper, it's more constant, it's forever," she continues. "You know what I have stuffed in my closet?"

I grin. "A battery-operated friend?"

"That too. Next to my unused wedding dress."

Sucker punched. "Why do you keep it? Are you still in love with him?"

She shakes her head. "Nah, it's been more than six months. I was this close"—she holds her thumb and forefinger a fraction of an inch apart—"to throwing eggs at his car when he dumped me. I was angry, still am, I think. But I'm not in love with him."

"If you ever feel the need to make good on the eggs part, I can help you. I have excellent aim."

"I know. You were the one who introduced me to the world of throwing eggs when Johnson bailed on me."

"That's right." Shit, I'd better come clean. "In

the interest of honesty, Johnson didn't bail on you. I might have scared him off."

"What? I was about to sign us up as dance partners for the end of year dance."

"Yeah, and I had it on good authority that he was a lousy dancer. He just wanted to kiss you."

"We were twelve," she exclaims.

"Yeah. Boys lose their brain to their penis about one year earlier."

"I can't believe this." She shakes her head, but smiles, elbowing me. "You're such an ass."

"Was protecting you. I'm not even going to say I was sorry."

"Any other times you protected me?" She shoots daggers with her eyes at me.

"Now that you mention it, remember Smith?"

She groans. "The guy I was working with on the chemistry project, who mysteriously dropped out and found another teammate?"

"That's the one. He'd made a bet with his friends that he'd be your first kiss."

"What if I wanted him to be?"

Sucker punched for the second time in less than ten minutes. "He wasn't good enough for you. None of them were."

"I see. It's a good thing I moved, then, or I would have never dated."

I'm about to remark that she wouldn't have gotten engaged or hurt if that was the case, but I sound too much like a caveman even to my own mind. She looks at me with a mix of amusement and annoyance.

"So why are you keeping the wedding dress?" I ask.

"Trying to sell it, haven't found a buyer yet. I had some interest right when you arrived at the clinic, but she ended up not buying it. It's weird having it in my closet though. It symbolized a big chunk of my hopes and dreams, and now it's just the reminder of another failure."

I lean over to her, tilting her head up.

"You're not going to kiss me again, are you?" she whispers, licking her lips.

"No. Just wanted to say, don't think of it as failure, Jonesie. It was experience. He wasn't man enough to fight for a woman like you."

The more time I spend with her, the more I want to be that man who fights for her. So what if I don't have a great record with women? I never wanted to make an effort before, and damn it, I want to now. Emilia makes me want things I never wanted before, and I don't want them with anyone else. I want them with her. But I'll take it slow. If she needs me to be her friend for now, that's what I'll be.

I rise to my feet, stretching my back. "I'll go now."

"Oh." She's evidently disappointed.

We leave the porch, and as we make our way through the house toward the front door, I say, "I'll send a company driver on Monday morning to get you to the clinic."

"What? Oh, my car. I'll just take the bus."

I cock an eyebrow. "You'll need at least twice as long with a bus."

"True, but it doesn't matter."

"Emilia—"

"Max!"

"I'll send a car for you, and that's that."

"You're unbelievable."

"I just promised Grams I'll take care of you."

"And now you're playing dirty."

"I've been known to do that to get my way. I'm just looking out for you." I push a strand of her hair behind her ear and her entire body hums at the skin-on-skin contact. She licks her lower lip, noticing too late that I'm eyeing her mouth.

"Don't fight me," I insist.

"Okay. Thank you. I hoped you'll stay a while longer." She stands awkwardly in front of the open front door.

"I can go back to being just your friend on Monday, Jonesie. If I stay any longer today, I'll kiss you again, no questions asked."

"See you on Monday." Her eyes widen, and she gnaws at that delicious lip of hers. How the hell am I supposed to spend time with this strong, sweet, all-around amazing woman and not kiss her again?

Chapter Twelve

Emilia

I sleep badly on Saturday night and even worse on Sunday. I toss and turn the entire night, the memory of Max's lips on mine giving me hot flashes. Damn that man can kiss. Dragging my hands down my face, I turn to look at the clock. It's five in the morning. Giving up on the idea of sleep, I leave my bed, hop into shorts, put on my gym bra and a shirt, and go for a run. It usually helps me clear my head, but now, the longer I run the more I think about Max. With a jolt, I realize I'm about to see him in a few hours. With another jolt, I remember we'll be doing water exercises today. Me and Max alone in a swimming pool. This will be interesting. I realize I haven't seen him shirtless until now, even though his soaked shirt on Saturday highlighted his toned, delicious body. A small voice at the back of my head says *This will be a disaster*, but I do my best to ignore it.

The driver arrives at seven o'clock sharp, as promised. When I start telling him the address of the clinic, he politely informs me Max already gave him all the details.

He nods curtly, opening the door for me. After I slide inside the car, I find a brown bag with my name on it. Immediately, I pry the bag open, revealing the contents. A book! Not just any book, but the first volume in the Chronicles of Narnia series, which was my favorite book as a kid.

I'm about to ask the driver about it, then decide to ask the source directly. Grinning, I fish out my phone from my bag and text him.

Emilia: You just made this book junkie happy. I'd lost my copy of the book and never got around to buying another one.

His reply is almost instant.

Max: I know, saw all the other volumes in your library except this one.

Licking my lips, I hover my thumbs above the screen, wondering if I should bring up Saturday's kiss. Maybe it would help clear the air. Then I remember our second session together—the last time we attempted to clear the air—and I decide to take a much less straightforward way.

Emilia: So is this a talking book?

He doesn't answer. Stomach in knots, I peer out the window, resting my forehead against the cool glass. As I watch the gray clouds hanging low on the sky, adrenaline strums through my veins. I'm so lost in the beautiful view that I jump in my seat when my phone finally vibrates.

Max: What's that supposed to mean?

I type back as fast as I can, my fingers

prickling with excitement.

Emilia: When you want to tell me something, but don't know how, so you send a message through things.

As soon as I press Send the little dots indicating he's writing appear, and I hold my breath.

Max: All books have messages in them. That's the point.

Emilia: Smartass. You know what I mean.

Max: Ah, not really. But if it would say something, it would be along the lines of Sorry, I'm not sorry.

What the heck?

Emilia: You are confusing me.

Max: Ha! That was my goal.

Emilia: Care to elaborate?

Max: Saturday you said all men were easy to figure out. I thought I'd raise that bar of yours a little. I'm going to a meeting now. See you in a few hours.

Pushing my phone to one side and grinning from ear to ear, I mull over his words. When the driver drops me in front of the clinic, I have a weird pep in my step as I walk inside. From this day on, I will call it the Max Effect.

I have two patients before my scheduled session with the man of the day, and for the first time in a long time, I can't fully concentrate on my patients. I go through the motions, keeping an eye on them, but my mind is elsewhere, reliving that all-consuming kiss from Saturday.

After I finish with the last patient before Max, I head to the hall adjacent to the clinic, where the swimming pool is. Unlike the many training rooms, we only have one pool, but we make sure to only book one patient at a time to ensure *intimacy*. The word is strangely ironic in this case.

Since I still have a few minutes until our session begins, I do a few laps in the water. Swimming usually has a calming effect on me. The touch of the water usually cools my head, but all it does today is remind me of Saturday morning, of the two of us in the ocean.

Something shifted between Max and me, and it has as much to do with the kiss as with the way he spoke to Grams. He was gentle and kind, and I didn't think he could possibly get deeper under my skin, but he did. Pushing myself out of the water, I stand on the cold tile and rearrange my hair, pulling it tighter into a bun.

"If this is how I get to see you from now on, sign me up for lifelong therapy, Jonesie."

I swirl around, and holy smokes and fire. Max is wearing nothing but swim shorts, and he is hotter than anyone has the right to be. I knew from the first time I saw him that the man works out. But seeing him almost naked.... Yummy. He is *ripped*. He has a stomach that is all but perfect, and I try—and fail—not to gawk at the light trail of hair starting from under his navel and descending further down until it disappears in his shorts.

"I get that you like what you see." Max wiggles his eyebrows, sliding into the water. He leans on his back, floating, giving me a perfect view of his sculpted abs. My fantasy is running wild conjuring images of his package.

Slowly I lower myself in the water and then swim until I'm right next to him, but careful enough not to touch him. His presence in the pool unnerves me. The pool is too small, I tell myself. But I have the suspicion that even an Olympic-sized pool would still appear too small. Max has the kind of presence that feels *too much,* no matter where he is.

"You're okay," I tell him.

Far from appearing offended by my non-compliment, Max chuckles. He's now standing in the pool. "You can try to play it cool all you want, Emilia. I know what you're thinking."

I put my hands on my hips. "And what's that?"

"That I'll be starring in your dirty dreams," he says confidently.

"You already are."

The second the words are out, I clap my hand over my mouth. My entire body feels aflame. I'm surprised the water around me isn't boiling. I don't dare look at Max, instead keeping my eyes on the edge of the pool. His uncontrolled rumbles of laughter fill the room. And they are damn addictive. A chuckle bubbles out of my throat, and before long, I'm laughing so hard, I'm in danger of cracking a rib.

"Please, forget I ever said anything," I say

once I've calmed down somewhat.

Far from obliging me, Max asks, "Are you having a dirty daydream right now?"

"No." My answer would be more believable if it weren't accompanied by a grin, damn it. But being around this man makes me smile. His easygoing, fun way is addictive.

"Yes, you are," he insists. "Difficulty speaking, heavy breathing, I get it. My naked body usually causes this reaction."

Caught.

"Let's start the session," I say in a serious tone. "You are wasting your hard-earned money talking."

Max is beside me after two strokes across the water. "It's worth it to see you blush."

"What are you doing?" I whisper to him. "Saturday we agreed on...." My voice trails off as I realize we didn't actually agree on anything. I just *word vomited* my romantic failures, and Max said nothing.

A devilish smile takes form on his face. "We agreed on nothing. I thought long and hard about you this weekend."

I ignore the way my body sizzles long and hard at his words. Swallowing, I say, "Care to share any conclusions you've reached?"

Max purses his lips as if considering it. "Nah, I think I'll let you fret a little longer. You look delicious when you do it. How about we start the exercises?"

Going through the session proves to be a challenge. The routine for water exercises resembles the one for normal exercises, in that I first perform the exercise, and then my patient repeats it, and I stand nearby, making sure they perform the exercises correctly. The major difference is that a layer of clothing is missing now. Which means I get to stare at and touch Max's bare skin for an hour. Sixty minutes that are both torture and bliss. I sense his gaze on me the entire time, which heats up every nerve ending in my body. Putting some distance between us would be a good idea, except I can't since I'm guiding him through the moves. If I'm honest, I'm not sure distance would help. I can feel his presence even when he is across a room.

"You did that on purpose," I accuse when Max does a simple exercise wrong for the fifth time.

"What? I just don't know how to do the exercise."

"You can't do a simple leg bend?" I counter.

He shrugs, a smile playing on his lips. Max is enjoying himself immensely. "I'll do it much better if your hand is on my thigh."

"Jesus," I mutter, keeping my hands firmly behind my back. "What's gotten into you today?"

"You're standing in this pool, looking irresistible, and all I can think about is how fucking incredible you tasted on Saturday."

I think I might have had a mini orgasm just from hearing him speak like this.

"Max, please do your exercises."

As he finally complies with my request, I step back, feeling victorious. Except then I see the way his chest and ripped muscles contort, and I realize I'm the one who lost.

"You survived the session," I announce when he's done. "You're free to go."

"I have an idea. Let's race. Twenty pool laps."

"I do laps every day. You can't keep up."

"Wanna bet?"

This makes me pay attention. I should have known he has an ulterior motive. "What's the bet?"

"I win, I get to kiss you again."

His gaze is heated, but I feel bold. "I win, you don't mention kissing again. Ever. *And* I get to kick your ass."

"Deal."

"Fine, let's do this. Prepare yourself, Bennett."

I swim with a vengeance, putting one arm in front of the other, propelling myself forward. I am consciously aware I'm not going at my full speed. When I finally touch the end of the pool, I pull myself up, gazing around me. There is a twinge of disappointment as I see Max a few feet behind me. Maybe some part of me wanted to lose. Goddammit.

Max notices I won and stops swimming, instead straightening up and walking toward me, the water rippling around him, caressing his skin. I can't help noticing the way the sinewy lines of his abs flex when he moves.

He advances until he's inches away from me, completely invading my personal space. He's so close my breasts squish against his chest. Instantly my nipples turn to stone. His arms are at my side, palms firmly planted on the edge of the pool. Being trapped between his arms gives me a sense of security, which is ridiculous, because I'm in danger of falling for his charms.

"I won. That means you can't kiss me," I say in a low and unsteady voice. Every inch of my body longs for him, almost painfully so.

"Don't worry, Emilia. I won't kiss you again until you ask me to."

Until. Not unless.

Somehow I find my voice. "What makes you think I will?"

"You want to. You would never have taken the bet otherwise."

"Maybe I just wanted a chance to kick your ass."

"You wouldn't have taken that chance if a part of you didn't want the kiss."

"Know-it-all."

Max tilts his head to the right, scrutinizing me. "I don't know if I can be just your friend. I'll try, but as you can see, I'm failing repeatedly."

"You don't seem to try very hard." Nervously I lick my lower lip, and Max follows the movement with his gaze. His proximity does unspeakable things to me.

"That's right. I'll be honest with you, Emilia. Until now I didn't make an effort in my relationships, and now I think I know why. I couldn't see them going anywhere. But with you... it's different."

"What are you saying?"

"That you're fun, sweet, and always on my mind." He lifts his hand to cup the side of my head, then drags the backs of his fingers down my cheek, moving them along on my jaw. He stops short of touching my mouth. "Part of that is desire, but it's more. I like to be around you, to see you smile. To *make* you smile. You've grown into an amazing woman, Emilia."

"Stop being such a fancy-pants charmer," I whisper.

"You have no idea how much I'd like to charm this bathing suit off you. But I'm not bullshitting you."

I know he's not. He's kept that boyish honesty I loved about him—even if it annoyed me at times, such as when he informed me my pixie cut sucked. Now, though, I have no idea what to do with his information, and judging by his expression, neither does he.

"Max, I...."

He puts a finger on my lips, silencing me. Unfortunately, feeling the warmth of his touch awakens all my senses. I become painfully aware of my hips grazing against his muscular thighs, of our mouths being only a breath away.

"Don't say anything," he says. "We'll just see

where the pieces fall into place."

His eyes have that glint of mischief and determination I know too well. Only now he decidedly delivers it in a very grown-up Max way, which warms my heart... and other parts. Instantly, I know all bets are off.

Chapter Thirteen

Emilia

My grams always used to say, "when one door closes, you kick the shit out of every other door and window, until one opens."

Her own version of *when one door closes, another one opens.* She was never a believer of good things just falling into one's lap, and she raised me the same. So when the repair shop informs me that my car's repairs will be twice as much as I anticipated, I allow myself to panic and fret for a few hours, and then I make a plan. I call a few of my patients who asked me if I'd be willing to do sessions at their homes, and offer my services. Home sessions are usually a pain in the ass, because I don't have all the necessary equipment, but it can work in easier cases. I end up with three evenings booked. It'll be a stretch fitting everything in, but I'm in no position to turn anything down.

What's a girl to do when she has too much on her plate? Arm herself with her two best friends and a sugary, caffeinated drink while on lunch break at work. At least this girl does. My version of wine and a girls' night out.

"You are insane," Evelyn says, and Abby nods vigorously as we enjoy a coffee on our lunch break on Tuesday. We're in the small backyard of the clinic. It's a beautiful April day with the sun shining almost unnaturally bright. Except for two snow-white clouds, the sky is a divine shade of blue. I wish I could be outdoors the entire day, soaking in the light and warmth of the sun. It's beautiful.

"No, I'm trying to pay for my car's repairs," I reply.

"You need to let off steam, or at least have a breather now and again," Abby insists. They both offered to help financially, but I vehemently refused. That's not what friends are for, and I don't take handouts.

"I know what you need," Evelyn says wickedly. "I bet Max wouldn't mind helping you let off steam."

"Yeah," Abby says. "His Royal Highness seems eager enough." Abby has a slightly unhealthy obsession with royal families and uses that moniker for men who pass her gorgeousness test.

"That's between His Maximum Hotness and me," I volley back, surprising both of them.

"What's that supposed to mean?" Evelyn asks. I told them about the kiss on Saturday.

"I have no idea," I admit with a sigh. "But the moniker fits him. He's just… he makes me feel so many things at the same time. Too many."

"That's a good thing," Evelyn insists. "Don't be afraid to feel, Emilia."

A lump forms in my throat. "I'm not. What I'm afraid of is losing him. My friendship with Max was always my happy place as a kid, and it is now too. Risking all that to calm down my hormones feels wrong."

Evelyn and Abby exchange a glance, which tells me they've spoken about this at length. When they don't say anything in return, I have the slight suspicion they might be up to something. Just as I'm about to question them, my phone buzzes with a message from Max.

Max: Random thought—coffee tastes better with cinnamon. Had it today for the first time. You should try it sometime too. How are you?

I love it when he sends me messages about little nothings. Even as kids, we used to meet up after school to tell each other about our day.

Emilia: Great. Managed to get some side gigs to pay off the car repairs.

Max: What? You're already working full-time... I want to help.

Emilia: You can make me laugh. Helps me let off steam.

The moment I send the message, I know it was a wrong choice of words.

Max: Consider it done. Love hearing you laugh. BUT, and I'm just putting it out there, I know much better ways to let off steam.

Looking up from my phone, I find Abby and Evelyn staring at me. Giving them an enigmatic smile, I head inside the clinic.

***

Over the last sessions of his therapy, the chemistry between Max and me gradually gets out of control.

"What are we doing today?" Max asks at the start of the very last session. Today it's just him and me in the training room.

"Mattress exercises," I inform him, pointing to the mattress on the floor.

"Great. They're my favorite kind."

"Really?" I frown at him as he lowers himself on the mattress. He hasn't shown much enthusiasm for any exercises until now. "Which ones are your favorites?"

"All of them. Doggy style, missionary, you name it. Which one is *your* favorite, Jonesie?"

My ears turn red, and I immediately avert my gaze. "You are shameless."

"I'm being told that at least twice a day." He says this with so much pride, it's ridiculous.

Sighing, I shake my head. "Let's start with leg bends. I will watch you and correct you when you're doing it wrong."

He pins me down with his gaze for a brief second, igniting every cell in my body. Determined not to back down, I stubbornly hold his gaze, even though my breath becomes shallower by the second. Eventually, he lies on his back and starts the exercise.

"No, no," I correct. "You can't push your lower back against the mattress." I wedge my hand between the mattress and his lower back. "Your back is not allowed to touch my hand."

As Max resumes the exercise, I can't keep my wandering eyes from taking in the movement of his sinewy muscles. Damn it. I have officially upgraded from ogling to eye fucking him.

"You're going to strain your eye muscles from over exercising them, Jonesie."

Busted.

The next exercise is trickier because I have to ensure that neither his shoulder nor his hip lift off the mattress while he lifts and bends both his legs. The easiest way to accomplish this is to hold one hand on his hip and one over his shoulder. Which means I'm leaning over him, practically putting my boobs on his chest, my mouth dangerously close to his. As Max bends his leg, his knee brushes lightly against the side of my ribs. Heat spears me anew, and I nearly bite my tongue. Damn it. How am I supposed to do my job if feeling his knee in my freaking ribs turns me on?

"You have beautiful lips, Jonesie," he says.

"Stop calling me Jonesie." Despite myself, I grin.

"But I can tell you that you have beautiful lips?"

"No, you can't do that either. My gym, my rules, remember?"

"I have an excellent memory, but when I have

a woman over me, I can't help myself."

This man is relentless. Can't he see what he's doing to me?

"I didn't take you for the type who likes women on top," I reply, feeling bolder than usual.

Max cocks an eyebrow, and then his lips curve into a smile. "I'd like you anywhere. On top of me, under me. To my side. I assure you I can perform in any position."

Giving up on the pretense of helping him with the exercise, I sit back on my ass, sighing loudly. He bolts into a sitting position on the floor.

"What are we doing, Max?" I ask.

"Pushing each other, waiting to see who will be the first to fall over the edge. I have an inkling it'll be me."

My question was rhetorical, so I wasn't exactly expecting an answer.

"I don't think I can be just your friend," Max continues, and I feel as if someone just doused me in cold water. "I thought I could, but evidently, it's not working."

I take a deep breath, trying to calm my racing heart.

"It's not just because I'm attracted to you, Emilia. I admit I am. Fuck, I am. I leave every session with blue balls, and I've jerked off so many times thinking about you lately that my right hand will fall off."

My eyes widen as an arrow of desire shoots right through me. Max isn't done though. He scoots closer to me on the floor, looking straight at me.

"When something good happens, the first person I want to share it with is you. When I know you're worried about something, I want to take that worry away from you."

"Max," I whisper weakly. "Why do you say all the right things?"

"Give me one reason why we shouldn't follow our instincts. Yeah, we're risking our friendship, but clearly we're not doing a great job keeping it platonic as it is anyway."

He's right. The past four weeks are proof of it, and damn it, I want to be with him, but I need to be honest with him first. This morning, I finally sold my wedding dress. Getting rid of it felt cathartic... and like a sign.

"I have so many issues, I could fill a mile-long list with them. On both sides," I say.

"Start firing. I'm ready to take notes. I can type seventy words per minute."

"Max—"

"Emilia."

I snap my head up to him. "I'm serious."

"So am I. Try me."

"I have daddy issues and abandonment issues," I say in a small voice. "Which are at the root of many other suboptimal traits and inadequate developments in attachment."

"Suboptimal what and inadequate huh?" Max glares at me. "That sounded very... cold and odd. Like something a self-help bullshit test would word vomit."

I blush violently. "I did first read that in a self-help test, and then I talked to the in-house therapist and my friend, Evelyn, who said about the same thing, albeit using friendlier terms."

Max reaches his hand out to me, placing it over my fingers, which are spread on the floor.

"Well, I'll say it in simple words. You've had bad luck. Your dad was an asshole, and you lost your mother. You also haven't had much luck with men. I could be cocky and say that it's a sign you had to wait for me, but I don't want to get ahead of myself."

I burst out laughing, and he laughs with me. God, I could listen to this sound the entire day.

"Told you I could make you laugh." Without warning, he cups my cheeks in his hands. "I have known who you are for fifteen years, Jonesie. All your fears, all your insecurities were there when I met you, in one form or another." With a smirk, he adds, "And you know my fears too."

"You hate small spaces." I claw myself out from his grip because his lips are far too close to mine. "That makes you so undesirable."

"Well, it does mean we could never have sex in an elevator or a broom closet."

"Two places which are very high on my list," I deadpan, though I break out in a sweat imagining the two of us doing the deed in a broom closet.

"Look, it's not like I have a great record with dating," Max continues. "Can't promise this will work. Maybe I'll screw up. Maybe you'll screw up.

Maybe we both will. We'll never know if we don't try."

I hug my knees to my chest, resting my chin on them and looking at the beautiful man in front of me.

"Let's grab dinner tonight," he suggests, glancing at the clock to our right. The session is almost up. "We don't have any sessions left, and we need to sort this out, Emilia."

"Okay, but I have a seminar I can't skip. I finish at nine."

"I'll pick you up when you're done. Text me the address."

"Okay."

We both rise to our feet, and Max kisses my forehead, placing one hand on the center of my back. I can sense the message behind his gesture, a soft encouragement to trust him. But he lingers with his lips on my skin for a split second too long, and the innocent touch turns into a sinful sensation, his mouth igniting me. Desire zips through me, and I'm suddenly hyperaware of all things Max: the very faint stubble on his chin, his masculine scent of wood and sea, the slight tremor in his chest… and mine. We're both seconds away from losing control.

When he takes a step back, we're both panting.

"See you tonight, Emilia."

YOUR INESCAPABLE LOVE

Chapter Fourteen

Emilia

The rest of the day passes by in a haze, and by the time I leave the clinic and head to the hotel downtown where the seminar is taking place, I have butterflies in my stomach. On the way, I call my neighbor Mrs. Wilson, thanking her again for agreeing to look after Grams tonight. She offered to sleep at our house, insisting that I stay out for as long as I want.

As I step inside the seminar room, the clock hanging on the wall in the front catches my attention. There are fifty-nine minutes left until Max picks me up. But who's counting?

I force myself to focus on the seminar, taking notes and already making a mental list of the patients who would benefit from the techniques presented. The second it's over I burst out the door and walk to the elevator, heading to the underground parking lot of the hotel, where Max texted me that he's waiting for me.

Just before the elevator doors close, John

steps inside.

"Emilia! Just the woman I was looking for."

"Hi," I say tiredly.

"How about that third date? It's Friday night, we can stay up late." He stands with his feet planted wide, and I have to move around him to push the button for the underground level. After pressing the button, I decide that bluntness is needed, since the man seems incapable of taking a hint.

"Look, John. No offense, but we weren't on any date. It was just two colleagues grabbing a quick bite."

His usually friendly expression morphs into a grimace of disbelief.

"Didn't occur to you to say that before I paid?" he bellows.

"It was cheap pizza. And you were the one who pretended to go to the bathroom but instead paid the bill. Both times." I can barely contain my anger now.

"Because I thought you were fucking coming home with me. You weaseled out every time."

"You're a jerk."

"I thought you were playing hard to get, or had some stupid three-date rule before sex. But you were just a tease, weren't you?"

The doors of the elevator open, and I quickly step out. John follows me. Damn it, Max is inside the garage. I don't want him to see John and get the wrong idea.

Swirling on my heels, I confront him in the

small space between the elevator and the open door leading to the garage.

"You read into it whatever you wanted. It was just pizza." My hands are curled into fists at my sides, and I'm shaking with anger.

"Women like you are unbelievable. You lead guys on, and then blame us." He shakes his head, spitting at my feet. "You're a fucking tease."

Right. I've had enough. "You're delusional, and if I were you, I'd shut up. I might be small, but I have a mean right hook."

Turning around, I step forward, wishing to put as much distance as possible between him and me. In my haste, I catch my heel in a small hole. Losing my balance, I hurtle toward the ground on one side. My right elbow and knee hurt like hell when they make contact with the pavement. Unfortunately I'm wearing a red, sleeveless shirt, and a pencil skirt short enough to leave my knees exposed. My left side is spared, but I'm in blinding pain for a split second. I think I just left a layer of skin on the pavement.

"Emilia!" Max calls. My eyes are blurry with tears of pain, but I see Max a few feet away, striding toward John and me. I push myself up as fast as I can, wobbling on my feet.

"Are you okay?" Max asks me in a gentle voice, and all I can do is nod in relief. The muscles in his arms tense as he brings his fingers to the side of my face in a slight caress.

John, who truly is an idiot, says, "So that's who you're teasing tonight. One word of advice.

Don't waste any money on her. She's not worth it. Just a fucking tease, this one."

Despite being in pain, I raise my fist. Max, who was already shaking with restrained anger, is quicker than I am. He turns to John. I blink once, and then Max's fist collides with the side of John's face. Since Max is at least a foot taller, the impact knocks John off balance. He barrels back a few steps, holding the side of his face with both hands.

"What the fuck?" he bellows.

"If a woman says no, she means it. Be a man and accept it." Max stalks toward him, and as he raises his hand—curled into a fist, again—John has the good sense to scurry away. Max turns to me, inspecting my right knee and arm. I have scratches on both, and they sting like hell.

"Emilia," he says softly. "I'm so sorry."

"For what?" I'm startled.

"For not stepping in earlier. I was distracted in my car, e-mailing my assistant, and then I saw the two of you arguing. Got here as fast as I could. That idiot—"

"He didn't do this," I explain. "I was in a hurry to get away from him and didn't look where I was stepping."

"I saw you stumble. It was the only reason that idiot still has teeth. He deserved that punch, though. For talking to you like that."

His words warm me on the inside, as does the half hug he pulls me in, careful not to touch my injured side. I sure could've punched John myself, but I'll be damned if it doesn't feel nice to have someone defend me and care about me.

"Thank you for defending my honor, knight in shining armor."

"Give me your phone," he says into my ear, pulling away.

"Why?"

"Phone," he insists.

"Jeez, you're such a caveman."

I push the phone in his hands. "What are you doing?"

"Putting myself on speed dial. When you need something, you call me. You want me to pick up food because you're sick? Call me. You want a quickie? You'd better call me. Shit hits the fan and or an idiot annoys you? You fucking call me."

"Are you mad at me right now?" I don't know if I should be pissed at him, or hug him. I wish I could do both at the same time.

"No, I'm worried. Seeing you on the floor scared the hell out of me. And now you have a bloody elbow and knee. Come on, I'll take you home."

I nod. "Sorry for tonight, about our plans."

"It can wait. I can wait."

Holding his big, warm arm around my shoulders, he leads me to his car.

"Do you have anything I can clean your wounds off with at home?" he asks after we're out of the garage.

"Yeah." As he veers into the street, I suddenly

change my mind. "I don't want to go home. Grams will worry if she sees the scratches."

"Okay. Do you want to go to my place?"

"Sure." I inspect the wound on my leg, which runs pretty deep, blood marring half of my knee. I can't see my elbow properly, but it burns.

We enter Max's apartment a short while later. After we both kick off our shoes, he leads me toward the enormous couch in the living room, gesturing for me to sit on it. If I weren't so focused on my wounds, I'd be busy inspecting my surroundings. As it is, I'm working hard not to whimper the entire time.

"Wait here, I'll bring something to clean off your wounds."

He returns almost immediately, holding a bottle in one hand and cotton pads in the other.

"This will sting," he warns, kneeling in front of me.

"I can do it." I attempt to snatch the cotton pads from his hand, but he shakes his head.

"Let me do this for you, Emilia. I want to."

Gritting my teeth, I brace myself as Max pours peroxide on the pad. He starts with my knee, and holy fuck.

"Agh. Damn it," I exclaim. "Stings so much."

"It's not deep," Max says, inspecting my wound. He repeats the process with my elbow, which stings even more than my knee did. As soon as he's done, I pull my arm back.

Max chuckles. "Show me your elbow. I want to check if there's any dirt left."

Stubbornly, I keep my arm back.

"Should I bribe you with sweets? Or more adult bribes? Vodka? My kind of mattress exercises?" His expression instantly changes to serious. "Sorry! That last part just slipped out."

"You've been throwing innuendos and flirting shamelessly for four weeks, but now you're sorry?" This downright mystifies me, considering he's been relentless until now.

"Yeah, but I'm cleaning off the wounds you got while trying to get away from a jerk. Innuendos are the last thing you need."

"What do *you* need?" I ask.

"Doesn't matter. You're the important one now. Not just now, as a matter of fact. Always."

For long moments, I'm too stunned to speak. His dark gaze holds mine, warm and reassuring.

"Wow," I say eventually. "You're something."

"What do you mean?"

"Let's just say I'm not used to men being this considerate." Sure, I've never settled for anything less than respect, but it seemed like I always had to demand it. None of the men I've been with put me first out of their own initiative, as if doing that somehow undermined their masculinity. Max is man enough to not only make me feel like he's putting me first, but also say it out loud with a sense of pride.

After placing the bottle of peroxide and the

pads on the coffee table in front of us, Max sits next to me on the couch, placing his hand at the small of my back.

"Told you! You've been around the wrong men. All the more points for me."

"Can't believe you're awarding them to yourself." Throwing back my head, I giggle heartily.

"You're so beautiful when you laugh."

The air between us charges instantly, as I become acutely aware of how close to me he is. Three inches, possibly less, separate us. He rests his forehead against mine, rubbing the pad of his thumb against my bare shoulder. The skin-on-skin contact sends a jolt scissoring through me until I intimately yearn for Max. I inhale his scent, desperate for more. I need to touch him... everywhere. I can't resist this man any longer. I want to be his. I want to know what it's like to be loved by him. It feels right, being here with him, and I can't be scared because something feels right.

"I can take you home," he says in a low voice.

"No." The small word has an atomic effect. Both our breaths grow heavier. His hand tightens on my shoulder, while my hand fists his shirt, pulling him closer to me.

"Are you sure you want this?" he asks.

"Are you trying to buy your way out of this?"

"No, just don't want you to do something you might regret tomorrow." As he moves the pad of his thumb from my shoulder down my arm, all the way to my wrist, I'm unable to hold back a moan.

"I knew you'd be all talk and no play," I say playfully.

"Those are dangerous words to throw around."

"I like challenging you."

"Sweet Emilia." He drops his head to my neck, resting his lips just above my collarbone. "I'm going to make you come hard tonight."

Cupping my face in his hands, he pulls me in for a kiss. It starts out tender, just a brush of his lips, but it's enough to set my nerve endings on fire. I sigh against his expert lips, hungry for more. He swipes his tongue over my lips in slow motion, making me ache everywhere for him.

"Max," I whisper, and I feel his lips curving into a smile against mine. I open my mouth, and he dips his tongue inside, exploring me. I relish the sweet torture, sighing in his mouth. Deepening the kiss, Max pushes me on my back on the couch, frantically undoing the buttons of my shirt. He unhitches his lips from mine, descending on my jaw and then the column of my neck. After he pushes my shirt off my shoulders and down my arms, being extra careful with my hurt elbow, he cups my breasts over my bra. My nipples pucker under the fabric, eager for skin-on-skin contact. Max moves one hand to the small of my back, searching for my zipper. In a matter of seconds, he pushes my skirt down, and then I'm in front of Max Bennett in my lingerie only.

"What are you thinking?" I ask as his eyes rake over my body. "You look like you're analyzing something."

"I am. Thinking which part of you I should start with. I want to devour every single inch of you."

"You have big goals for tonight, mister."

Max pushes a strand of hair behind my ear, putting his lips to my forehead. "You have no idea."

"Show me."

"I want you to tell me what you like, and what you need. No holding back."

I swallow hard, nodding. Suddenly, I feel bare in front of him. "Same goes for you."

Max leads me to his bedroom, holding my hand on the way. A shiver runs through me when I step inside, aware that another limit is blurring between us. This is his personal space. I'd inspect it more closely if I wasn't so taken with the man in front of me, who is still fully clothed. I must remedy that immediately.

"You have too many clothes on," I say.

"You're welcome to start taking them off." His eyes hold a challenge, as they always do. But the more time I spend with Max, the more I like every challenge he throws my way.

I start by removing his jacket, and then undoing the buttons of his shirt. I don't rush through the motions, instead taking my time with each button, knowing I'm driving him crazy. When his chest is finally bare, I inhale sharply, appreciating the view in front of me. This is a fine, fine man. His torso looks sculpted. I can't take my eyes off him, or my hands. I have a compulsive need to touch every inch of his skin, every ridge and every line. He is ripped, and feeling his chest rising up and down with frantic breaths does wicked things to me.

"I wouldn't mind if you hurried up, love."

"I'm taking my time," I tease him, but I undo his belt, pushing his pants and his boxers down. Now *that* is a sight to behold. I sit on the bed as Max stands in front of me. I palm his erection, moving my hand up and down, dragging my thumb across the tip.

"Fuck." Max tilts his head, and I watch his Adam's apple dip as he swallows hard. I've barely moved my hand a few more times when Max pushes me to my back on the bed, climbing over me.

He kisses along my collarbone, then drags his lips across the upper slope of my breasts just where the fabric of the bra meets my skin. At the same time, he drags his fingers across my thong-covered center.

"You soaked through your panties," he groans, intensifying the movement of his fingers. "That's so fucking sexy. You're sexy."

Abruptly, he pulls his fingers away, leaving me writhing. He undoes my bra next, the desire in his gaze intensifying as my breasts spill free. My nipples turn to hard nubs under his intense gaze, and a new wave of heat pools low in my body. Max feathers his palm over one of my nipples, while his mouth covers the other. Oh God... the heat of his lips is too much. I need him now. All of him. I push my hips against him wantonly, and his lips curve in a smile against my breasts.

"I need you."

"I want to make sure you're ready," Max murmurs.

"I am ready, I promise." If I get any readier than this, I might explode just by having his mouth on my skin.

Moving back, Max hooks his thumbs at the sides of my thong, pulling it down my legs and then discarding the fabric next to the bed.

My intimate spot pulses for him. As he leans forward, dragging his fingers through my glistening heat, coating my folds with it, he trains his eyes on me. They are hooded with desire, but I spot a glimpse of something else behind them too: kindness and gentleness, two things that are indisputably Max.

He drags his thumb from my entrance up to my clit, circling the sweet spot until my back arches off the bed.

"I need you inside me. Now," I say.

Max nods, leaning across to the nightstand and procuring a condom from it. Pushing myself up on my elbows, I watch him put the condom over his erection. *Oh, my.* Seeing him touch himself arouses me to no end.

Max positions himself between my legs, spreading my thighs even wider apart. He slides just the tip of him inside me at first, thick and teasing. He moves back and forth ever so slowly, not giving me more than the tip, offering torture and pleasure at the same time.

Then he enters me to the hilt, stretching and filling me until I feel like I'm about to break out of my skin.

"This is so good," he groans, levering himself over me, propping himself on his forearms. His lips find mine as he loves me faster, deeper, driving me crazy. "You like this, don't you? Feeling me inside you?"

"Yes, yes. I do."

His balls slap against the crack of my ass with every move, and the sound turns me on. Heat radiates from the spot where we are connected, spreading through my body, making my toes curl and my heart beat lightning quick.

Levering himself on one forearm, he slips one hand between us. When I feel Max's thumb circling my clit, I nearly lose it. I fist the bedsheet with one hand, meeting his feverish thrusts. My other hand roams on his shoulders and his back, caressing and grazing.

The pressure he applies on my bundle of nerves is damn near perfection. Tension builds in every cell in my body, fueled by his thrusts and grunts. Watching him come undone is almost as much a turn-on as his finger circling my clit. Before long my inner muscles clench around his length, a sign that I will succumb to an orgasm soon.

"You're so tight, Emilia." Max intensifies the rhythm of his thrusts, and I move my own hips in a frantic pace, seeking my release.

"So good." I dig my nails into his back as a

wave of pleasure sears me. Max seals his lips over mine, claiming me, and I cry my release in his mouth. The next few minutes are an excruciating pleasure. Max grips my ass cheek with his palm, driving inside me like a man possessed until he widens inside me, and he rasps out my name over and over again.

Still lost in the throes of bliss, I barely register that he moves away, probably to discard the condom. When he returns to my side, pressing his warm body against mine, I feel safer and happier than I ever have.

Chapter Fifteen

Emilia

When I wake up next morning, I don't open my eyes right away. For a few blissful minutes, I just replay last night's events in my mind, hoping I haven't been dreaming again. I ache everywhere though. Content that I have been visiting Smutland for real this time, I blink my eyes open, only to find Max next to me. His head is propped on an elbow. My breath stops for a split second as I remember how he made me feel. And then my haze-filled morning brain comes up with the reaction *Yum*.

"Morning," Max greets me.

"Hi." For some reason I'm incredibly shy, and I pull the cover over my breasts. Max cocks an eyebrow.

"No need to feel shy."

I give him a nervous giggle in return.

"If you're going to say last night was a mistake, I will kiss you until you change your mind." He scoots closer to me, looking beautiful, all man, and impossible to resist. "Actually, if you're going to tell me anything other than, *this was the best sex of my life*, you're gonna pay."

And just like that, he breaks the ice, doing away with my morning-after jitters.

"I admire your confidence. Are you under the impression that you can tell me what to think or say just because you were inside me?"

"Wouldn't dream of it," he says solemnly. "This is reverse psychology."

I wave my hand in a dismissing gesture. "Clearly you don't know women."

Max leans in closer, cupping my jaw. "I know you. At least, I knew Jonesie, the girl, now I want to know the woman. I want to know all there is to know about you." Putting his lips to my ear, he whispers, "I can be very persuasive."

"What does that persuasion include?"

"Spoiling you, lots of kissing, and hot sex."

"If I pretend to disagree with you all day will you do that stuff?"

"You little vixen."

Hooking an arm around my waist, Max pulls me to him until our bodies touch completely. We're naked under the cover, and feeling his warm skin against mine is about the best damn way to wake up.

"I wasn't going to say that last night was a mistake. You're right. We do have a good thing, and I want to be with you. Just don't hurt me, okay?" I ask in a small voice.

"I won't."

"And if at any moment you think that we're

not working out, just say it. I'll do the same. Promise to do it when you feel something is off. Don't wait until we can't work on it anymore. I don't want to collect wedding dresses." My throat nearly clogs at the mere thought of that scenario playing out, but I need to say it out loud. If there is one thing I can trust Max to do, it's to be up-front with me. I rarely show my vulnerable side to anyone, even Evelyn and Abby, but I can't seem to help myself with Max.

"You already dreaming about marrying me, Jonesie?" His voice is light, but my stomach drops.

"Crap. I didn't mean that…. I just—"

"Shh, calm down, beautiful. I know what you meant. I was just trying to lighten things up. I'd never do that. I promise." He caresses my cheek with the back of his fingers, and peppers the side of my jaw with kisses.

"Good." A knot unfurls in my stomach, and I feel as if a weight has been lifted off my shoulders. "Now, I still want you to make good on your threats. They sounded like so much fun."

"You're a demanding little thing."

"I might be a bit high maintenance," I admit. "I require a lot of laughter and orgasms."

"Happy to comply with both. But I have a requirement first."

"We're negotiating?" I ask in disbelief.

He purses his lips, as if he's weighing his options. "No, we're just exchanging information." He adopts a serious, businesslike demeanor, and I have a hard time reining in my laughter. "In order to comply with your requests, I need to know all of the facts."

"All right, fire away."

"Do you admit that last night was the best sex you've had?"

"It might make the top ten," I tease.

"There was definitely something that sounded an awful lot like 'I've never felt like this before' in there."

"Pfft," I say, waving my hand. "I could have been referring to many other things."

"Such as what?" he challenges.

"Such as the lovely Egyptian cotton I'm lying on." I wiggle my butt against the bed, and pat the smooth fabric of the sheet to make my point.

Max levers himself over me, propping the weight of his upper body on his forearms. "If you remember the cotton and not what I was doing to you, I have some serious improvements to do."

"I won't say no to that." I lace my fingers at the back of his neck, my forearms resting on the expanse of his broad, strong shoulders. "What improvements are you thinking about?"

"Making you come until you can't even remember your name," he whispers in my ear. Desire shoots right through me, singeing me.

"Oh, God, I want you," I murmur.

His eyes twinkle with a hunger that mirrors my own, and when he lowers his mouth to meet mine, I raise my head, meeting him halfway. This man will drive me crazy with desire. Max makes passionate love to me, and despite fighting to remain awake afterward, I drift off to sleep.

***

When I wake up next, the bed is empty. I grab Max's pillow, hugging it to my chest. It smells like him, and I love it. Sitting up on the bed, I inspect the room. Across from the bed is a double window, which allows in plenty of natural light. Since we're on the tenth floor, the view encompasses the San Francisco skyline. A few gray clouds hang low in the sky, a sure promise that rain will follow sometime today. Tearing my gaze away from the window, I take in the colorful green carpet, which contrasts with the elegant white furniture. On the nightstand next to the bed, I find a note from Max.

I called Mrs. Wilson this morning. She doesn't mind staying at your house the entire day, looking after Grams.

Something warm and powerful takes residence in my chest as I read the note over and over again. This means more to me than he can possibly know. Smiling, I descend from the bed, heading to the bathroom.

I take my time in the shower, and wash my hair as well, which turns out to be a bad idea a few minutes later, when I realize Max doesn't own a hair dryer. My hair tends to be on the wild side if I let it dry naturally. Oh well, nothing to do about that now. I go about finding Max, wearing nothing but a towel I wrapped around me.

Music blares from the living room, and when I get there, I discover it comes from some embedded sound system that extends to his kitchen. Nice. I could see myself cooking in this perfect kitchen. I inspect the glossy cabinets and the stove. It doesn't have one single scratch. It's perfect. *Too perfect.*

Over the music, I hear Max's voice from outside. He's on the balcony, and he's quite a sight, wearing low-rise jeans and nothing else. One hand holds his phone to his ear. I stay put for a moment, simply enjoying the view and wondering how lucky I am to be standing here.

Finally, my fingers begin to itch with the need to touch his gorgeous hair, or maybe his skin. I haven't decided which part of him I want to take advantage of first when I push the sliding doors of the balcony open. Max swirls around, looking me over from head to toe.

"James, I'll call you back later," he says into the phone, not taking his eyes off me. Then he clicks off.

"Now this is something I could wake up to every morning," he tells me. Taking a step forward, he cups my face, sealing his lips over mine in a hungry kiss. The kiss grows more passionate by the second, and before long, his arms are around my waist, and I lace my fingers at the back of his head. Without warning, he lifts me up, and I instinctively wrap my legs around his waist. He walks like this to the kitchen counter, accommodating me on it. At that precise moment, my stomach rumbles loudly, reminding me I haven't eaten anything for almost twenty-four hours.

"I'm hungry," I inform him unnecessarily.

Max places his palm across my stomach, chuckling. "Yeah, the announcement was pretty clear. There's a cafe across the road, and they have excellent breakfast."

"But I love your apartment so much. I don't want to leave it." I touch the sleek surface of the counter, sighing. "We can scramble something here. I can make something tasty out of any raw materials."

"Except that my raw materials are just last week's leftovers," he says with a smirk. "I think there's three-day-old pizza and a two-day-old burrito in there. If you look hard, you might even find some week-old pie leftover."

"You don't cook at all?"

"Nope."

"What good is it having a top-notch kitchen if you don't use it?" I inquire.

"That's what I asked myself when I saw the apartment. I bought it before I returned from London, and Alice helped decorate it."

"Ah."

"Yes. She insisted that a state-of-the-art kitchen," he says, making air quotes with his fingers, "is a must-have. I learned long ago not to fight Alice unless I absolutely have to. Anyway, I think I finally know what to do with the kitchen." His eyes spark with mischief. "I might not do cooking, but I'll happily do you."

His voice is low and throaty, fueling my own desire for him.

"Can you get your mind out of the gutter enough to feed us?" I ask, only half joking.

"If I have to."

Max smooths his hand down my hair, and I self-consciously realize that my hair is a wild mess. I don't have my usual hair products here, which means I can't tame the frizz of curls. I groan when I catch my reflection in the tinted black glass of the oven. My hair sticks in one million directions.

"This is such a mess." I desperately pat my palms down my hair.

"I like it," Max says. "I missed seeing it this wild."

I open my mouth, ready to fire back something sarcastic, but then I realize he's not joking. He holds my gaze in his for long moments before he leans in, his lips brushing my forehead. The chaste, sweet kiss fills me with warmth, and I rest my palms on his chest. As we stand here, sharing this quiet moment, it strikes me how different dating is when you do it with someone you've known since you were a kid. I know so much about Max, and yet, a side of him is completely new to me, and I can't wait to discover it.

"By the way, this week I worked with the investigators I told you about. They researched some potential partners. You want me to tell them to look up your father?"

Oh. I never gave him an answer on that

matter, and Grams has brought up the subject again twice.

"Yeah. I... I want to do this for Grams. It'll be good for her."

"What about you? 'Cause I think you'll end up hurt."

"Maybe it will be good for me too. Settle that score."

"You sure?"

"Yes."

Max nods once, kissing my forehead.

"Okay. Come on, let's shop for raw ingredients, and then you can charm me with your cooking talents," Max says.

"I have to change. Be back in a minute."

With the speed of the wind—or in my case, extreme hunger—I race to the bedroom, put on yesterday's clothes, except the panties, and then join Max in the living room.

"Wow, I never imagined you'd actually be back in a minute," Max says with appreciation.

"I always keep my word. I wanted to talk to you about something though.... I want to go back to the house tonight. I know Mrs. Wilson said she'd stay the entire weekend, but I don't want to stay away for so long."

"Okay. We can go to your house anytime you want."

We, not you. There was no hesitation in his voice. "Great. By the way, thank you for calling my house and talking to Mrs. Wilson. Can't believe it slipped my mind to do it."

"You deserve time off from all your responsibilities, Emilia. Cut yourself some slack. I'm happy to help."

Not knowing what to say to that, I just rise on my tiptoes and kiss the corner of his mouth. This man is worming his way into my heart with every word.

Max leads me to a nearby grocery store, and as we walk side by side, I can't help noticing the way he keeps a protective arm around my waist, or occasionally my shoulders, and walks on the side to the street. I lean into his touch all the way, soaking in the warmth and safety he radiates.

I go wild in the grocery store, buying enough food for six people, but I don't feel at all guilty. As we exit the store, we notice the drops of rain splattering on the pavement. A memory flashes before my eyes, of Max and me running barefoot through the rain, our feet sloshing through the mud. A low chuckle snaps my attention to Max.

"You're thinking about all those times we got dirty in the rain, aren't you?" he asks.

I nod. "We did like to get dirty a lot."

He leans in to me, whispering conspiratorially, "We still do, only now it's a different kind of dirty. Much more satisfying."

He takes my hand, and as we rush to his building, I relish every feeling Max awakens in me—the familiar and the new.

Once back in the apartment, I immediately head to the kitchen. The rain was light, just a few drops, so there's no need to change. I whip out a pan from his very well-stocked cabinets and start making pancakes. Max merely hovers around me, looking ridiculously out of place.

"How come you don't cook? I remember you distributed tasks evenly when you were kids."

Max scowls, having the distinct expression of someone who has been caught while doing something wrong.

"What I'm about to tell you is a secret," he says seriously. "I think only half my family knows this."

"Oh, what a secret. Do tell," I encourage, turning to him while keeping an eye on the pan.

"You remember Christopher, right?" The serious expression melts into one full of mischief.

"I think I do." I feign thinking hard for some seconds. "Tall, handsome—looks exactly like you."

"That's the one. Well, we didn't use our likeness just for pranks, we also exchanged tasks from time to time. Christopher is an excellent cook."

"What tasks did you do for him?" I ask suspiciously, turning the pancake in the pan.

"Mainly outdoors stuff. Cutting wood, mowing the grass." A short pause follows and then he adds, "Kissing his girl."

I gasp. "You didn't."

"I was actually trying to help him, at *his* request."

"And somehow your lips landed on hers? They have a will of their own?"

"Something like that," Max says with a self-satisfied smirk. "He was preparing some crazy romantic scheme, and he wanted it to be a surprise, so he asked me to pretend to be him with his girl for about an hour while he got everything ready."

"That makes no sense whatsoever."

"We were sixteen. It seemed flawless logic back then. At some point, the girl kissed me, and well, I was a horny sixteen-year-old. How could I resist kissing her back?"

He says this with such honesty that I can't help chuckling. "I imagine that went over very well with Christopher. Did he punch your sorry ass?"

"You could say that. It was the longest period we went without talking. Then we beat the shit out of each other and made up."

"Men." I shake my head, removing the perfectly cooked pancake, putting it on a plate, and starting with the next one. This is my favorite breakfast. "Why do you always have to solve things by fighting?"

"We're basic creatures. I think it's the fastest way to get the anger out of our systems."

"I see. Any other secrets you want to share?"

Max folds his arms over his broad, strong chest. "Nah, I think it's enough for today. Wouldn't want to scare you off."

"So first you got me in your bed, and now you're sharing the ugly stuff? You're smart."

He hooks one arm around my waist from behind, flattening my back against his chest, and I wiggle my ass straight against his crotch.

"You're a little devil," he whispers in my ear, raising goose bumps along my arms.

"I have my moments," I reply boldly.

Chapter Sixteen

Emilia

After breakfast, Max gives me the official tour of his apartment. I catalog everything in my mind, eager to discover more about him. Ironically, I already know more about Max than I did about any man I dated, including my fiancé. But most of my knowledge is about Max the boy. Now, in his apartment, I'm getting a snapshot of Max the man.

We're back in the living room, and I'm scanning it for a second time, when my eyes fall on a guitar case lying on top of a cabinet.

"You play guitar?" I ask in delight.

He follows my gaze to the case and grins. "Yep. Just one of my many hidden talents."

"What are some of the others?" I challenge, enjoying the easygoing banter. I feared things might shift into the weird territory after doing the nasty, but so far, I love this.

"Out of this world orgasms," he says confidently.

"Never thought it would be possible for you

to get even cockier." I head over to the cabinet and, standing on my tiptoes, I blindly reach out for the case, with the intention of pulling it down. Max rushes next to me in an instant.

"Careful, it's heavy," he warns, and pulls it down himself.

"I take it you haven't played in a while?" I inquire.

"Since college, but it's a nice keepsake." He places the case on the floor, and as he retrieves the guitar from it, a nostalgic look crosses his features. I sit on the couch with my feet tucked under me.

"Tell me more about the guitar thing. Is it just a thing you started to draw in chicks?" The question was meant tongue-in-cheek, but red splotches appear on his cheeks.

"What can I say? You know me well. Took lessons in high school, was in a band in college."

I shrug. "Not many women can resist a man with a guitar."

"And you're one of them?"

Heat rises to my face, and by the satisfied grin on his face, it shows.

"Do you want to play me something?"

"Nah," he replies. "I think I want to make you blush for a while longer."

I flip him the bird. "Well, play me a song while you're at it."

"Bossy, I like it."

"If you can't beat them, join them."

Max sits on the couch next to me, holding his

guitar. He watches me with warm eyes as he strums his fingers over the instrument. From the very first sound, I perk up. He is talented. The song is soft and melodic, and the hair at my nape rises as I listen to him. He is so calm and inviting, as if this comes naturally to him. Then he surprises me by humming along to the music, and now every hair on my body stands on end as I listen to him, watching his lips move. Right at this moment, he is utterly irresistible to me. The urge to lick his lips, and more intimate parts, hits me hard.

"Wow," I say after he's done. "You're great at this."

"What did you expect?"

"Men like to impress. I thought you were just talking big."

"You need to give me more credit, Emilia. But I can show you big." He wiggles his eyebrows suggestively. I ignore him, because I genuinely want to know more.

"Tell me about the band."

He leans back on the couch, lacing his fingers at the top of his head. "We were five guys in college. Decided to have fun together. We were well liked, and scored a few gigs in local bars. We even had some interest from agents and a record label that wanted us to do an album."

"What happened?"

"The others went to record the album, but I didn't stay in the band. Started working with my brothers."

"Why didn't you want to play professionally?"

"It was a lot of fun, and a way to relax. I always knew I wanted to work at Bennett Enterprises." There is no hesitation in his voice.

"I admire your decisiveness. It took me a while to know I wanted to be a physical therapist."

Max surprises me by smirking.

"What?" I press.

"Alice and I were talking about you a few years ago, taking guesses at what you might be doing. My guesses were doctor, physical therapist, or vet."

"You know me better than I know myself, then." The recognition sparks something deep inside me. "You're happy with your job?"

"Very. I know the business inside out, especially after being in London and building everything up there."

"That must have been hard."

"Yeah, but I had a lot of capital to set everything up. Sebastian and Logan are the geniuses of the family, though. Pippa, too. They started with less than one percent of that capital way back when, and pulled it off. Not only pulled it off, but they had profits early on. I didn't have to take on a single cent in student loans. They paid off college, expenses, everything. Same for the rest of my siblings. I didn't have a care in the world. Still don't, as a matter of fact."

It dawns on me why he never questioned a different career than working at Bennett Enterprises.

Family loyalty. That was something I didn't fully grasp as a child, though I was envious of the way they always had each other's backs. I'm proud to see that sense of loyalty lasted over the years, intensified even.

"What's with the smile?" he inquires.

I shrug one shoulder. "I learned a lot about you today."

"And what's that?"

"You love your family and your job, are a lousy cook, and kiss your brother's girl if given the chance. Not to mention you look hot playing the guitar."

Max pulls my feet in his lap, cuffing my ankles with his hands. "I especially like how you formulated that last part. Not, *you play the guitar well*, but *you look hot playing the guitar*."

"You misunderstood. Great voice plus great notes equals hot. It's a girl thing. And your fingers looked mighty hot strumming those cords."

My man's lips curve up in a delicious smile. "Now I see where you're going with this."

"Finally. Thought you'd never take the hint." I lift up my skirt a tad, offering him a peek of my thigh.

"I'm a simple man," Max replies, his fingers feathering around my ankles, making me shudder. "You have to tell me what you want."

Licking my lips, I lift my skirt even higher, until my intimate spot is almost visible. His eyes zero in there, and then widen.

"You're not wearing your thong," he says on a groan.

"I'm not."

"You've been walking around like this all morning? Even at the grocery store?"

"I have," I confirm, pushing my skirt up to my waist, watching with delight as his composure slips away. Parting my legs, he leans to me, peppering my inner thighs with kisses before lashing his tongue against my sensitive flesh. My thighs quiver as my hips lift up infinitesimally from the couch. He rims his thumb along my entrance, dipping his tongue inside me once.

"Max. More," I whisper. But instead of obliging me, he straightens up on the couch, grinning devilishly.

"That's your punishment for walking around commando and not letting me know."

"Tease," I accuse him. "I'll have my revenge on you."

Chapter Seventeen

Max

Monday evenings at Blake's bar have become somewhat of a regular thing. He opened it a few months back, and in the beginning, we just came once in a while, but now it's almost every Monday. It's a slow evening for him, and it gives us all a chance to catch up with each other. I do see and talk to some of my brothers on a daily basis at the office, but we talk about work stuff, mostly. Right now, part of the gang is here: Logan, Sebastian, Christopher, and Blake, obviously. Of the girls, only Alice made it. We're all sitting at a table near the counter, including Blake. He wears many hats since he opened this place—kicking ass on the business side and mixing drinks from time to time.

"I won't bring you another round," Blake says. "It's a workday tomorrow."

"Since when are you so responsible?" Sebastian asks him.

"Since I'm supposed to keep my customers in check," Blake answers, as if barely believing that's his role. "I used to hate bartenders who refused to give me more to drink, and now I'm one of them."

"Cheers to karma doing its job," Logan says, raising his glass of beer. "Good job on this place. I looked over the numbers you sent me. They're great."

Blake widens his eyes theatrically, opening his mouth, feigning shock. "Did you just pay me a compliment, Logan? I'll mark this day on the calendar."

Logan flips him the bird and everyone at the table bursts out laughing, Logan included. He used to scold Blake and Daniel on a regular basis, mainly because he felt our little brothers were wasting their potential, which they were. But now Blake runs his bar, and Daniel is doing a feasibility study on opening his own business.

"How come Nadine, Ava, and Pippa didn't make it?" I ask the group at large. Nadine is Logan's fiancée, and Ava is Sebastian's wife.

"They're all at Nadine's store," Logan replies. "Trying out the new collection."

"And you're here because?" I tease Alice.

She shrugs, answering with a serious expression. "You need some female supervision. And I am catching up with them later. I saw photos of Nadine's new collection. It's to die for, especially the ones with lace around the waist."

That sounds like pig latin to me, and by the confused looks on my brothers' faces, I'm not alone. I judge dresses by their length, amount of curves they show, and ease of removal.

"She's very talented and hardworking," Logan says proudly. It occurs to me that for the first time, I'm not tempted to throw a witty retort at him for walking around like a puppy in love, with the obsessive need to tell the world how great his woman is. In fact, I understand where he's coming from. Another first. *Emilia Campbell, what have you done to me?* The desire to discover everything there is about her hits me hard. This woman makes me feel things I didn't know existed. From the first time I was buried deep inside her, I realized I'll never want anyone else. Better not mess this up.

Blake is still Blake, though. "Logan, we all know how great Nadine is and that you're happy and yadda yadda yadda. No need to hear it for the hundredth time. Same goes for you, Sebastian."

Logan and Sebastian flip Blake the bird, while Alice and Christopher look at me with shit-eating grins. Oh, hell no. No way am I throwing myself to the wolves.

"Anyone have time to go over to our parents' next weekend and help them redo the fence?" Sebastian asks. "Ava and I are going to Lake Tahoe with these two." He motions to Logan.

"I can do it," I say at once.

"I'll go too," Christopher adds.

Even though more than ten years have gone by since Sebastian started providing for our parents, they still haven't adjusted to having money... or free time. As a result, they constantly find something to repair or renovate, and do it themselves. They live with the mantra *Why pay someone if you can do it?*

Since my dad's accident last year when he fell off the roof, my brothers and I pitch in whenever they have a renovation project. Leaving my parents alone for too long is dangerous. They get... *ideas.*

Currently I'm not in my parents' good graces because I convinced my brothers to buy a company jet, which I admit was a splurge, but what the hell? To Mom and Dad it was a waste, but they'll come around eventually.

"Great," Logan says.

We chitchat for another half an hour before Sebastian, Logan, and Christopher leave. Blake, Alice, and I are the only ones left.

"I'm going behind the counter," Blake informs us. "My bartender looks like she could use some help."

Alice and I raise our eyebrows in unison. His bartender, a beautiful blonde, is mixing drinks for the three customers waiting at the counter, clearly not needing help. By the lustful look on my brother's face, he's referring to another kind of help.

"Blake!" Alice says sharply.

"You're sleeping with her?" I blurt out. "Don't be stupid. Stay away from your employees."

"I'm not taking this shit from you, Max," Blake says simply.

I straighten up in my seat, now genuinely concerned for my brother. "Blake, I'm not just giving you shit. You're opening a can of worms for sexual harassment lawsuits. It's not worth the risk. You've done a great job with the bar, and it has a great reputation. Do you want to drag that in the mud with scandals?"

He shrugs, but by the creases on his forehead, I can tell he's not dismissing my warning.

"You *know* how to play the big brother card with Blake," Alice says after Blake leaves the table. I grew up watching Sebastian and especially Logan play the big brother card, and I had time to observe what works with each of us. Logan leads by example—he does what he preaches, which means we listen to him... mostly. Blake and I have a different type of relationship. He pushes me to try reckless things, like skydiving, I try to keep him from doing too many stupid things. What works with Blake is pointing out what he has to lose, which in this case is the bar's reputation.

"I hope he'll stay away from that girl," Alice says. "Speaking of girls—"

"No. You don't get to question me about Emilia."

Alice grins, leaning in over the table. "I was about to say I'll be going too, so I still have time to stop by Nadine's shop."

Ugh... talk about setting myself up.

"So?" she presses.

"So what?"

"Anything happen? And don't think I haven't noticed that you went radio silence all weekend and ignored my three calls."

"Fine, I was with Emilia. We're dating."

My sister's expression lights up. Out of nowhere, she changes places, moving to the chair next to me and hugging me.

"What's this for?" I'm confused as hell.

She lets go of me, patting my shoulder and kissing my cheek. "Going after your girl. Better to go after who you want than carry a torch forever, wondering if it would work out."

"I haven't been carrying a to— Wait a minute."

Alice is being suspiciously un-Alice like. Her cheeks are pink, and she smiles coyly. She isn't coy. Not ever.

"Are you talking about me or about you?"

"About you!" Alice says sharply, but the pink in her cheeks intensifies.

"Don't lie to me."

"I'm not... exactly." She taps her fingers on my beer glass. "Fine, I was talking about me, but I'm not going to tell you who he is."

"Which means I know him." I run a list of possible candidates in my mind, and curse. None of them is good enough for my sister.

"Do I have to beat him to a pulp? Actually, you know what? I'll do it now and you can answer later. Just give me his name."

"Oh, for the love of God. That's why I never tell you people anything. You act like cavemen."

"Instinct. Nothing to do against it."

"I'm pretty sure there are women out there

whose brothers don't want to abuse anyone she might want to date."

"If there are, I don't want to meet them. So tell me."

"There's not much to tell."

"Apparently there's years of history."

"Doesn't matter. He's out of the country anyway for God knows how long."

That should narrow it down to... half a dozen potential bastards.

"Stop trying to guess who it is," Alice says, correctly interpreting my silence.

"So why haven't you...? Did anything happen at all.... Is it just a crush or...?" Man, I suck at this.

Alice grins, hugging me again. "You suck at talking about feelings, but thank you for trying."

"So?"

"Well, I've been carrying that torch for a long time, and let me tell you, it *consumes* me. I can't make a relationship work with anyone else, and I think it's because I'm not trying hard enough."

"Because of the torch," I state. For a brief moment I do wonder if I've carried a torch—as my sister calls it—for Emilia since I was a kid, and that's why I never made an effort to be in a relationship before her. I dismiss the thought. I would've known if that was the case. Even I can't be that clueless.

"Yeah."

"Does he know how you feel?"

"Not sure." My sister looks unhappier than I have ever seen her, and that reason alone makes me want to deck the guy. I'm used to Alice either being bossy, teasing, or a bubble of joy. This is... hard, and I don't want to see her like this.

"How long's he gonna be out of the country?" I ask.

"No idea," she replies, shoving a handful of chips in her mouth from the bowl in the center of the table. I mull the situation over in my head, trying to formulate any advice. Part of me wants to tell her to just forget the idiot. If he hasn't caught on about her feelings, he's not good enough for her. But I know Alice. She's relentless. She never gives up, and she won't let go of this unless she's absolutely sure there is nothing more she can do.

"How about this: make your play whenever he's in town. If it works out, fine. If it doesn't, I'll give him a black eye. At least you'll know where you stand."

"Can't believe it. One of my brothers telling me to go after a man instead of flexing your alpha muscles and telling me no man's good enough?"

"That would only make you want him more."

"You know me too well."

I kiss her forehead. "True."

"Sounds like a plan," Alice exclaims. "You don't suck at giving advice on love as much as I thought."

"That's supposed to be a compliment?"

"Of the highest order." She tips up my beer glass, drinking the very last few drops.

"You just had to drink mine instead of

ordering a new one, didn't you?" I ask.

"Yep. It's more fun to steal yours. Now I really have to go if I want to make it to Nadine's. God knows I can use some girl time."

"Emilia has no time for girl time," I find myself saying.

Alice, who was in the process of rising from her chair, sits again. "She has that much on her plate, huh?"

"Yeah. She works full-time as a therapist, takes jobs on the side so she can pay a caretaker for her grandmother during the day, and looks after her grandmother herself on evenings and weekends. There's a neighbor who sometimes helps her out, but...."

"Maybe I can help. Let me know when you want to take Emilia out next time, and I can watch her grandmother. Not sure how much she'll remember me, but... I liked her. She was a force of nature back in the day."

"But you're busy," I counter. "You're running a restaurant and opening another one."

"It's not a problem."

"Alice, if you do this, you can steal my food and drinks all you want, and I'll never be mean to you again," I say, kissing her forehead. Out of my three sisters, Alice is the one hardest to predict. She can go from spitfire to the loveliest person in a split second. Her nurturing side might not be as obvious to others as Pippa's, but it runs just as deep. I shouldn't play sister favorite, but Alice and I always had a special bond.

She smacks my shoulder. "Don't you dare not be mean to me. It's our thing. Now, I have to go meet the girls. I want to try one of those dresses with lace at the waist. Maybe one with crinoline too."

And here she goes with the pig latin again.

***

Emilia

"You need to give me the recipe for your beauty treatment," Abby says on Tuesday as we're in the clinic's break room, nursing cups of coffee. Evelyn is with us too. She lies on three chairs, with her arms bent under her head.

"I slept well this weekend, that's all," I mumble, not willing to spill the beans. Abby and Evelyn never have any qualms about dishing on details about their private life, but I've never felt comfortable doing the same. Now more than ever, I feel as if I should keep quiet, as if what Max and I have together might disappear if I tell anyone about it.

"Girl, I bet you haven't slept at all," Evelyn says knowingly, sitting up on one chair. "Did you and Max finally get down and dirty?"

Heat creeps up my cheeks, and Abby's eyes widen. "Do tell."

"Yeah, I spent the weekend with him," I admit. They exchange knowing glances, and I suspect

I'm missing something.

"How was it?" Evelyn asks.

I shake my head vehemently. "I don't share details, you know that."

Abby springs to her feet, pacing the small foyer. "That's not fair. You told us all about Dickhead, and we were good friends and listened to you. But we need to hear some good stuff too."

"Yeah, come on," Evelyn urges. "Give us something."

I'm racking my brain for a good excuse to leave my interrogators, when my phone vibrates with an incoming call. My lips instantly form a grin when I see who is calling. *Max.*

Adopting an apologetic look, I hold up the phone. "Have to take this."

I walk a few feet away, but I can still hear their whispers.

"Aww, look at her. She never had that look on her face when Dickhead called," Abby says.

"It's almost dopey," Evelyn adds.

"I did tell you it was a good idea to stop that elevator." Abby's words make me stop in my tracks and turn to them.

"You what?" I sputter.

"I thought you said you needed to answer the phone," Abby says.

"You really stopped the elevator?" I grip my phone tightly, but as I watch the two of them, my annoyance melts into amusement.

"Well," Evelyn replies, eyeing her feet, "I

thought it would give the two of you a push."

"How do you even know how to stop the elevator?" Now I'm fascinated in earnest.

Evelyn doesn't miss a beat. "I watch a lot of movies. He looks like he cares for you, Emilia. Really cares for you," Evelyn says. "So we wanted to see what happened if the two of you were stuck with each other in a small space for some time."

"But nothing happened. You two are confusing me." Belatedly I realize the phone in my hand has stopped ringing.

"That's the point," Abby exclaims. "He was the perfect gentleman."

"That sealed it for us," Evelyn adds.

I bite back a laugh, deciding on the spot not to tell them about Max's borderline phobia of small spaces. They only tried to help, after all. In their own weird, juvenile way.

"Just don't do it again," I warn them. As if on cue, my phone rings again. This time, I do pick up.

"Sword, or bow and arrow?" Max asks. "You'd better pick the right one this time."

"You know what, since your obsession with weapons is still on, I think I'll choose a shield. You preparing to attack me?"

"Oh, I am. You can choose the battlefield."

"How gallant of you. What are my options?"

"Bed, kitchen counter, car. Theater."

"Theat— What?"

"I had actually called you up to ask you if you'd be up for watching a movie tonight. But now that you've sidetracked me, I'm open to discussing the other battlefield options."

Laughter rumbles out of me, open and unrestrained. "Can't tonight. Mrs. Wilson has been great about staying with Grams on Saturday, but I can't ask her again," I say regretfully.

Max doesn't miss a beat. "I talked to Alice. She said she'd be happy to spend some quality time with Grams tonight."

"Oh. Are you sure she doesn't mind?"

"Not at all. She always liked Grams, and she wants to help out."

"You and Alice are great." That's an understatement, if I'm honest. But if I say anything more than that, I might become too emotional. This isn't something people offer lightly. "Thank you."

"What time will you two be at my house?"

"Eight sounds good?"

"Great."

"You still have time to choose between sword and bow and arrow until then," Max says.

"I'm sticking to my shield."

When I click off, heading back inside the clinic, my smile feels dopey even to me.

***

I'm in a frenzy from the moment I arrive home. Preparing for my outing with Max is just one part; the other is preparing Grams for spending the evening with someone she doesn't know. Yeah, she knew Alice well as a kid, but I have no idea if she'll connect the dots when she sees her as an adult. Grams seemed to be her old self when I entered the house, which lifted my mood, right until she asked if there's any news about my father. I told her Max is helping us find him, and now I'm worried that she'll get her hopes up.

Ten minutes before Alice and Max are supposed to arrive, Grams becomes absent again, lost in her own world. By the time I hear a knock at the front door, I've worked myself into a ball of stress.

"Jonesie!" Alice exclaims when she sees me. I survey her from head to toe. She doesn't look even remotely like the girl I remember. She has a mix of romantic elegance and tomboyish charm that is unique to her. She's wearing a knee-length navy blue dress, while earrings in the form of the sun and the moon hang on her ears. Her dark brown hair is almost waist-long. I can't quite point out the tomboyish part. Maybe it's her smile, which resembles Max's almost to perfection. The man in question hovers behind her, looking up to no good.

"So nice to see you again, Alice. What did you bring?" I point to the bag in her hand.

"I brought some ingredients for Grams's famous banana pie. Thought I could ask her to show me how it's done. Tried it a million times, the cook at my restaurant a trillion times, but the one Grams used to make is still the best. I read up today that people with Alzheimer's feel more at ease around strangers if they do something familiar together. I didn't think Grams would recognize—"

I hug her, cutting her off midsentence. "You are lovely. Thank you."

"For the love of all that is holy, Jonesie! I'm a hugger, but don't strangle me."

"Sorry." I pull back, grinning at her. "Thanks for coming tonight."

"Hey, once an adopted Bennett, always an adopted Bennett," she says, referring to the old moniker the family gave me because I was at their place so often. "Even though you technically cease to be one if you get down and dirty with one of us."

"Alice!" Max admonishes.

"What?" She shrugs. "Not saying anything you two don't know."

I blush furiously as both of them step inside the house.

"Ignore her if she annoys you," Max whispers to me, smiling. "That's what I do."

"I heard you," Alice says, striding inside the living room without looking back. Ah, how I love the banter between siblings.

It takes almost half an hour to explain to Grams that Alice will be watching her.

"Grams, you can show her how to do your famous pie," I say for the twelfth time. The information seems to finally get through to her, and she walks with Alice to the kitchen.

"We don't have to go if you're not comfortable leaving Grams with Alice," Max tells me, sneaking up behind me.

"It's okay, they'll do great. Sorry it took so long."

"Hey, from where I was standing, I had a great vantage point directly to this." He pinches my ass, kissing my temple. His way of lightening up the mood. "I like seeing this nurturing side of you with your grandmother. It's sweet."

Sighing, I listen intently to Grams and Alice in the kitchen. They seem to be happily working together. As patient as Max was this evening, I'm afraid all this is going to wear on him eventually... that he'll throw in the towel and choose someone who has less responsibilities. My fiancé, Paul, seemed to be holding up with everything just fine, until he bailed. *Damn it*. It appears that getting rid of the wedding dress didn't do away with my insecurities.

"What are you thinking?" he asks the second we leave the house.

"Nothing," I answer quickly.

"I know that look, Jonesie," he says, nipping at my earlobe as we come to a stop in front of his car. "It ain't nothing. I'm a pest, remember? I'll nag you until you tell me."

"You're more like Alice than you know," I murmur. "I have to choose my battles with you."

"Yeah, you do."

"I just.... I was wondering if all the complications in my life will grate on you eventually, and you'll look for something easier."

Max jerks his head back, his expression hard. "Listen to me. If you'd let me, I'd do much more to help with Grams. But you have a mind of your own, and I respect your wishes. You know what I want? I don't want easy. I want you, Emilia."

"Wow. You're good with words," I say in a low whisper.

His lip curves in a delicious smile, a sure sign we're moving to playful territory. "Now, that's not all I'm good with, am I?"

Joining in on his game, I frown, feigning thinking hard. "You're a decent guitar player and popcorn-shopper."

"Interesting choice of non-compliments." He flattens me against the car door, invading my personal space.

"Were you expecting something else?" I tease.

"I don't want to put words in your mouth," he whispers in my ear. "Though I'd like to put something else between your beautiful lips."

A white-hot current zips through me, electrifying every cell in my body. Amazing how he can make me feel emotional, laugh my ass off, and then heat up for him in the span of minutes.

"You're getting ahead of yourself," I tell him, barely containing my grin.

"Nah, just know my strengths. Let's go, Jonesie. I have some promises to make good on."

Chapter Eighteen

Emilia

The next two weeks are the stuff dreams are made of. Alice watches Grams a few evenings when Max and I go out during the week, and the two of us spend some quality time with Grams during the weekends.

"Girl, you're going to drive him crazy," Evelyn comments, nodding at me. We're on our lunch break, and we are in a small shop close to the clinic, where I am trying on dresses. Max and I are going on a date after I finish my sessions, and after I carefully inspected my closet yesterday, I decided I need a new dress. I paid for the car repairs last week and had some extra cash left over.

"I love this dress," I say, doing a full turn in front of Evelyn, who is sitting in a comfortable armchair in front of the changing room. The dress is light green and fitted in the upper part, showing the curve of my waist, while the lower part is voluminous. It doesn't have any kind of straps, but as I tug on it a bit, I confirm that it won't slide downward, leaving my boobs hanging out mid-date. I bet Max would love that though. I also bet he'll make a comment about it in no time. Just conjuring his naughty smile in my mind, and imagining his even naughtier thoughts when he sees me dressed like this, makes me giggle. This man has been forever on my mind lately.

"Do you have the shoes to go with it?" the vendor asks, appearing next to me. She's a small thing, even smaller than I am, but she has the most perfect blonde hair I've ever seen. I pick up from the floor the bag I brought with me, where I stuffed my shoes.

"Here they are." Retrieving the shoes from the bag, I hold them up for Evelyn and the vendor to see them. They both seem unimpressed. "What?" I ask defensively. I love these shoes: classic, black leather peep toes with a five-inch heel. Yeah, they *are* old. Like college-freshman-year old. But they are in good shape... mostly. The leather is a little chipped on one of the heels, but you have to look really close to see it.

"What shoe size do you wear?" the vendor asks.

"Nine and a half," I reply.

"I have just the shoes you need," she announces, flinging her shiny blond hair behind her. What I wouldn't give to have such hair.

"Bring them here," Evelyn says at the same time I say, "No, thank you."

"They are on sale," the vendor says. "Seventy

percent off."

"In that case, I'd love to see them."

After the vendor leaves, Evelyn says, "It's okay to splurge on yourself from time to time. I can't believe you still have those old things." She'd know all about them, since she was with me the day I bought them.

"I only wear them on special occasions," I say.

She crosses her legs, laying her arms on the armrests. "Well, now you can set them on fire. You need new ones. Stop feeling so guilty about pampering yourself a little."

Pursing my lips, I swallow my reply, merely admiring the dress in the mirror. When the vendor brings the shoes though, my resolve breaks.

"These are perfection," I comment while stepping inside them. "And they fit me." My legs appear interminably long in them, and they work for this dress. The reduced price tag convinces me to buy them. I'm pampering myself without breaking the bank, *and* I'll blow my man's mind tonight. Win-win. "I'll take them."

"You look radiant," Evelyn says as I'm changing into my old clothes after the vendor leaves to pack the dress and the shoes. "You love him, don't you? He definitely looks at you like you're walking on water."

I pause in the act of putting on my jeans, leaning against the mirror. The curtain of the changing room keeps her from my view.

"I don't want to rush anything," I reply, which is not much of an answer.

Of course, Evelyn calls me out on it. "That's a lazy-ass way to avoid answering. It's okay to love and accept love, Emilia."

"Evelyn, I asked you to come with me to give me your opinion on the dress, not to psychoanalyze me."

"Can't help it. It's my job."

As Evelyn and I walk out of the store ten minutes later, there is a pep in my step all the way back to the clinic.

The afternoon goes by in a flash. Mrs. Deveraux is my last appointment.

"You look glorious, girl," she tells me. "Tell me your secret. New diet. Wait—new man?"

Blushing, I nod. "Yeah, the friend you saw about a month ago."

She whistles loudly, bending to do her back exercises. "Is he as good as I predicted he'd be?"

I blush even more violently. "He's fantastic."

"Girl, I'm jealous. Make sure you tap that as often as possible. There comes a time when you'll only be able to do it as often as your arthritis allows you to."

"Mrs. Deveraux," I admonish. At her faux-innocent expression, I add softly, "You don't have arthritis."

"No, but my partner does. My former one did too." She eyes me curiously. "Back to you. How did you go from he's just my childhood friend to sleeping with him?"

The question makes me pause. "It just felt right."

"He's a hot piece."

"He sure is," I agree. In a lower voice, I add, "And he truly is fantastic in bed. The sex is amazing."

Mrs. Deveraux gives me the thumbs-up. "I knew it."

"Now, let's return to our exercises."

After the session, I shower quickly and dress in record time in my new acquisitions. Even my hair is cooperating today, the usual frizz missing. I'm almost done applying makeup when my phone vibrates.

Max: I'm at the reception desk. Evelyn cornered me. She looks like she's about to give me THE TALK. Rescue me.

Instantly, butterflies roam in my stomach, my knees weakening a little. Oh boy, and I haven't even seen him face-to-face yet. Taking one last look in the mirror, I head out to meet him, walking with determined steps, like a woman on a mission. I find Max and Evelyn chatting a few feet away from the reception desk, and almost burst out laughing. Evelyn definitely has the *don't hurt my friend or I'll kill you face*. To his credit, Max appears to be his usual, laid-back self.

"Don't scare away my date, Evelyn," I say. Max's head instantly snaps in my direction, and I take immense pleasure in the way his eyes widen, even darkening a notch, as he looks me up and down.

"Merely making sure he knows someone has your back," Evelyn explains. I love this girl so much. "Now, I'll leave the two of you and go on with my boring evening. Have fun. I'll be living vicariously through you."

With that, Evelyn heads out of the building. Max loses no time pulling me into a side corridor.

"Is there anyone else left in the clinic?" Max asks. There is a light scruff on his chin and cheeks, and it looks mighty sexy on him. I never thought scruff and business suits would go together, but Max definitely proved me wrong. Then again, Max looks good wearing anything. Or nothing. I especially like him when he wears nothing.

"By this time everyone's usually gone. Abby must be somewhere around, since she's in charge of closing. But don't get any crazy ideas," I warn.

"Define crazy." Max stops right in front of me, cupping the side of my face with his hand. His eyes zero in on my lips, and I lick them in an almost unconscious gesture. He swallows, and the way his Adam's apple bobs down and up makes my knees weak. Dragging a thumb across my lower lip, he leans closer until his mouth covers mine. The kiss is explosive. Our tongues lash against one another in a frantic rhythm, while our hands explore. Mine roam over his chest; his are everywhere. My waist, my thighs—the upper part of my inner thighs. *Holy hell.* When his fingers nearly reach the fabric of my thong,

I break off the kiss.

"This," I whisper. "This is crazy."

"Oh no, Emilia. Backing you against the wall and making you scream for me would be crazy." His head is burrowed in my neck, and his hot, labored breath caresses my skin. One of his hands is still on my waist. "You make me go from zero to full hard-on in seconds. What am I going to do with you?"

"Whatever you want," I whisper.

"Is that so?" His lips trail up my neck until they reach the lobe of my ear. "Don't give me carte blanche, Emilia, because I *will* take you up on it." When he gently tugs at it with his teeth, heat singes my center.

"Max…."

"I'm one kiss away from having my way with you here. Or in that elevator around the corner."

This brings a giggle out of me. "I thought elevator sex wasn't in the cards."

"Right now, I'm reconsidering it."

Pushing him away, I step back. "Keep your dirty thoughts until after our dinner. Where are your manners, Bennett?"

"You make me forget I have any."

"Let's go," I say, because his eyes still have that dangerous glint that sends delicious shivers down my back.

As we step out of the building, we find Mrs. Deveraux smoking and pacing in the small park in front of the clinic.

"Is anything wrong, Mrs. Deveraux?" I ask her.

"No, dear. Just waiting for my date to pick me up. Have fun with yours." She gives Max an exaggerated wink, which makes him frown.

"Err, why did your patient give me the sex wink?" Max asks once we're out of her earshot, looking somewhere between surprised and panicked.

"She told me from the very first time she saw you that you'd be a stud in bed for sure."

Max lightens up considerably at this. "How could she tell?"

"Apparently there's this way you walk that made her awesome-sex radar pick up."

"And here I thought I actually had to prove my worth to women by doing the actual deed. Turns out, all I have to do is walk around."

"Sorry to disappoint," I say cockily, "but I think Mrs. Deveraux's level of wisdom can only be acquired with age. You still have to prove yourself to us youngsters out here."

Max doesn't reply, merely kisses the living daylights out of me, right in the middle of the sidewalk.

"There's no sweeter challenge than proving it to you," he whispers in my ear, making me shiver. As he leads us to the car, Max places a protective arm around my shoulders and I interlace my fingers with his.

"Why are you smiling like that?" he asks, kissing my temple.

"I'm just amazed how you can go from sexy beast to protective boyfriend in just a few minutes."

"Hey!" He shoves the side of his hip playfully against mine. "I can wear both hats at the same time. For example, now, I'm thinking about how easy it is to feel you up in this dress. I have free access below, and I bet if I pull it down, I'd have a wonderful view of your tits."

"Haha! When I bought it, I wondered how long you'd last until you made a comment about it. We didn't even climb in your car yet."

Max shrugs, and as we come to a stop in front of his car, he opens the door for me. I love the gentlemanly side of him. Damn it, I love every part of him.

"I have a dirty mind. Always have, always will," he says before closing my door.

We drive in silence to the restaurant, and as the car veers on a street snaking along the shore, I press my nose to the window.

"I love the ocean so much," I whisper.

"I know. But you never told me why you love it so much."

"Not sure. When I look at it, I can almost believe that anything is possible, that the possibilities are endless."

"We can go on a cruise around the world one day."

My head snaps in his direction, his words reaching somewhere deep inside me. "That's incredibly sweet of you. But I don't think we could take so much time off from work."

He smirks. "The wonders of modern technology. I can do most of my work from anywhere if I have cell phone reception and Internet. And you can take a break."

"You know I can't afford one."

"Emilia," he says in a measured tone, keeping his eyes on the road, "I know you're stubborn, but I do have more money than I could need in this life, and I have every intention of sharing it."

"I don't take handouts." My voice is strong and unwavering.

He groans. "Jesus, we'll always fight on this."

"Probably," I say, but smile to myself as one word bounces around in my mind. *Always.* Can I really allow myself to hope that there will be an always for us? When twenty-eight years have shown me that the only constant is disappointment?

I push those sad thoughts out of my mind as we arrive at the restaurant a while later. It's on a cliff high above the sea, and all the walls are made of glass. The view is amazing, the atmosphere is romantic and intimate, and I might never want to leave.

"Wow," I exclaim once we're sitting at our table. "How can such a place exist?"

"A friend of mine opened it as an experiment."

"I like your friend already."

As we scan the menus, Max's phone buzzes. He takes it out of his jacket with the clear intention of shutting it off. Then he frowns, and instead puts it to his ear, mouthing *Sorry.*

"Max Bennett," he says into the phone. The voice at the other end speaks rapidly, but I can't make out the words. "Okay, keep me in the loop." After clicking off, he shoves the phone back into the pocket of his jacket.

"Max? Is something wrong?"

"Let's order." His words are clipped and heavy. I don't like seeing him like this, but I will let it go for now. Maybe he'll cool off in a few minutes. The waiter jots down our order, returning quickly with our drinks.

"You know you can tell me anything, right?" I ask Max once we're alone. "You don't have to, but you can."

He takes one sip from his glass before answering. "That was the detective who is searching for your dad."

Oh. Now I wish I hadn't pushed.

"What did he say?"

"That he's got three good leads. One in Chicago, one in Wisconsin, and one in Quebec, Canada."

My heart leaps to my throat. "Three? He narrowed it down to three in such a short time?" My father's name is Julian Campbell, and he shares the name with a few thousand others.

"Not necessarily. He says they look like possible matches, but he's still researching other leads."

I remain quiet, my eyes fixed on the candle between us. Sweat breaks at the back of my neck, and I have the distinct feeling that someone is poking the inside of my throat with a needle.

Max reaches for my hand over the table. "Tell me."

How can two simple words carry so much weight? Hesitantly, I place my hand in his, soaking up the warmth and reassurance he radiates.

"I don't know what to say," I explain.

"Anything that's on your mind."

With other men, I kept my cards close to my chest. But Max makes this impossible, even if I wanted to. Maybe it's because we have so much history, but there is an inherent trust between us that I didn't have with other men.

"I don't know if this is good news or bad."

"Do you want me to stop the search?"

"No, not at all." He watches me with an expectant expression, and I decide to open up. "I don't remember much about him. But on the day of Mom's funeral, I overheard him fighting with Grams. He told her he hadn't signed up to be a single father and raising me on his own was too much work, that he hadn't wanted me in the first place. " I have never shared this with him. In all our years of friendship when we were kids, I kept this to myself. Looking back, I think it was because I felt ashamed, as if it was my fault he left. My voice is uneven, but I force myself to keep talking. "And then when my fiancé bailed, he said something very similar, that being with me felt more like work than a relationship. It felt as though I wasn't worth fighting for, like I didn't deserve love. And now I've turned into an insecure mess."

"No, now you finally trust me. Thank you for telling me this. Explains a lot. I admire you even more for wanting to find him to make Grams happy."

I give him a small smile.

"Just to make one thing clear. You deserve love, and you are worth fighting for. You are an amazing woman, and it's a damn honor to be your man. I don't take that for granted. I don't take you for granted. You deserve everything, Emilia."

"So do you, Max."

Sighing, I try hard to swallow the love declaration that's on the tip of my tongue. *It's too soon.* Sometimes I think Max knows some deep parts of me better than I do. He didn't seem shocked or taken aback by my admission. I think that is because he saw my wounds a long time ago, and was looking for the right balm for them. When we were kids that meant being my friend, making me laugh and come out of my shell. Now… now he's saying all the right things.

A recognition strikes me and the surprise is such that it knocks the wind out of my lungs. I've been in love with Max Bennett since I was nine years old. I just didn't know it.

A startling noise jolts me out of my thoughts, and I discover I'm shaking with equal parts giddiness and nervousness. One day I will share this realization with Max, but now it seems too soon.

"Sorry," Max mutters, checking his phone. When he pushes it back in his jacket, he's frowning.

"Anything wrong?" I ask, wishing I could wipe that crease off his brow.

"Work stuff. We want to expand in Brazil, and I'm having trouble bringing their distributors to the negotiation table."

"I have full confidence you'll succeed," I assure him. "What other countries are you expanding into?"

"Mostly European ones. We got into France while I was in London, and last week I sealed a very good deal with some high-end retailers in Germany."

The waiter interrupts us, bringing mountains of food, and we exchange no words afterward, concentrating on the treats in front of us. Our dinner is delicious, and I discover Max loves clams. He ordered a double portion as his main course, explaining that he'll skip dessert instead. So while I'm savoring my stracciatella and chocolate ice cream, he's eating the last few clams, attacking them with a boyish enthusiasm.

"I always thought clams look too much like a pussy to enjoy them." I freeze the second the words are out of my mouth.

Max chokes on his bite and bursts out laughing, not calming down for a few long minutes. A few guests from the other tables have turned to us.

"Sorry," Max explains to them through chuckles. "My girlfriend here is very funny." Turning to me, he says in a low voice, "I can't believe you said that."

"Me either, even though it's true. But let's forget it. Clam talk is off the table."

"How about pussy talk?" he whispers. "Is that on the table? How about under the table? Or in the shower, on the bed. We can steer clear of any tables."

"Stop, or I'll drown in embarrassment. There are people around us." Granted, his voice is low enough that they can't hear, but I feel like my cheeks will catch fire soon.

"Why don't you check the situation under the table? It requires your attention." His gaze holds so much heat that I instantly ache for him, especially once I make sense of his words.

"Max," I admonish, my cheeks on fire.

"Do you know what hearing the word pussy from your mouth does to me?"

"Obviously it made you laugh," I mumble.

"It made me hard."

***

Those words bounce around in my mind, messing with my senses for the entire journey back home, which I'm certain is much shorter than it should be. Max is driving like a man possessed. When we finally reach his apartment, we wordlessly give in to our desire, not even making it to his bedroom.

He kisses my jaw and the column of my neck,

biting me gently at the base of it. Damn if that's not a turn-on. I dig my fingers in his arms to show my appreciation, then run my hands down his chest feeling him up shamelessly.

"I will make you feel so good tonight that you won't want to leave my bed ever again," he murmurs against my skin.

His voice is inviting, and everything about him beckons to me. His eyes, full of kindness and desire alike; his hands, searching and comforting at the same time. With every kiss and every word, he carves himself a place in my heart. He hoists me up on the counter in the kitchen, undoing the zipper of my dress, which falls to my lap, leaving my breasts exposed to him. His nostrils flare as he takes a sharp inhale.

"I've wanted to do this the entire evening." His thumbs caress the sides of my breasts, making my insides instantly tighten. Every word coming out of his mouth feels like a sinful promise. My body hums at his proximity, yearning for more of his touch. But Max doesn't seem to be in a hurry. His thumbs still torture the sides of my boobs in the lightest of caresses. Such a simple movement, such a devastating effect.

"O-okay," I stutter, drawing in a deep breath.

"Put your arms on my shoulders and wrap your legs around me." His voice drips strength and masculinity, a combo that makes me inherently trust him even though I don't know what he intends to do. I do as he says, and without warning, he lifts my ass off the counter. I tighten the grip of my legs around him, lacing my fingers at the back of his neck.

"Don't worry," he says, as if sensing my thoughts. "I won't let you fall."

"I know," I whisper. Max leads us to the bedroom, putting me on the bed, removing my dress and thong. Wordlessly he removes his own clothes as well, and as I watch him reveal more and more of his skin, I can't help a little movie playing in my mind.

"Why are you smiling?" he inquires.

"I was imagining you as a stripper."

Max chuckles, but doesn't stop removing his clothes. "You have a dirty little mind, Emilia."

"You need a stripper name." I frown, tapping my jaw with my forefinger, feigning to be thinking hard. "The Amazing Max?"

"That's too tame. How about Orgasm Machine? Or—"

"You need to earn such a name first," I tease, flaunting my hand as if he couldn't possible deserve the nickname.

"Challenge accepted. Lie on your back."

I do as he says, now looking forward to his sweet torture even more than before.

"Spread your legs for me." The commanding tone in his voice sends tendrils of heat low in my body.

"What if I don't want to?"

"Oh, you'll want to."

We engage in a battle of stares, and he wins of course. I spread my legs and he settles between them, lounging over me.

Max peppers my chest with kisses, my nipples puckering almost painfully, begging for his attention. He licks the sides of my breasts with the tip of his tongue.

"Your skin tastes so sweet."

My hips buck off the bed as need sears me, but Max takes his damn time, nuzzling one nipple and then the other.

Finally, finally he descends with his kisses, lingering around my navel for a few excruciating seconds before going further down. But then he proceeds to kiss my inner thighs, completely ignoring my center. I writhe and moan as his lips nuzzle the soft skin of my legs.

"Max, please."

"You're so wet," he murmurs as he drags his thumb up and down my entrance, making me shudder. "I love seeing you like this."

He lowers his head and when his lips touch my sensitive flesh, my entire body ignites. I hold my breath as he sucks gently on my clit while thrusting one finger inside me, moving it in and out at a frantic pace. Needing more, I buck my hips, looking to meet his thrusts.

"Stay still," he commands.

"No can do," I whisper. "I—"

Abruptly, Max pulls his hand away. I sigh in protest, feeling betrayed.

"Every time you don't do as I say," he explains, "I will stop what I'm doing."

I pout, letting know his words don't make me happy, but I secretly enjoy this little game of his. Which I'm certain he knows.

Placing my hips back on the bed, I nod, licking my lips for good measure. His eyes darken instantly, and he rewards me by sliding two fingers inside me. He mimics the act of making love with his fingers, his mouth expertly suckling and nipping at my clit until I come, harder than I ever have before.

"One."

I barely have time to register what he means before I feel one stroke of his tongue right under my entrance. A white-hot shudder thunders through me as I realize he's counting orgasms. As he licks me all the way to my clit, I become so wanton and aroused, I don't know what to do with myself. My flesh is still tender from my orgasm, and Max's mouth gives me as much torment as it offers me pleasure. Time to return the favor. Placing my palms on his shoulders, I push him away. He cocks an eyebrow, but I just shake my head, rising to my knees. He's in the same position. I take advantage and run my hand once over his muscle-laced torso. Then, lowering my head, I lick him once from his navel up on his chest. Max grips my hair gently, pulling me up until our eyes are almost level.

"Turn around," he commands. His eyes have a spark of dominance that strike right in my core.

"Okay."

No sooner is my back to him than he says, "Lie down on your stomach."

I'm shaking with anticipation as I follow his instructions. My tender nipples hurt as I touch the bedsheet. Before I realize what's going on, Max shoves a pillow under my center, lifting my ass up. Having the length of his erection against my ass cheek sends sparks of desire along my nerve endings. Not being able to see him or anticipate his next move makes this waiting game all the more thrilling. Then I feel his hot and humid mouth at the base of my spine, trailing up my back until he kisses my neck.

"I will be so deep inside you, Emilia," he all but grunts into my ear. His fingers reach down, coaxing my clit, which is still oversensitive from the last orgasm. I come in one minute flat, biting into my pillow. "Two."

My entire body is on fire as my orgasm still pulses through me, but I want him. All of him. He's making me insatiable.

"I need you inside me, Max. Now."

A strange sound reverberates from my left, as if Max is rummaging for something on the nightstand. The sound of ripping foil follows. *Condom.*

The anticipation is killing me. My flesh is still so tender, I think I will explode the second he enters me. When he slides the tip inside me, a shiver runs through my entire body.

"You're so tight." He slides inside me to the hilt, coaxing a whimper out of my mouth. "Oh, fuck, Emilia."

I pulse around him already as I push myself into him, needing more. Needing everything. We give in to the throes of passion without restraint. The sound of flesh slapping against flesh resounds in the bedroom, intermingled with our moans and groans. I place my palms on the mattress to steady myself as wave after wave of pleasure sears me. Pressure builds deep inside me as every inch of my body tingles with the need for relief.

"Fuck," Max says on a groan. "You feel too good. I'm going to come soon."

His words are like a match, lighting my senses on fire. As he widens inside me, my insides clench tightly, and my orgasm races through me at the same time Max finds his release. He remains on top of me for long minutes, drawing deep breaths. Having his hard chest against my back and his strong arms at my sides is amazing. We're both at peace, at least until I decide to be naughty and squeeze my inner muscles around his softening erection.

"What are you doing?" he inquires, propping himself up on an elbow.

"Giving him a small thank-you hug for all the great work."

"I see. He hasn't done such great work if all he deserves is a *small* thank-you, though."

"Never said that."

"I'm curious, what would be a *big* thank-you?"

"You'll know it when you see it. Or feel it," I reply playfully.

A few minutes later, he lies by my side and I

nudge against him, finding my favorite spot—between his shoulder and his chest, with my nose resting in the crook of his neck. He drapes his arm around me, and I feel warm and safe and loved. I want to stay here forever.

Chapter Nineteen

Emilia

Max and I spend the next week wrapped in a bubble of our own making. While we don't manage to carve out time for another actual date, he stops by during my lunch break a couple of times. We finally agree on a cozy night in at my house on Friday evening, but when the day arrives, I'm forced to text Max and ask for a rain check.

Emilia: Sorry, nasty stomach bug. Need a rain check

Grams was down with a nasty stomach bug last night. She's marginally better now, but unfortunately I caught the bug too. So I'm hugging my toilet seat, emptying the contents of my stomach for the third time in two hours. I don't even have anything left to throw up, for God's sake. It has to stop at some point.

"Violet, honey, should I do something?" Grams asks, standing in the doorway of the toilet, her silver-gray hair hanging in sweaty curls. Normally, hearing her call me my mother's name would bring me to tears. As it is, I can't even muster the energy for that. I don't know if the sting in my throat is from the stomach acid or from fighting a sob. I'm a freaking mess.

"It's okay. Go to sleep, you need it after being sick last night." It's barely eight o'clock, but she needs her rest. Grams shifts her weight from one foot to the other, resembling a lost child and not my strong grandmother, before nodding and disappearing from my sight. I can't help thinking how this situation would have looked more than one year ago. I would have looked after Grams when she was sick, and she would have done the same when I was unwell. But now even the slightest change in her routine turns her upside down, and I'm taking care of both of us. I don't mind at all, but just for today, I want my Grams back. The old Grams. Feeling my stomach heave again, I lean over the toilet. Nothing comes out, but I don't dare move away. I reek of vomit, but I'm too exhausted to even rise to my feet and make it to the sink and clean my face.

I have no idea how long I stay like this, with my head on the cold tiles of the bathroom, curled in a fetal position. My stomach is rumbling violently again when the buzz of the door echoes throughout the house. *Go away.* There's no way I can pull myself together long enough to make it to the door. I listen intently for sounds that would indicate Grams is opening the door, but the house is silent. My own fault, I suppose. A while ago I convinced her to use earplugs at night, so she won't be bothered by the sounds of the street.

Whoever is at the door buzzes twice more before giving up. I sigh against the tiles, wishing they were softer. The side I'm lying on is starting to ache. I'm weighing my chances of making it to the bed when a loud sound from the living room startles me. I wince so violently that I knock the top of my head against the toilet.

"Owwww."

"Emilia? The back door was unlocked," Max's voice sounds from the living room. "Where are you?" My stomach recoils at the sound.

"I'm in the bathroom. Don't you dare come in here."

Which is exactly what he does, of course. I try to scramble into a sitting position, but all I manage is to hit my head against the toilet again. Stupid toilet. Why is it standing in my way?

"Holy shit," he exclaims when he steps inside, which I suppose sums the situation just about right. I'm lying on the floor, reeking of vomit, and I might have two concussions from hitting the stupid toilet bowl. Max holds two small bags with pharmacy signs on them.

"What are you doing here?" I ask on a groan. "I texted you saying I need a rain check."

"Because you're sick." Holding up the bag, he adds, "I went to the pharmacy and bought everything they had for stomach bugs, which isn't much. The pharmacist says it's important to let it all out."

"It's all out, trust me. If anything more comes

out, I'll be vomiting my intestines."

"Where is Grams?"

"Sleeping. She's okay now."

Max crouches next to me. My first instinct is to push myself away so he can't smell me. I decide against it because there's a high chance I'll smack my head against the toilet bowl again, and I think I might pass out this time.

"Let's get you cleaned up," he says softly, pushing a strand of hair that sticks to my cheek out of my face. Vomit clings on it. I want to die.

"Max, please go. I don't want you to see me like this."

"Are you insane?"

"I've hit my head twice against the toilet, so I can't rule out the possibility. I'm very embarrassed right now."

He sits next to me, propping my head on his thigh. I'm marginally better, because his thigh is softer than the floor. Not soft enough though, because my man works out too much for that.

"We've seen each other when we had measles. This is nothing in comparison," Max says.

"What are you talking about? We never had measles. I didn't at least. Maybe you had it after I moved."

"Yes we did. That time when we had red spots everywhere."

"That was chicken pox, Max."

"Whatever."

I move my head slightly, flinching when my

stomach burns anew. *Oh no.* This can't be happening again.

"I still can't believe we had it at the same time," I mumble.

"Can I tell you a little secret? I gave it to you on purpose."

"Huh?"

Weirdly enough, I remember that time crystal clear. Probably because it was a sunny spring, and Max and I were locked inside the house for what seemed like an eternity. We were ten, and the evening before I came down sick, he snuck into my bedroom to bring me some stickers I forgot at his house. When I woke up, I had five red, painful blotches on my body.

"I already knew I had chicken pox when I came to your house," he says, as if reading my thoughts. "Mom forbade me to leave the house. When I realized I'd be stuck inside for weeks, I decided I didn't want to be alone. Mom even moved Christopher to another room so he wouldn't get sick."

"You had half a dozen siblings in that house, but you chose me?"

"What can I say, Jonesie, there was no one I'd rather be sick with than you."

"Wow." I swallow my laughter for fear that any chuckle and giggle might be accompanied by my stomach acid. "You chose me to give chicken pox to. That's really romantic. Hate to burst your bubble, though, but you didn't have anything to do with it.

The incubation period is ten to twenty days, so I contracted it long before that."

"Well, damn."

We had fun, even though we were sick. Mrs. Bennett convinced Grams that it was better if I stayed at their house until I got healthy again, because I needed care and Grams couldn't take so many days off. Since Christopher was moved to another room, I got to share a bedroom with Max. The boys had bunk beds, and even though the top one belonged to Max, he let me sleep in it, because I wanted it so badly.

"It's different now, Max. We're dating. You're supposed to think I fart rainbows and never have morning breath."

"You're delusional."

"All the more reason for you to go home and do something fun on a Friday night," I insist.

"That's not going to happen. You'd better get used it."

"Ugh, I don't even have the energy to fight you."

"Excellent. I win by default then."

He runs his palm on my back in circles, and God, it feels good.

"What's in the other bag?" I ask, realizing one of the bags doesn't have a pharmacy sign on it.

"Some cheese crackers. I'd bought them for Grams before you told me you were sick. I remember she liked them. She still does, doesn't she?" he asks, glancing down at me.

"Stop being so considerate about everything," I tell him without thinking.

Max cocks an eyebrow. "Why?"

Sighing, I admit, "I'm not used to it. I don't know how to react."

"You mean to say I wasn't considerate before?"

"No, no. You always were sweet to me, but now it's different, because...." My voice trails off when I catch his smile. "I'm not making any sense, I know."

"You are, Jonesie. Because I *know* you." He places a kiss on my forehead that shouldn't make the skin on my entire body heat up, but it does any way. This man deserves a medal for not even cringing at the way I smell. I can barely stand myself. "It has to do with the farting rainbows bullshit. You think that because I got in your pants, I'll suddenly become some kind of jerk."

I cover my face with my hands. Through my fingers, I say, "I'm sorry. I know it's not fair to hold you to the standard the jerks in my past have set."

"Actually, I have no problem with it. They've set the bar so low it makes exceeding your expectations very easy."

"Wow, when you put it that way." I chuckle, and immediately I regret it because my stomach heaves.

Max shrugs, pointing to the bag of crackers. "Anyway, I was just being self-absorbed. I thought my chances of Grams chasing me out of the house with a broomstick would be lower if I brought her favorite crackers."

"I love it when you're being self-absorbed."

"You're mine, Emilia. Get used to me being around all the time."

Mine. The word rolls back and forth in my mind, goose bumps rising on my skin. I like the sound of it. It makes me feel safe and hot and bothered at the same time. I never thought the two feelings could coexist. But if there is a man on this planet who can achieve the impossible, I have full confidence it's Max. Almost instinctively, I lean against him, resting my head on his chest, close to the crook of his neck.

***

Max

"Don't you want me to move you somewhere more comfortable?" I ask her.

"Nah, moving makes me want to throw up."

Damn, hadn't thought of that. But there must be something I can do to make her feel better. "Let's get you cleaned up."

Emilia grunts, but nods. "Just don't forget that I can't move too much."

Carefully, I prop her up on her ass, and that's when I see the traces of vomit on the front of her shirt. She tries to cover them with her hands, offering me a mortified smile.

I remove her clothes one by one, and there is nothing sexual about this moment. We're quiet as I wash her, rinsing her skin and her hair. Afterward, I intend to carry her to the bedroom, but no sooner do I lift her in my arms that she says, "Oh no. Put me down, quick."

She makes it to the toilet in the nick of time. I hold her hair back while she throws up.

"I'll sleep here."

"Won't Grams need the bathroom over the night?"

"Nah, she sleeps like a rock until morning. I'll stay here. It doesn't make sense to leave. You can sleep in my bedroom," she tells me after rinsing her mouth over the sink while I hold her.

"Stayin' right here, sweetheart." I lie down on the floor, patting my chest, indicating for her to place her head there.

"I don't know if I should. What if I throw up on your shirt?"

In a stroke of genius, I remove my shirt. "Problem solved. Clever tactic to get me to strip, Jonesie."

She chuckles, leaning next to me, perching one leg over me and resting her head on my chest. My dick twitches when I feel one of her boobs against the side of my torso. *Forget it, Bennett. You're not getting laid tonight.*

"Thank you for staying here with me," she says softly.

"Hey, I'm spending the night with a beautiful,

naked woman in my arms. Couldn't get any better."

Well, it could. The floor is damn hard, but my woman finally seems comfortable, so I'm not moving even if my back will kill me tomorrow. Emilia traces some lines on my abs with her fingers, which further endangers the situation below the belt. *Damn it.*

"Why do you have to be so perfect?" she murmurs. "I have to get you to drink lots of beer."

"You want me to have a beer belly?" I ask in confusion.

"Yeah. We must do something about your pretty face too. Make you uglier. Or maybe cover it up with a thick beard."

"Why?"

"So no one can steal you from me," she whispers, hiding her face from me. I barely stop myself from kissing her senseless to show her how much she means to me.

"No one will, Emilia. I want to be happy, and lately that means making you happy."

Chapter Twenty

Emilia

On Tuesday I'm well enough to present myself at the clinic, but I'm on a diet of toast the entire day. I don't trust my stomach at all. The weekend was a blur of stomachache and multiple close-ups of my toilet bowl. All I distinctly remember is Max's warmth and patience as he took care of me. I didn't think this man could get under my skin any deeper, but he did.

I have a silly grin on my face the entire day, which garners me curious and skeptical glances alike from my patients. Yeah, I probably seem like a madwoman to them, especially because I chuckle to myself from time to time when I remember tidbits of my conversations with Max. There's no bonding like spending an entire night together on the bathroom floor. That night, the entire weekend, in fact, meant a lot to me. I'm in this so deep, it scares me.

In the afternoon I have a half hour break because one of my patients cancelled at the last minute. I take advantage and walk to a bench outside, hoping to soak in some sunrays before the sun sets. On the way there, I catch my reflection in a mirror. I have dark circles under my eyes and my skin is two shades paler than usual. I lost five pounds over the weekend, and even though I resemble a zombie more than a living person, I have a certain *glow* I haven't seen before. I've never understood the concept of someone glowing until now. I must be losing my mind. Maybe that's why they say *madly in love*.

Lying on the wood bench outside, I close my eyes, smiling at the sun. The wind is downright cutting, but that's why I have a thick jacket today and I brought a cup of tea with me, which I am nursing in silence. Seconds later, my phone rings. My first instinct is to ignore it, but I change my mind as soon as I peek at the screen and notice the name of the caller. Max.

"If you were anyone else, I would have completely ignored you," I tell him instead of hello.

"Glad to hear I have special status. I wonder why that is."

"Mmm, might have something to do with your fantastic kissing abilities."

"I see. Any other abilities you might want to single out?"

"Nah, nothing else stands out," I tease him.

"I'll keep that in mind. Why did you want to ignore phone calls anyway? Your workday's over."

"Not exactly. I'm on a short break. I rescheduled some of yesterday's patients for today."

"You're overworking yourself." His voice has

changed from playful to hard within an instant. I shift to a sitting position, my back hurting a notch from the hard surface of the bench.

"I need the money. And I'm healthy." I take a few sips of my tea, waiting for him to bring up the reason for calling. When he doesn't say anything, I press, "Did you call for any reason?"

"Well, now that you mention it. I'll ask you something, and you have to say yes."

I chuckle, but make sure my voice is firm when I reply, "You can't boss me around, Max."

"Doesn't mean I won't keep trying."

"What's the matter?" My stomach tightens as I wait for his answer.

"My family is getting together at Pippa's house Thursday for dinner, and I want you to come with me."

Instantly I leap to my feet, fueled by a burst of energy. Unfortunately I also spill a good amount of the tea on myself. Thank God it was only lukewarm. "I'd love to. I can't wait to see your family again. I have to talk to Mrs. Wilson, but I think she'll say yes."

"You do know they'll drill you about us, right? I'll ask them not to, but—"

That makes me chuckle. "If your family is anything like I remember it, it won't work."

"They're exactly the way you remember them."

"Can't wait to see them again, anyway."

"All right. But if you hear the words

matchmaking or wedding, don't get too scared."

My hands clasp tighter, one around the cup, the other around the phone. "What?"

"My family has been on a mission to matchmake everyone. Long story, I'll tell it to you when I see you. Just don't worry if you hear the words. They're being tossed around very casually in my family."

Despite myself, I grin. Of course they'd be tossed around casually in the Bennett household. Jenna and Richard Bennett are the picture-perfect example of a happy marriage. For me, the child of a loveless marriage, those two words seem as real as the possibility of finding a unicorn in my back yard. My fiasco engagement reinforced that view for me.

"Can't wait to see everyone again," I tell Max honestly.

***

Max picks me up from the clinic Thursday evening. He's wearing jeans and a simple black shirt.

"Such a gentleman," I tell him as he opens the door to the passenger seat for me.

"Nah, was just looking for an opportunity."

"To do what?" I'm momentarily distracted by the patch of chest showing through the unbuttoned top of his shirt. A naughty impulse to lick that spot shoots through me. *Hot damn*. No man has ever had this effect on me.

"This."

Before I realize what is going on, Max tips his

head to mine, parting my lips and kissing me thoroughly. There is nothing tentative about it. He's claiming every inch of my mouth with ferocity, his passion dizzying me.

"Max," I admonish as we both come up for breath. "We're in front of the clinic. What if someone sees?"

"What if they do? All they see is me kissing my woman."

My woman. I like the sound of that. A lot. Still, that doesn't mean I'll let him get away with it.

"It's not professional. They won't take me seriously if they see me kissing a man as though I'm about to climb him. I worked hard at building my reputation."

His lips curl up into a half smile. "You want to climb me?"

"That's the only piece of information you caught from all I said?"

Max doesn't answer, instead holding my gaze in a silent challenge. It takes every ounce of my restraint not to burst out laughing, but I hold my ground. A few heated seconds later, he places a chaste kiss on my forehead.

"By the way, I forgot to congratulate you on scaring the crap out of John. I was at a seminar yesterday, and he avoided me the entire evening."

He steps back, and I notice his features have hardened. "You went to a seminar where John was?"

"Yeah. He's attending a lot of the same seminars I do."

"Why didn't you tell me?"

"I wasn't aware I'm supposed to ask for permission," I say dryly, now working to put distance between us.

"That's not what I meant. But I don't want you to be around him."

Instantly, I boil on the inside. "You can't dictate—"

"Damn it, that's not what I'm doing. I'm concerned for you, and that moron—"

"He insulted me. That's all. I agree he's an idiot, but he's not a danger. And as I said, he was avoiding me."

"Emilia—"

"No." Pulling myself to my full height, I look him straight in the eyes. I can go toe to toe with him. "I'm sorry, Max, this isn't how things are going to be. I have a career I worked hard for, and I will continue to do that. You need to keep that caveman in you in check. I won't have any of this."

Seconds of loaded silence pass before Max lets out an audible breath.

"I'm sorry, you're right. That was out of line." He runs an agitated hand through his hair. "When you said his name that image of you on the garage floor popped in my mind, and I lost it."

"So we're on the same page?"

"We are, but let's get one thing straight. You are mine to protect."

I try hard not to melt at his words. "From real threats, Max, not imagined ones."

"We agree on that."

I rise on my tiptoes, giving him a quick peck on his lips. "We just had a couple's fight."

He grins at this. "We didn't do too bad."

Opening the car door, he gestures for me to enter it.

"By the way, the neurologist said he can see Grams tomorrow evening," he says a few minutes later while we're speeding through the city.

"That's great." I finally convinced Grams that it'd be good to get another opinion on her medication. "Thank you." Needing to switch to a lighter topic, I ask, "Who's going to be at Pippa's house?"

"My entire family. Even Summer. She's been in Italy the past couple of months, but she's back now. Worked for a museum there. "

"Sebastian's wife and Logan's fiancée and Pippa's husband will also be there?"

"Exactly."

"So, what was that about matchmaking?"

Max doesn't miss a beat. "Mom wanted grandchildren for a while. Since none of us kids were in serious relationships, she took the reins into her own hands. Didn't really work out. Eventually Pippa took over from Mom, and she was surprisingly successful."

"Who plotted to bring Pippa and her husband together?"

Max gives me a startled look. "How do you know anyone did?"

"Just a hunch. I know your family. Meddling isn't a one-sided activity."

"Sebastian's wife, Ava, and Logan's fiancée, Nadine. I think Alice was involved too."

"I see those girls fit right in with the Bennett clan. Can't wait to meet them."

We fall into companionable silence, and I can't help smiling as I remember the family dynamics and how I always wanted to be part of the clan. I loved Grams, but there was something undeniably magical about the large, loud, and lovely family.

When I snap out of my memories, we've veered left into a quiet residential area in San Francisco. I've never been here before, but I can see the appeal this has for families. The streets are large and lined with thick, old trees, which cast a comfortable shade while still allowing in plenty of sunlight.

"They just moved in here last week." Max fills me in. "It took forever for them to find a house. Here we are."

Wow. Pippa and Eric Callahan's house is a thing of beauty. Spanning two levels, with a warm brown roof on top, it seems plucked out of a fairy tale. The house is huge though, a U-shaped building surrounded by a garden so large one could fit half the clinic inside.

"Why is it so large?" I ask as we walk up to the front door. "Eric has just one daughter, right?"

Max told me Eric was a widower and single

dad to a daughter when Pippa met him.

"Yeah, but I think they are planning on having even *more* kids after the twins," Max says with a fake shiver.

"You afraid of kids, Max Bennett?" I tease.

"Not exactly, but three sound like a handful already."

The front door opens before we have a chance to knock, and Jenna Bennett greets us. She looks every bit the woman I remember, plus a few wrinkles and white strands of hair. Her eyes haven't lost any of their kindness, nor has her smile.

"Max, thank you so much for bringing this lovely girl today."

She pays no further attention to her son, instead pulling me into one of those bear hugs I fondly remember. She smells like flowers and honey, and I could stay in the circle of her arms forever.

"It's so good to see you again, Emilia." She lets go of me, patting my shoulders. "I can't tell you how many times I wondered what became of your family after you moved away."

I had thought of the Bennetts often enough after I left. To know Mrs. Bennett also thought about us warms me on the inside.

"Mom, you can catch up with Emilia later. Let's say hi to everyone."

Mrs. Bennett nods, leading the way. I give him a speculative look as I walk with him behind her. Remembering his warning, I wonder why he's so eager to face them all. Maybe he has a plan.

The house is as beautiful on the inside as it is on the outside. Decorated in a simple yet elegant fashion, Pippa's eclectic spitfire and warm personality is visible in every corner. Mrs. Bennett leads us along a long corridor, which opens into a huge living room. Almost all eyes are on Max and me as we step inside, and I feel myself shrinking under their scrutiny and curiosity. My gaze immediately finds his father, Richard Bennett, looking as sturdy as I remember him, if a little tired. He was the best father figure I could have hoped for growing up. On one memorable afternoon when I was twelve, he came over to my house and taught me how to paint the front door, saying I should know how to properly paint. I asked him if he was teaching me because I had no dad who could do it, and he kindly told me that every girl should know how to paint, that he'd taught Alice and Pippa, and would teach Summer too when she was old enough.

"Eric, Ava, Nadine, this is Emilia," Max says.

I shake hands with the three of them, and then with Eric's daughter, Julie. The girl's age surprises me—she seems to be around thirteen, almost a teenager. Max never mentioned her age, so I supposed she was a small child. But this means Eric had her when he was very young. His story—the loss of his wife, and then his dedication to raising his daughter as a single father—hits a little too close to home.

I'm exchanging a few words with Julie when Max addresses the rest of the room. "Everyone else, you already know Emilia. Yes, we're dating. No, you can't pester her with questions. And I forbid everyone to say the words wedding and matchmaking."

I stare at him incredulously. This was his *plan*? Even I can tell how much shit his siblings are going to give him for this. I recognize Sebastian, Logan, Summer, Blake, and Daniel easily. The twins have wide grins on their faces as they shake their heads. I nearly choke when I see the person standing next to Blake. Christopher. *Holy smokes*. I knew he looked exactly like Max, but the impact of that fact became clear only just now. He's the same six feet of hotness as my man. I look away quickly, but still catch Christopher's self-satisfied smirk.

"Well, now that my genius brother made it awkward for everyone," Blake says, "we can move on. Nice to see you, Jonesie."

One by one, I greet everyone, making small talk and wondering how everyone grew up to be so attractive. Summer was a kid last time I saw her, but she's grown up to be a beautiful woman. This family has damn good genes. No sooner have I made the rounds than Summer and Alice each grab my arms, pulling me to one side.

***

Max

"When are we eating?" I ask Pippa as I follow

her to the kitchen, my stomach rumbling already.

"I'll check on the roast beef right now. I ran a little late with preparations."

"You're still cooking?" I ask in alarm.

"I'm pregnant, Max," she says as we enter the kitchen. "Not sick. And Eric cooked. I'm just checking on things."

"Yeah, but you should take it easy. You've been organizing your move and stopping by the office every day, and you're about to give birth. Slow down."

Pippa sighs. "The doctor says that moving and walking should help my water break. I am supposed to be due next week, but I barely even feel Braxton-Hicks contractions. And it'll probably be a delayed birth."

"But, but—they are twins. There's two of them, and not much space. Shouldn't they be in a hurry to come out?"

"Over 50 percent of twins are born preterm, and being overdue doesn't happen very often, but it does occasionally." My sister whisks a fork out of the sink, then proceeds to walk to the oven. "Let's see if this beauty is cooked."

"I'll check."

"You're adorable, but if I let you decide when it's cooked, we'll starve."

"Not true. I'm an expert at ordering takeout. And this can't be so difficult." I take the fork from my sister's hand, opening the door of the oven. Pippa smartly steps to the side, but I don't. The wave of heat hitting my face makes my eyes water.

Grimacing, I wipe the moisture from my eyes. "You could've warned me."

"Nope. Payback for always weaseling out of your cooking duties when we were kids."

Pippa chuckles, giving me instructions on how to check if the roast beef is done. Turns out it's not, so my sister feeds me some cold leftovers in the meantime. We sit at the small wooden table in the center of the kitchen.

"So," Pippa begins. "What's the deal with Emilia?"

I groan. "I thought I said—"

"We're not supposed to pester her on this issue, so I choose to pester you. I want to hear all about you and her."

"Make sure to speak loudly," Blake adds, appearing out of nowhere in the kitchen. "We all want to hear."

"Who's we?" I ask, dumbfounded. I answer my own question as Alice steps into view as well.

"Were you eavesdropping?" Pippa asks the two of them with a grin.

"No, we followed the smell of the food," Blake replies. He and Alice sit in the two remaining empty chairs at the table, whisking the plate of leftovers from me. My stomach is still empty.

"But we couldn't help overhear you say that you didn't plan on pestering Emilia," Alice tells Pippa. "Don't worry, Summer and I did it for you. She's head over heels where our brother here is concerned."

I look at Blake for help, but the bastard is just stuffing his face with my food.

"Girls," I say in a firm tone. "Keep out of it. Emilia and I are taking it one day at a time, enjoying getting to know one another. I'm not going to tell you anything more."

Alice raises a brow. "You've known each other for almost twenty years."

"Things are different once you get in a girl's pants," my brother supplies helpfully.

"What he said," I reply. "Only I wouldn't have phrased it like an asshole."

Blake shrugs, helping himself to more leftovers from the fridge.

To my astonishment, Pippa says, "Okay, we won't meddle."

"No offense, but I have a hard time believing that," I say.

Rising from her chair, she paces around the kitchen, patting her enormous belly. "I think you're right. You both need time to learn each other. You were tight as kids, yeah, but now it's different. Just be careful. Don't hurt her."

"What's that supposed to mean?" I feel as if someone punched me in the gut.

"It means you haven't had a serious relationship before, and men usually need one relationship—"

"Or ten," Blake chimes in.

Pippa glares at him before focusing on me

again. "Or more, until they get it right. From what Alice said, Emilia has a lot on her plate without heartbreak on top of it."

A loaded silence follows before Blake bursts out laughing. My sisters and I all turn to him.

"What's so funny?" I ask him.

"Man, Pippa couldn't push Sebastian and Logan hard enough, and she's actually warning you not to mess up." Leaning back in his chair, he places his hands at the back of his neck. "I guess it just feels good not to be the only one on the receiving end of warnings all the time."

Ignoring the stab, I focus on Pippa. "I won't hurt her. This isn't some sort of trial or fun for me. I'm serious about her. I've never felt this way about other women. Maybe that's why I didn't make an effort before."

Blake rolls his eyes, but my sisters have strange expressions on their faces.

"I'm serious about Emilia," I repeat. Pippa and Alice exchange glances before they both burst out laughing and high-five each other. "What's going on?"

Alice props her head in both hands, grinning widely. "You got played, that's what's going on. You wouldn't tell me much when I questioned you at Blake's bar, so I thought it would be best to hand the reins to the queen." She points to Pippa, bowing her head mockingly.

"I knew the only way to make you talk was to attack you," Pippa says simply.

"So wait, this whole *don't hurt her crap* was a ruse?" Blake asks, visibly disappointed.

Alice shrugs. "It got him to tell us what we wanted to know. That he's serious about her."

"I thought you were on my side, Alice," I say accusingly.

She jerks her head back. "Whatever gave you *that* idea?" She and Pippa share another malicious look. They manage to play me every single time. How is this even possible? Yet as I look at my two sisters half in awe, half annoyed, the warning—real or fake—does gnaw at me. What if I do end up hurting Emilia?

***

Emilia

The dinner is delicious. After we finish stuffing our bellies, we all head to the area of the living room housing two enormous L-shaped couches. Eric immediately arranges the cushions behind Pippa's back so she's comfortable, and it's clear he's doting on her all the time. They are precious together.

"Nadine and I have news," Logan says after everyone's seated. "We finally set our wedding date. It's in September."

"Congratulations." Ava hugs Nadine tightly, smiling at Logan. Everyone takes turns congratulating them and pestering them with questions about location and other details.

"Nothing's set in stone," Nadine repeats with infinite patience. "But I'd like a small wedding at the old ranch, like Pippa's."

"Yeah, not gonna happen." Logan kisses her forehead, patting her leg. "I want a big splash. I thought we'd agreed on it."

"We're still negotiating," Nadine tells the room. "But from time to time I like to let him think he's won."

Everyone roars with laughter, and Ava whispers to me, "That's the secret with the Bennett brothers. Always let them believe they're in charge. Ouch." She all but leaps off the couch, rubbing her arm vigorously where a grinning Sebastian pinched her.

"Emilia has enough experience dealing with Max," Mrs. Bennett says knowingly. "They were inseparable as kids."

"Yeah, you were at our house all the time," Christopher says. "You were the first adopted Bennett."

"What do you mean the first?" I'm genuinely confused.

"We use that nickname for other good friends who became close to the family. You started the trend," Christopher explains, and it's the weirdest feeling, as though I'm talking to Max, but also *not* talking to Max.

"I started a thing?" I whisper to Max. "I'm so proud of myself right now."

Max places an arm around my shoulders as he delves into a talk with Blake, who sits on the other side. I smile, soaking in his warmth and the energy and happiness floating in the room. A while later Eric and Pippa give us a tour of the house, which is as impressive as I imagined when I first saw it from the outside.

"I still can't believe you're a painter," I tell Summer honestly as Max and I are preparing to leave. Summer and I are outside, a few feet in front of the door, while everyone else is still inside. She's showing me photos of her latest creations on her phone. "They are amazing. I especially like this one. The sunflowers are gorgeous."

"You can have it. Tell me your address and I'll send it tomorrow."

"I couldn't. I'm sure you sell them for a lot of money."

"I always gift family and friends any paintings they like," Summer says sweetly. "If you don't tell me your address, I'll ask Max."

My eyes widen. "I see the bossy trait runs in the family."

"That it does," Max booms behind us. Grinning, I swirl around on my heels and place my palms low on his chest. Unable to help myself, I allow my hands to roam up to his neck, my body humming at his nearness, at feeling his hard muscles beneath my fingers. I'm about to give him a quick peck on the lips when I register the color of his shirt: dark green. Max was wearing a black one. I freeze on the spot. Raising my gaze, I notice the slightly shorter haircut. *Oh, no, no, no.*

With a trembling voice, I ask, "Is there any chance you changed your shirt and got a haircut in the span of five minutes, Max?"

"Wrong brother, sweetheart. But don't stop on account of that. My brother owes me. Still have to kiss his girl once to get even. Feel free to continue to feel me up. I was enjoying it."

"Christopher," Summer says briskly. "Not funny."

I'd forgotten she was here. Stepping back, I drag my hands down my face. I can't believe I almost kissed my boyfriend's twin brother. I've never felt more ashamed in my life.

"What's going on?" The voice belongs to Max himself, and he sounds pissed. Rightfully so. I stare at a spot on the floor, unable to meet his gaze just now.

"You just interrupted a near-make-out session," Christopher informs him. Nudging me with his elbow, he says, "If he annoys you too much, you can always dump him and take me instead."

After the awkward moment passes, Max and I bid Christopher and Summer good-bye and walk to the car in silence.

"I'm sorry," I murmur once we're inside his car. Instead of gunning the engine, Max slips his thumb under my chin, lifting it.

"Look at me," he says in a soft voice. Biting my lower lip, I do as he says.

"It took me a while to realize it's him." The

second I utter the words, I want to take them back.

Max groans. "I'm gonna punch that little fucker."

"No, you're not. He's your brother. You can't be jealous of him."

"I'm jealous of my own damn shadow when it comes to you, Emilia." His gaze is so intense, I swear it has the power to set every cell in my body ablaze. "You are mine."

I nod, licking my lips. He follows the gesture with his eyes, dragging his thumb across my mouth. "Your mouth is mine." His hand drops to my waist, reaching between my legs. "Your body is mine. Everything."

"Everything," I agree. Max claims my mouth, turning my knees weak with the power of his kiss. Energy zaps through me and our surroundings blur as my entire being focuses on the spot where our lips touch.

"Someone's naughty," Max says when we come up for air. One look down reveals that my nipples are showing through my flimsy dress.

"It's your fault."

"Because I'm so irresistible?"

Grinning, I decide to tease him now that we've put the critical moment behind us. "Because you brought me into a house full of sexy men. There are some incredible genes in your family. Your brothers are all panty-dropping gorgeous. Especially Christopher."

"Really?" he deadpans, his eyes serious. God,

riling him up is such fun.

"Hmm. I have a hard time deciding which one of you is hotter."

"You're too naughty for your own good."

I shrug one shoulder. "Nothing you can do about it tonight." We agreed that he'll drive me home, but won't stay the night, because he has a very early meeting tomorrow morning. But he'll stay at my house tomorrow and Saturday. I sense I'll get plenty of payback for teasing him.

"Wait until tomorrow."

Chapter Twenty-One

Emilia

"Thank you for coming to our house on a Friday evening," I tell the neurologist the next evening as he steps inside.

He shakes hands with Max, Grams, and me and then the four of us walk to the living room. Once we're seated, he focuses on Grams, who is very much herself right now.

He goes into detail about Grams's medication. We see her usual doctor about every two months, because as the disease progresses, some of the pills lose their effectiveness or the goal of the treatment shifts.

The most heartbreaking part of every visit though, is reading out loud *the List*. Grams writes on a piece of paper every single thing she feels has worsened in her mental health since the last visit to the doctor. I keep a list of my own.

"And last week," Grams concludes, "I got lost in my own damn house."

I bite down on my lip, my eyes stinging. The doctor watches Grams with kind, warm eyes, nodding.

"How long until I completely lose my mind?" she asks him bluntly. I startle in my chair, and Max, who sits next to me, puts his palm at the small of my back. The reassuring gesture is exactly what I need to keep strong.

"Mrs. Campbell," the doctor tells her gently, "every patient is different. The new medication should help mitigate some aspects, such as the headaches you told me about."

But it won't help you not get lost in your own house.

He doesn't say the words out loud, but they hang in the air like a thick fog. After writing down the prescription for her new set of pills and giving us some more helpful pointers, he leaves. Max walks him to the door, while Grams and I remain seated in the living room, the usual sadness that follows a doctor visit rearing its ugly head again.

We order some pizza, and I can't take my eyes off Grams during dinner. She is lost in thoughts, and I'm convinced she's slipped away from us when she surprises me. "Emilia, any news on finding your father?"

Sucking in a deep breath, I swallow the last bite. "The detective is trying to locate him. I'll let you know as soon as I have a definite answer."

"Thank you for doing this. Both of you." She looks at Max and me with adoration before returning to her dinner. After she's done, Grams excuses herself, saying she wants to go to bed early.

Once we're alone, Max and I move to the couch, and he pulls me in his arms.

"That was rough," he murmurs.

"Yeah. I think the worst is knowing what's coming and not being able to stop it. I don't even know how to comfort Grams anymore."

"You're doing a great job just being here for her." Pushing a strand of hair away from my face, he adds, "And wanting to find your father for her. You're amazing."

My insides tighten, fear clouding my thoughts. "Let's hope that'll turn out okay."

"Do you want to talk about it?"

"No. It'll just put me in a bad mood, and it's not going to help anyway. I guess until I meet him, it's not worth fretting about it. My plan is to actually fly wherever my father is and meet with him before telling Grams anything. I don't want to get her hopes up in case things go wrong. I hope they don't." With a sigh, I add, "Thank you for being here tonight."

"Anything you need, Emilia. I mean it."

I lay my head against his chest, playing with my fingers around the buttons of his shirt. "Can you tell what I need now?" I ask playfully.

"A distraction," he says without missing a beat. "Which I am more than happy to provide."

Without warning, he stands, lifting me in his arms. We're quiet as he carries me to the bedroom, but I manage to sneak my hand between our bodies and cup his already hard length with my hand.

"I'll show you."

Carefully placing my feet on the floor once we're in my bedroom, Max runs his hand through my hair, twirling a strand around his fingers.

"You've become quite the little vixen," he says.

I look him up and down, notice the thin trickle of sweat on his forehead, the desire in his eyes. "I like the effect that has on you."

In a fraction of a second, he hooks an arm around my waist and hoists me up against the wall.

"You drive me crazy," he whispers against my skin, his low and husky voice raising goose bumps on my neck. He slips his fingers under one of my straps, pulling it down my shoulder, baring my skin to him. Stepping closer into my space, he dips his head, feathering his lips on my shoulder. Moaning, I tilt my head to the side, giving him better access as he brings his lips to my neck, ascending to my ear. Every inch of me clamors to be touched, kissed... loved by this beautiful man who is claiming more of me with every word and every look.

My hands find the hem of his shirt, slip under it, and feel up his gorgeous abs.

"Greedy girl."

"Always. I'll always be greedy for you."

He nudges my legs open with his knee, his hand already undoing the zipper at my back, pushing my dress down my arms. The fabric falls to my feet, leaving me naked and exposed.

"Look at you, all beautiful and ready." He looks me up and down with a hunger that sends a jolt right through my center. He doesn't even have to touch me. His gaze is all I need to be on fire. "What should I do with you?"

"As long as we can keep quiet, whatever you want." My own voice is breathy and needy.

"Dangerous words, love." He smiles devilishly before grabbing both my wrists with one hand and pinning them above me, leaving me defenseless. But if there is any man I want to be defenseless with, it is him.

"You'd better make good on your promise."

He kisses me like a man possessed, swiping his tongue over my lips before dipping it in my mouth and exploring me until I'm trembling in his arms.

Instead of continuing with his delicious kisses, he steps back, scrutinizing me with those mesmerizing eyes of his.

"What are you doing?" I complain, pouting.

"Deciding which way to make love to you tonight."

Wow. That was incredibly sweet and hot.

"What are the options?" I work to make my voice as neutral as possible, but I don't fool him.

"Wouldn't you like to know?"

"I don't get a say in it?"

"Nope."

Right. Time to gain a little more control over the situation. Closing the distance between us, I undo the top few buttons of his shirt, planting a kiss after popping open each new one.

"What if I want you to do all of those dirty things going on in your mind?"

"Feisty." His voice is low, and I detect a hint of a shake in it.

"You bring out a side in me I didn't know I

had," I say honestly.

"Back at you, Emilia."

His thumb touches my lip from one corner to the other, and then he does the same with his tongue. Sealing his lips over mine, Max grips one of my thighs, grazing it with his nails. He needs me just as badly as I need him. His hand descends to my ass, cupping my cheeks and pressing me against him. I moan as I feel how hard and ready he is for me.

"Max...," I whisper.

"Fuck, I need you."

I turn to putty in his hands as we remove each other's remaining clothes at lightning speed.

"Sit on the bed," he instructs, which I do. Watching his erection in front of me is too tempting. I wrap my hand around it and swipe my tongue once over the head. Max lets out a deep groan, gripping my hair with one hand.

"Fuck, that is sexy," he says on a moan as I take him in my mouth as deep as I can. "You're sexy, Emilia."

Unhitching my lips from him, I crawl backward on the bed, keeping my eyes trained on him.

He leans over me, his hand sliding down between my thighs.

"You're so wet and beautiful, Emilia. I could come just from watching you."

But he's not just watching me. His palm is wrapped around his erection, moving up and down. He presses the thumb of his other hand on my clit, circling the bundle of nerves. Watching him please us both is possibly the most erotic moment of my life. Need splinters me, making me ache for him to the point where it's almost painful. He places my feet on his shoulders, lowering himself until his beautiful face is level with my center. Without unhitching his thumb from my clit, Max dips his tongue inside me once.

I swallow a moan, flattening my back against the bed, pushing my hips forward. When he dips his tongue again, I'm positive I'm one second away from making love to his face. His expert mouth feasts on my swollen flesh, nipping and lashing until I am ripe for him. My fingers find the soft curls of his hair and I tug at them gently, greedy for more of him.

"I want you," I whisper. "Inside me. Please."

He straightens up, retrieving a condom from my nightstand. Holding my gaze, he sheaths the condom over his erection. He pushes his length across my folds, touching my clit in the process. My thighs quiver, an unbearable tension forming in my center. Unable to wait any more, I push myself up, gripping the base of his erection and positioning it at my entrance.

"Taking control. I like this." Max enters me in one swift move, pushing in so hard, he sends me into a tailspin. My inner muscles instinctively clench against him.

"Max. So deep." I bite down on my lips, stopping the incoherent string of words.

"I'll never tire of hearing that."

Max runs his hands up and down my legs while moving faster and faster. I won't last long, and neither will he.

"Touch yourself," he commands. I lower my hand to my clit, all shame or restraint forgotten. I move my hand at a frantic pace, feeling pressure building inside me.

"This is the sexiest thing I've ever seen."

I writhe and moan, begging for my release as my climax builds inside me. Sweat breaks out on my forehead as I increase the pace of my fingers, just as Max increases the speed of his thrusts. Every thrust brings me closer to the edge. When my orgasm finally engulfs me, I swallow my cry of pleasure, his name on my lips.

***

Max

The next morning I wake up before Emilia. She is sprawled on the bed, her leg swung over me. For a brief second, I consider waking her up and giving her a quiet orgasm instead of a "good morning," but that would be selfish. She is peaceful and beautiful in her sleep, and all I can do is look at her and wonder how it can feel so right to have her here with me. What was I doing before? How could I have known she existed and not gone after her? She wrinkles her nose in her sleep, pushing a rebel strand of hair off her face, and I can't resist placing a soft kiss on the tip of her nose. She's just too damn cute. She wrinkles her lips this time, then turns her head in the other direction. The message is clear: no morning sex. Yet.

I leave the room as quietly as possible, heading to the living room. Grams is nowhere to be seen, so I assume she's still sleeping. I'm about to go off and buy breakfast when I remember that Emilia actually cooks, so she might have breakfast food already.

An idea strikes me while opening the fridge. Grams and my girl love pancakes, and I bet they have the ingredients for it. I'll be the first to admit that I lack in romantic ideas, but I'd bet Emilia would love it if I made her some pancakes. How difficult can it be to make them?

I search for a recipe on the Internet, and then get to work. Twenty minutes later, I realize that making pancakes is not as easy as it seems. The pan looks like I can throw it away, the resulting pancakes are nothing more than burned shreds, and I cannot figure out where it all went wrong for the life of me.

Groaning, I pull my phone out of my pocket and dial Alice's number.

"Morning, little brother," she answers, her tone chipper as usual.

"Hey. So, I need some help. I made pancakes and ended up with a burned pan. Not to mention the contents looks like someone ate it up and threw it up."

"Eww. Thanks for the visual. You're making pancakes? Why?" After a brief pause, she squeals into the phone, nearly deafening me. "You're making them for Emilia?"

"Yep. Just tell me what to do. How do I fix this?"

"I can't believe you negotiate million-dollar deals for Bennett Enterprises but can't make pancakes."

"No one's perfect," I deadpan. "I should've called Summer."

"I'm not sure she knows about pancakes."

"Yeah, I thought so too, which is why I ended up calling you." I try to scrub the thick, black crust off the pan, but it sticks to it like glue. Definitely belongs in the trash. I'll buy them a brand-new one.

"Always lovely to hear I'm not your first choice."

"Alice," I say in a warning tone.

"Right, you want to know what to do."

"Yeah."

"One: clean up. Two: go buy some pancakes."

"Your faith in me is astounding." Looking at the mess in front of me, I say, "But you're right. Thanks."

After the line goes static, I clean up the crime scene, get dressed, and venture out to buy half a dozen pancakes. When I reenter the house, I find Emilia awake and in the kitchen.

"Keep your voice low," she says. "Grams is still sleeping."

"Stop whatever you're doing," I tell her. "I bought breakfast."

She turns around, smiling devilishly. "But I have breakfast stuff. I can even make pancakes."

"Yeah... about that...."

"What?"

She whirls around, looking at the stove intently. "It smells of burned stuff."

So much for my cleaning skills. She opens the dishwasher, and then looks in the garbage, where I tossed the pan.

"You tried to make pancakes?"

I realize I have no choice but to come clean. "I did. That's the result, so I went to buy some."

"You're adorable," she says. "You didn't have to do it."

"Thought I'd give being romantic a try. Obviously didn't work out."

Emilia walks up to me and laces her hands at the back of my neck, giving me a quick peck on the lips. "Whoever said buying breakfast isn't romantic?"

"Are you being nice to me just because I bought your favorite pancakes?"

She shrugs, a coy smile spreading on her face. "You'll never know."

"Here is a test for you. You'll only get your sweets after you give me a proper kiss."

"You mean this was a half-assed kiss?"

"It was an *I can't wait to get it over with so I can have my sweets* kind of kiss. I want an *I'm getting wet* kind of kiss."

"You're awfully presumptuous."

"Can't help it. Comes along with the package."

"Fine."

She rises on her toes and gives in to my kiss. Then she steals the bag out of my hand and hurries to the kitchen. The little vixen.

"I feel a little used right now," I inform her.

"Oh, feel free to feel very used. I'm in pancake heaven."

I watch her eat, barely restraining myself as she makes delicious sounds.

"You're doing this on purpose, aren't you?"

"Teasing you? Making you sweat?" she asks with a grin. "Of course I am."

"Two can play at this game, Emilia," I say in a low tone. She merely gives me a coy smile, concentrating on her food.

"Thank you," she says softly once she's done. "For breakfast, and for yesterday. You mean a lot to me."

She sighs and frowns, as if she's considering her words. "I didn't have the courage to put myself out there again after my fiasco engagement. But with you, everything feels so right that I'm almost afraid something bad will happen, just because it has to."

Stepping closer to her, I drag my fingers down her cheek, focusing on her eyes. "Get those silly ideas out of your head. Before you, I thought there was something wrong with me for not making any relationship work. But with the wrong person, it will never feel right. You're my right person, Emilia."

She offers me a heartfelt, delicious smile. "And you are mine."

Chapter Twenty-Two

Max

One week later, on Friday, I'm convinced I've lost my mind. Yeah, that must be it. Otherwise, why would I have a book about pregnancy open on my computer at work? Sometime today I started researching late births and Braxton-Hicks, and fell down the research hole. In the meantime, I found out late first births are normal, but there are about one thousand other things that can go wrong during a pregnancy. Why do women put themselves through this? And to think Mom went through this *seven* times. I should close the damn book, but reading it is like watching a car wreck. It's bad, but I can't look away.

A knock at my door jolts me out of my reading.

"Come in." I immediately minimize the book on my screen. If anyone sees it, they'll think I've lost my balls on top of losing my mind. Christopher walks in.

"You're a genius," he says. "Brazil just informed us they'll fly to San Francisco to negotiate with us. We just have to set up the date."

"About damn time."

"They're gonna ask for blood to give us placement in their stores."

"I'll give them what's fair, nothing more or less." Yes, we want to enter their market, but we're not going to overpay for it. Christopher sets a stack of papers on my desk. "Get back to me after you look through these. There are—" He bursts out laughing out of the blue. What the hell? Then I notice he's looking at my computer screen. Shit. I minimized the window with the book, but the title is still visible.

"If you're gonna give me shit for this, there is the door," I inform Christopher, who doesn't stop laughing.

"I don't have time to give you shit right now." He's already backing out. "But I'll keep it on my to-do list."

"Mr. Bennett, don't forget about your lunch meeting." My assistant peeks inside my office just as my brother leaves. I'm meeting Emilia for lunch. "You have reservations in ten minutes."

"Thank you, Laney. I'll be on my way."

My assistant heads back out, and just as I rise from my seat, my phone rings. The name of the detective in charge of finding Emilia's father appears on the screen.

Placing the phone to my ear, I ask, "What's the news?" What I like best about Detective Ferro is that he's a no-nonsense guy. He hates small talk as much as I do.

"I tracked him down."

"Are you sure it's him?"

"One hundred percent."

"Good. E-mail me all the information, and I'll take it from here."

As I stride out of the office, I wonder how best to break this news to Emilia. I don't see how this can be anything but bad. No matter how I spin it, she'll be hurt. Knowing Emilia, I'm sure deep down she believes her scum of a father will have some good reason for leaving. Maybe I'm a cynic, but I strongly believe some people are assholes just because. And I want to protect her from people like that, even if it's her own father. Still, this isn't my call to make. If she wants to go through with it, I will be there for her, ready to comfort her or punch the moron, depending on what the situation calls for.

Emilia waits for me in front of the building, wearing jeans and a shirt that clings to her, showing off enough skin to make my mouth water.

"Hello, handsome," she greets me. "I missed you." She adds those last few words in a lower voice, as if she's ashamed.

"I missed you too," I assure her. I'm beginning to think that even if I saw her daily, it still wouldn't be enough. Her pupils dilate at my admission, as if she wasn't expecting it. The honesty in her eyes is raw. Does she know how rare that is?

I lean down to kiss her, and she rises on her tiptoes to meet me halfway, flattening her tiny body against me. As I hook my arm around her waist, she's never seemed more fragile or beautiful. I love this woman, and I'll do anything to protect her and make her happy. When she pulls back, her eyes glint with hunger, and not of a sexual nature.

"Can't wait to get to the restaurant. I'm starving," she says, confirming my thoughts. There's nothing more satisfying than realizing I know my woman so well I can read her like an open book. I want to anticipate her every need and fulfil it. Right now, she needs food. No way I'm breaking the news about her father to her on an empty stomach. Growing up in a full house taught me that things could go south fast when everyone's hungry. As an adult, I've been in enough meetings that solidified that point of view. Food first, bad news later. I might sneak a session of lovemaking in between too.

The restaurant is two blocks away from the office, so we walk there.

"You're always doing this," she murmurs.

"What?"

"Keeping an arm around my shoulders and walking on the side of the sidewalk that is to the street. Like you want to protect me from cars or something."

I kiss her temple, pulling her in closer. "I want to protect you from everything. Cars, bad people, bad dreams. As far as the arm on your shoulder, I'm just looking for any opportunity to touch you."

"I see. So you're a protective opportunist. I think I like you, Max Bennett."

"Like me? What can I do to upgrade that?"

She frowns. "Huh?"

"I love you, Emilia."

She stops in her tracks, and her shoulders tense under my arm. I hadn't planned to spring that on her like this, in the middle of the street. Hell, I hadn't planned anything at all. And now that she's silent, my stomach starts twisting.

"I have a feeling this should have happened in a different environment. Candles would've probably helped, but when it comes to romance, you've got the wrong brother."

Jesus, I'm rambling like a teenage boy. Why isn't she saying anything?

"Do you mean that?" she whispers, looking up at me and licking her lips.

"Yeah, not one romantic streak—"

"No!" she interrupts. "The other thing."

"Oh, yeah. I do. I love you."

Her shoulders relax on the spot, and my stomach loosens. Dragging my thumb across her lips and then cupping her cheek, I zero in on her eyes, wanting to read what's going on in that pretty little head of hers.

Her lips lift up at the corner in a smile. "I've loved you since I was nine."

Holy shit. So much for always being able to read my woman.

"You've been holding out on me."

"Not really." Biting her lip, she leans into my touch. "It's just something I realized recently."

"Mmm, my burned pancakes made quite an impression on you, then." Tilting her head up, I kiss her wildly. Before I know it, I push her against the wall of the nearest building, feasting on her delicious lips.

"Max." She pushes me away, out of breath. "You can't kiss me like that in the middle of the street."

"I just told you I love you, and you admitted you've been hung up on me for nineteen years. We can do whatever we want."

"You're twisting my words." She slaps my shoulder, darting out her tongue. On a whim, I bite her gently on her tip. "Ouch. What was that for?"

"You just made me a happy man, Emilia."

"You'll bite my tongue from now on when you're happy?" Her grin is contagious.

"Maybe."

"I think you need to reassess your reactions, mister."

I still have her trapped against the wall, and there are endless possibilities to what I could do to her. But there is a street full of cars behind us, and the sidewalk is bustling with passersby.

"What *do* you want me to do to you when I'm happy?" I ask her. "I'm not letting you go until you say it."

She eyes one of my arms and then the other, as if assessing her chances of escaping. But my palms are firmly pressed against the wall at her sides, caging her in between. She makes a "come here" motion with her finger, and I lower my ear to her mouth.

"I don't know about that… but I do know what I'll do to you. Drive you crazy." After a brief pause, she adds in a barely audible whisper, "Go down on you."

Jerking my head, I step back, gawking at my spitfire of a woman, who never talks dirty. Hell, even now, she's blushing. But as she slips away from me, I recognize this for what it was: a ploy to make me lower my guard—or in this case, my arms.

"Earned my freedom," she says sassily, still blushing. "Let's go have lunch, Bennett. You're starving me."

Yep, she's definitely full of surprises today. "Let's go." Taking her hand, I lead the way, wondering if she plans to catch me off guard with her womanly wiles again today.

***

Emilia

We're sitting in a remote corner of the busy restaurant, and we're halfway through lunch when I have the hunch Max wants to tell me something. His brow has been furrowed for minutes now, and he's chewing his food slowly, as if he's searching for the right words to break some bad news to me. Maybe he wants to take back his love declaration. My heart clenches at the thought, and suddenly my burger tastes like paper. I've been on the receiving end of a love *retraction* before, and it stung like hell. But my feelings for Paul weren't nearly as strong as they are for Max. What if he's concluded he said it too soon? Or maybe I scared him off with my own admission. Or maybe I'm just overthinking this, and his serious demeanor is because he has a lot on his mind at work. I'm about to ask about that when Max's phone starts buzzing.

"Sorry, it's Pippa," he mouths to me, placing his phone to his ear. "Hi."

Pippa speaks quickly on the other end, but I don't catch a word.

"I'm at Lenny's right now with Emilia, eating a burger. I can pass by your house tonight and—" He stops midphrase as his sister speaks quickly again. "Okay, sure, you can join us."

"Anything wrong?" I ask after he places the phone back in his jacket.

"Nah, she's just looking for an excuse to move as much as possible. She's supposed to be due this week and is supposed to stay at home, but...." He leaves his sentence unfinished, shaking his head. Some twenty minutes later, Pippa shows up at our table.

"Emilia," she exclaims, pulling me into a hug. She smells divine, a mix of jasmine and mint, and she has a warmth that is all hers.

"Not so tight," I whisper, trying not to squish her belly while returning her hug. "We don't want to disturb the little ones."

"Oh, don't worry." Letting me go, she says,

"Nothing disturbs them. They're so happy in here they refuse to come out." She eyes Max pensively, then asks him, "What are the chances of getting rid of you so Emilia and I can catch up? We didn't get to talk much when you came to my house."

"You want to talk about me?" Max asks, eyes narrowed.

Pippa rolls her eyes, sitting next to her brother. "You always think everything's about you."

"If it's not about me, then I can stick around," he says smugly.

"God, you're stubborn. Fine, stick around. If you two are done eating, can we take a walk? I already ate. I just came by to see Emilia."

I point to her protruding belly. "Won't you get tired carrying them around?"

"Oh, trust me, I'm tired. But the doctor said that moving around can help the water break. I swear that I'll walk these babies off."

"Let's walk then," I say.

The three of us head outside, and Max leads us on a quiet side street, lined with trees offering comfortable shade. A few minutes into our walk, Pippa's eyes widen, and she stops midstride. "I think my water just broke."

"Holy shit. What do you mean you think?" Max asks, and his eyes are even wider than Pippa's. In fact, unless I'm gravely mistaken, Max is in full-blown panic mode, while Pippa is glowing. "I don't see any water."

Pippa snorts. "You've been watching too

many movies, Max. That's not how it works."

"How does it work, then?"

Pippa sighs. "If you really want a visual, it's like peeing yourself a little."

"So what do we do now?" Max asks, looking from Pippa to me and then back at her.

Pippa rubs her belly, smiling widely. "*You* won't have to do anything. I, on the other hand, will go anywhere from zero to twenty hours of hell."

"You look strangely happy about it," I remark.

"It's been a long nine months," she explains. "Now, I should call my husband to let him know the good news. Can't wait to have them out."

"Yeah, but we need to get you to the hospital for them to get out. You can't give birth here." He is breathing in and out quickly in an obvious attempt to calm himself.

"Right, Max, can you come here a second?" I pull him by the arm a few feet away from his sister.

"You need to calm down," I tell him. "You'll just make her panic."

"Why *isn't* she panicking? Why is she so calm? That can't be *normal*."

"I heard that," Pippa says loudly.

"I meant for you to hear it," Max retaliates. This isn't going to go very well.

Pippa opens her mouth, but instead of words, a gasp comes out. She touches the side of her belly with one hand, turning the other one into a fist.

"Contractions?" I ask, hurrying back to her

with Max on my heels. She nods, gasping again.

"Holy shit." The words belong to a terrified Max. "Are you in pain? Don't forget to breathe."

"Brother, I love you, but you're no good at calming me down," Pippa says.

"Max," I say calmly. "Let's go to the hospital."

"Yeah. Should I call an ambulance?" he asks frantically. Pippa and I exchange amused looks.

"No need," I tell him. "You can drive us. Where is your car?"

"In the garage at the office."

"Go get it. Pippa and I will wait for you here." I point to a bench under a tall, thick tree.

"Okay," Max says. "I'll be back right away."

Fifteen minutes later, we are speeding on the streets of San Francisco. I'm sitting with Pippa in the back, timing her contractions.

"We have a lot of time," I tell her in a soothing tone. "The contractions are seventeen minutes apart. This is still early labor."

"Can you tell that to my brother?" Pippa asks, glancing worriedly at Max. "He drives as if the end of the world is coming."

As if on cue, Max honks loudly, making both Pippa and me jump in our seats.

"Get out of my way, you moron. I have a hospital to get to," he bellows before honking again.

"He's losing it, isn't he?" I ask Pippa, who nods and attempts a smile, even though it turns almost immediately into a grimace from the pain.

She nods. "Why don't you try calming *him* down? I think I'm calmer than he is."

I shift to the edge of the seat, placing my hand on Max's shoulder. Surprised, I discover he's shaking slightly. Poor guy, he's going to hyperventilate before we make it to the hospital.

"Max," I say in a calm voice. "Everything will be fine. Calm down."

He answers by honking at a car that just slipped in front of us. "Drive faster, you asshole. If my sister has the babies in the car, you will be sorry."

"Max," I try again. "The babies won't arrive in the car. The contractions are far enough apart that we will make it to the hospital in time even if we're stuck in traffic."

Max doesn't even seem to hear me. He has both hands on the wheel, grasping it so tightly that his knuckles turn white.

"This is going well," I mutter, sliding next to Pippa again.

"Men are weird creatures," she says. "You should see Max in a negotiation. He's usually the calm one, when even Sebastian loses his cool."

"But his nieces are already making him lose his cool." I grin at this, suddenly wanting to hug Max.

"Can you do me a favor and call Eric again?" She called him while we were waiting for Max on the bench, but he didn't answer. "I'd do it, but if I have a contraction while talking to him, he'll panic even more than Max."

She hands me her phone, Eric's number already on the screen.

"Ah, we finally found the one word with the power to bring men worldwide to their knees," I say as Max goes on another honking chorus. "Childbirth."

***

By the time we arrive at the hospital, Pippa's contractions are more frequent.

"Those babies are in a hurry to come out," I tell her, jogging next to her as some nurses wheel her to a room. The nurse helps her change into a hospital gown and then lie on the bed. This is a birthing room, which looks very homey and comfortable. The birth will take place in this room. I hover next to her, unsure what to say or do. Max is in the hallway, pacing around and calling his family, but I'm not sure he'd be of much help if he were here with us.

"I've been waiting to hear that for weeks now. But damn, it hurts." Pippa grits her teeth as yet another contraction makes her jolt. After it passes, she unexpectedly grips my hand.

"Promise me you won't let anyone else except my husband stay in here during the delivery."

I'm about to tell her that knowing the streak of stubbornness running deep in the Bennett family, I'm unlikely to be able to stop them if they put their minds to it. But Pippa's grip is tight, and her eyes are begging.

So instead of protesting, I say, "I promise. No one else besides your husband and the hospital crew will stay."

She lets go of me, visibly relaxed. Madness reigns for the next half hour. I get hold of Eric on the phone, and he panics the moment I utter the word labor. He arrives shortly afterward with his daughter, Julie.

They go directly to Pippa, and then Eric turns to a nearby nurse, questioning her, while the girl remains by Pippa's side, fear and excitement warring on her lovely face.

Sebastian and Ava arrive next. He sits on the edge of his sister's bed, chuckling and evidently trying to distract his sister from the pain. The rest of the family trickles in, and after each of them pokes their head in, they scatter outside in the hallway. Max and I are in the hallway as well, sitting and holding hands. I can't help feeling as though I'm intruding on family time.

After a while, a nurse announces Pippa is ready for delivery. A pale Eric kisses his wife on the forehead.

"I'll stay in here with you," Alice declares. Pippa opens her mouth, but she can't make out more than a few words before she cries out in pain from another contraction. Now I understand why she appointed me as her spokesperson. Great foresight on her part.

"Alice," I call, stepping forward, "Pippa insisted that she only wants Eric inside with her."

"But I—"

"No negotiating," I say firmly. Alice narrows her eyes at me, then at Pippa, and nods.

"Men are such pussies," Alice whispers to me as all of us except Eric leave Pippa's room. The Bennett men are all awfully quiet. "They beat their chests, but childbirth scares the shit out of them."

"It really does, doesn't it?"

Once the door to Pippa's room closes, everyone is silent.

I find Max pacing around an adjacent empty hallway, looking far calmer than in the car, but still not quite himself. His shoulders are hunched with tension, and his arms are folded against his chest. I don't like seeing my man like this.

"Hey," I tell him. "Everything will be all right."

"There are about one thousand things that can go wrong during childbirth, and I read them all this morning."

"You what?"

"Pippa told me on Friday how the babies might be late, and I started researching about that."

"And somehow you ended up reading an entire book?" I can barely hold back my grin. Max is the most adorable man in the world.

"Yeah, don't mock me."

"I wasn't about to."

"Liar."

"Fine, I was about to. But only because I think it's very sweet."

"Don't tell anyone else." His warning tone tips me over the edge, and I burst out laughing.

"Why, would it endanger your alpha male status?"

In an instant, Max pulls me to him, trapping me against his hard chest. "You're too sassy for your own good today, you know that?"

"I'm just fascinated by you, that's all."

"And now you're trying to talk your way out of it."

"Whatcha gonna do about it, Bennett?"

By way of answering, Max seals his lips over mine, kissing me thoroughly until we hear someone clear their throat behind us. We pull apart, and I avoid looking at the nurse who admonished us. She continues walking down the corridor, and when she's out of sight, I turn to Max.

"If I'm too sassy, you're too shameless today. What's with all the public kissing?"

"It was one nurse, and I wouldn't care if the entire hospital would be watching. You're mine." *Can't argue with that.* Max pulls me into his arms, and I lay my head against his chest, breathing in his scent.

"Max, is it all right if I stay?"

"What do you mean?"

"It's a family thing... I'm intruding."

Max cups my face, kissing my forehead. "You're not intruding. I want you here. I need you."

"Are you sure?"

"Yeah. I want you to be part of my life. *Every* side of my life."

His words reach a place deep inside me, and I'm too emotional to say anything more than, "Okay, I'll stay."

"Thank God, because I also need you here to keep me sane."

I grin at this. "So you admit you were acting a little out of it on our way here?"

"A little? You're being polite. I was like a damn maniac. The more I think about it, the more embarrassed I am."

"You were so adorable, I was debating whether to kiss you or punch you to calm you down."

"Interesting choices." Tilting his head to me, he adds, "Lucky I had you with me. Wait. How come you can be here? What happened to your appointments?"

"I called the clinic and asked them to cancel everything for the afternoon." That means a hefty loss of income, but I wouldn't have missed the birth of the twins for the world. Max seems to be reading my thoughts.

"But you're counting on the income...."

I shake my head. "I'll find a way. I'm happy to be here with you and your family."

Elena and Mia Bennett-Callahan are born at 6:14 and 6:26 p.m. on a beautiful May day, and they are the most adorable babies on the planet. I instantly want to cuddle them, but there is a long line of Bennetts in front of me waiting to do the same. The doctor in charge tells us that both the girls and Pippa are in perfect health.

"Look at them," Max says a while later, tapping the window to the nursery where the newborns are. "They're the most beautiful kids in the room." He says this with such pride, as if they were his. He puts his arm around my shoulders, and we watch the sleeping babies for a long time. It's warm and cozy here in his arms, and I don't want to go. Turning my head to him, I observe him in silence. To my astonishment, I discover that his eyes are a little glassy.

"Max," I ask tentatively. "Are you crying?"

"No, I have something in my eye."

"In both eyes? You big goof."

"Shut up." He pulls me into a bear hug from behind, flattening his chest against my back, resting his chin in the crook of my neck. I can't quench the desire to make fun of him, even though I'm melting as I'm experiencing this sensitive side of him.

"I suppose I'm not allowed to say anything about this to anyone either."

"No."

"Fine, your secret is safe with me. After all, I never told anyone about that time you were bawling your eyes out when we saved the pups."

"I was having an allergy to dog hair."

"Which you conveniently never had again," I volley back.

"I swear to God, if you don't stop with this

right now—"

"You'll do what?" I challenge, looking forward to his reaction. Challenging him has brought me delicious paybacks in the past. Max doesn't disappoint. He pulls me away from the window of the nursery room and into a neighboring corridor. Then he pushes me against a wall and kisses me raw.

"Mmm, I think I'll annoy you some more," I tell him. "Your I'm-annoyed-with-you kisses are the best. I'm surprised you even took the time to pull me to this corridor."

"Of course, I couldn't let the babies see me kissing you against a wall."

I chuckle. "What?"

"It's not good for them to see that."

For a split second I'm convinced he's pulling my leg, but no, he's all serious.

"Let me get this straight. You don't care if you kiss me in front of my clinic, or in the middle of the street, or in front of the nurses here, but a room full of babies can't see us?"

"They're impressionable."

That's it. I can't hold the laughter in anymore. Giggles bubble out of me, loud and uncontrollable. "They have no idea what's happening around them, Max."

"You can never know. What if it influences them in some way? I'm not taking any risks."

Ah, I foresee Mia and Elena having to deal with one too many overprotective uncles. Max will probably lead the pack.

"Do you want to spend the night at my place?" he asks me. "I need to sleep next to you tonight."

"Sure, let me just call Mrs. Wilson." She's been helping out a lot lately. Caressing his cheek, I kiss him softly. I need to sleep next to him tonight too.

Chapter Twenty-Three

Emilia

Something is different between us when we walk inside his apartment. Maybe it's the fact that we experienced the birth of the twins together, but I feel much closer to Max. He and I have experienced many things together throughout our history, but this was different, special.

In the dimly lit living room, Max wraps his arms around my waist. His lips touch mine, soft, warm, and demanding. I push my body against his, needing to be even closer to him. Fisting the fabric of his shirt, I sigh in his mouth.

Max leans his forehead against mine, and we just enjoy each other in silence. As I sense his warm breath on my skin, my age-old desire for motherhood kicks in hard. I know it's not just because I was looking at a room full of babies, but also because I'm finally with the right man. One who makes me feel safe and loved, with whom I laugh about the silliest things. One whom I trust with all my secrets and wishes.

"I'm jealous," Max says. "You just had an entire conversation in your head, and I wasn't part of it."

"Stop reading me so well. It's unnerving."

Kissing my forehead, he steps back, surveying me from head to toe.

"I'll do something else then," he says in a low voice, full of promise. He removes my shirt, kissing my neck as the fabric falls to my feet. Not one to waste time, I turn around, undressing him as well, until we're both just in our underwear.

I can't help giving him the once-over. God, I don't think I could ever tire of watching him. Taking my hand, he leads me to his bedroom.

"Lie on the bed," he commands. His words spur a primal need inside me, and all I can do is nod. Shaking with desire, I do as he says, and he leans over me, threading his fingers through my hair.

"I love your hair," he murmurs.

"It's wild today." I shimmy underneath him, my legs wide open, my inner thighs cradling his groin.

"That's what I like most. And your lips. They are perfect." He strokes his thumb against my upper lip and then the lower one. Feeling bold, I open my mouth, sucking on his thumb, grazing it with my teeth. Max sucks in a sharp breath. "I love every part of you. Especially your feisty side."

"Figures," I tease, pushing him slightly off me so I can have better access to his neck, which I lavish with kisses, biting it gently.

"I want you." His fingers curl around a few strands of my hair, and then he cups the back of my head. "You're so beautiful, Emilia." Then he seals his mouth over mine. His tongue invites mine to a ferocious dance, one to which I give in willingly—almost desperately. All my senses are hyperalert, as if the sheer power of his kiss has awakened them to life. The scent of his skin is intoxicating, the heat of it almost too much to bear. Even this—lovemaking—is different tonight. With every touch and every word, he reaches deeper inside me, in places I haven't allowed anyone. But I welcome him, and I hope he'll stay forever.

Abruptly, he pulls back, his hands feverishly undoing the clasp of my bra. I sigh as my breasts spill free from the confines of the fabric. Max wastes no time, running his thumb around one nipple while licking around the other one. And damn, that tongue of his is magic. He descends further down with his mouth on the valley between my breasts, stopping at my navel. His hands tug at the hem of my panties. I have the slight suspicion he'd like nothing better than to yank them down, but for some reason holds back.

"You soaked through your thong," he groans, his gaze zeroing on the spot between my legs. I open my legs further as an invitation. Max strokes me with one finger, and feeling the drenched fabric against my sensitive skin is too much. My hips arch off the bed, seeking reprieve.

"Max...," I whisper, needing his touch.

Wordlessly he peels off my panties, doing it slowly, teasing me. When I'm finally completely naked before him, he gives me a once-over.

"I will make you feel so good." Lowering his head, he peppers kisses on my inner thighs, drawing little circles with his tongue, inching closer and closer to my slick spot. He lashes his tongue once over my folds, and I quiver. When he takes the ripe flesh between his lips, suckling gently on it, I nearly come out of my skin.

"Max, ah!" Words escape me as I'm lost to sensation, a million daggers of pleasure searing me. When his thumb circles my clit, I'm nearly delirious. "This is. Yeah... perfect." He dips his tongue once inside me, and then again. I fist the sheets with both hands to keep myself from doing something crazy... like making love to his mouth, or entire face.

I needn't have worried, because Max pulls away, leaving me cold and aching for him.

"You going to get rid of those boxers or what?" I tease.

He tilts his head to one side, as if considering not to. Oh hell, if he plans to torture me some more, I'll rip those boxers off him myself. But Max is a smart man, and as usual, seems to be reading my thoughts. So he drops his boxers, putting a condom over his length. I lick my lips at the sight of his thick shaft.

Bringing his erection dangerously close to my entrance, he rubs himself against my inner thigh. I shiver as I feel his hot, hard length against my skin.

Watching me straight in the eyes, he drags his tip up to my clit, circling it once. Energy strums through me, manifesting in a shiver that makes me quiver from head to toe.

"I need you inside me," I whisper. "I ache, Max."

He gulps, his Adam's apple bobbing down. And then he enters me to the hilt in one swift move. I gasp, the sensation overwhelming me.

"You're so big," I whisper as my insides stretch around him. When I hear him chuckle, I blink my eyes open. He watches me with a playful expression.

"You definitely know what I want to hear." Leaning forward over me, he levels himself on his forearms and eases himself in and out of me in a maddening rhythm. "You like it deep, and wild and fast."

"Yes." Wrapping my legs around him, I dig my heels into his ass cheeks, pushing him closer to me.

He cups my jaw, giving me a chaste kiss. Looking me in the eyes, he changes the rhythm, easing in and out of me slowly. Needing to touch as much of him as I can, I place my palms on his chest, feeling the way his hard muscles flex as he makes sweet love to me.

"I feel closer to you tonight than before, Emilia," he whispers. In his eyes, I see the same array of emotions running through me: love, fear, uncertainty, and a wish to be all in. It's more than either of us was banking on, but it's wonderful.

"Me too."

My release builds slowly, starting from my center and firing up all my nerve endings, sending my vision and all of my senses into a tailspin.

Chapter Twenty-Four

Emilia

I wake up alone the next morning, and briefly wonder if Max is trying to cook breakfast again. No smell of burned food lingers in the air though, so I suppose all is right. Muffled words reach my ears, and I realize Max must be on the balcony, even though I can't see him on the portion of the balcony that stretches in front of the bedroom.

Whistling to a catchy tune I heard yesterday on the radio, I leave the bed. After a quick shower, I realize my clothes are in the living room, and if I'm honest, I'm in no mood to wear them right now. But I can't join Max on the balcony stark naked. Hmm. I might not have any clothes here, but Max has a closet full of them. Time to... borrow some.

After searching for a good fifteen minutes, I end up wearing a white office shirt. Since it's large enough for two of me, I roll the sleeves to my elbows and wrap a belt around my middle. The shirt is long enough that it covers my butt almost completely, leaving only a tiny spec of ass cheeks visible. Perfect for not attracting stares from neighbors, and for tempting my man.

When I enter the living room, Max is sitting on the sofa, reading on his laptop. I walk on my tiptoes, wanting to surprise him, but he catches me midstride.

"You wear my clothes well."

"How did you know I was here?" I ask, pouting.

He doesn't miss a beat. "I have an Emilia sensor. Goes off whenever you're nearby."

"Really? Where is it, if I may ask?"

He waggles his eyebrows. "You can do more than ask. You can kiss it, lick it, ride it."

"You are truly the most shameless man I've ever met."

"I openly admit it."

"You say that like you're expecting a prize," I say suspiciously, joining him on the couch.

"I was hoping my honesty will earn me that ride. Any chance?"

He woke up awfully self-assured this morning. Some teasing is required. "Only after breakfast, Bennett. Or coffee at least. Not awake enough to enjoy everything."

He holds his palms up in mock disappointment. "I can't believe you just said that."

"Hard rule for me. Coffee before orgasms." My face breaks into a grin, and it's all Max needs. He jumps my bones, covering my neck with kisses, his erection pressing against my inner thigh. "I see your sensor is working overtime."

"Always, Emilia. Always."

"I have a surprise for you," Max says a while later as we're sharing breakfast. After making love, we ordered in.

"Ooh, I love surprises," I say. "Except, wait, it's not a slug, is it?"

On a memorable sunny day after we'd finished the school year, Max came running to my house, informing me he had to show me something, that he had a surprise for me. I was beyond excited, stomach full of butterflies and all, and followed him, jogging. My grand surprise turned out to be a cave full of slugs. Slimy bodies sprawled on bare stones. I had nightmares for months.

"No, I like to pride myself on making better surprises these days." He grins devilishly for a split second, before his face goes serious. "Though I'm not sure if this is a good or bad surprise."

"Oh."

My stomach twists as I wait for him to speak. He chews the last bite of his sandwich, takes a sip of coffee.

"Max?"

"I spoke with the detective who's on your father's case yesterday. He called before we met for lunch, but then too many things happened and I forgot to tell you. "

Lowering my eyes to my empty plate, I draw in a deep breath. "And?"

"He found him."

"Where?"

"New Orleans. He gave me his home and work address."

I snap my head up. "I thought he had it narrowed down to—"

"None of those were the right one."

"But he's sure the one in New Orleans is?"

He nods, scrutinizing me. "I still suck at surprises, huh?"

"No, I.... Thank you for doing this."

"Talk to me, Emilia."

"I don't know how I feel."

"You don't have to do anything with this information. You don't—"

"I want to go to New Orleans," I say at once. "I want to talk to him, ask him to come see Grams. I think it'll be good for me too. I'll look up tickets online later."

"We can take the company jet."

For a few seconds I'm too stunned to say anything. I'm not sure what surprises me more. That he's putting his company's jet at my disposal, or that he wants to join me. As usual, Max anticipates what I'm about to say.

"Before you can protest, yes, I'm coming with you, and yes, using the company jet is not a problem," he says.

"I never knew you could be bossy and sweet in the same sentence, but you outdid yourself, Max Bennett."

"When do you want to go?"

"When do you have time?"

"Let's go next weekend. I have meetings on Saturday, but we can fly out Saturday evening and come back Sunday."

"Okay. Next weekend it is."

***

"Wow." I exclaim a week later when Max and I step inside the jet. It's large enough for sixteen people, and looks far more luxurious than a regular airline plane.

"What can I say? We like to travel in style."

"I've never heard you mention it before."

"That's because I don't like to brag. Anyway, it was a smart decision to buy it for the company. We have enough people traveling back and forth the entire time. Having our own plane made sense. When teams fly out they can use the time in the air to actually be productive."

"You don't need to defend the choice to me," I say, giggling as we sit next to each other.

"Sorry, it's a habit. Had to work hard to sell the idea to Sebastian and Logan. They thought it was an unnecessary luxury. You should have seen my parents' faces when I told them about it. I told them it's for work. Now, using it for personal reasons when it would otherwise be parked in the hangar—that's just making the most out of my assets."

"You're such a little devil."

We spend the first hour of the flight talking about New Orleans and what we're going to visit there, but we don't talk about my father. There isn't much to talk about... not now; maybe after I meet him. My stomach twists painfully as I try to imagine how it will go. I can't help the sense of foreboding that has taken up residence inside me. Max threads his fingers through my hair, looking at me with questioning eyes. I shake my head, kissing his knuckles.

"You should get some sleep," he says, getting out his laptop.

"Won't you sleep?"

"Nah. The distributors from Brazil were supposed to come in two weeks, but then they moved the meeting to Monday morning."

"This Monday?" I ask, stricken. "Max, why didn't you tell me? I know how important this deal is for you. We could have postponed."

"Doesn't matter. I'll just work on the materials for the meeting now and on our flight back. Go to sleep."

It's late, and it'll be early morning when we land in New Orleans, so we should both get some sleep... or try to.

***

"I think I have a love-hate relationship with New Orleans," I exclaim the next day.

"Already?" Max asks with a smile.

"Yep. Hate the heat. Love the beignets." We're having breakfast inside the famous Cafe du Monde, and I'm on my third beignet. These things are addictive. I'm also on my fourth coffee, because I didn't sleep a wink last night.

"Emilia, you should slow down. Too much coffee and sugar is a bad combo."

Stuffing my face with the last bite of beignet, I frown at him. "How do you know?"

"You forget I have three sisters, the eldest one who drilled into us boys the importance of sugar and caffeine. I also know what happens when she has too much of both."

"I need the energy. We still have to finish visiting the Quarter. Let's go."

Since my father owns a bar, I decided to visit there rather than go to his home. It's safer. The bar opens in the evening, so Max and I opted to visit the French Quarter in the meantime.

The area is a thing of beauty, and so different from everything I've seen until now. There are street artists at every corner, and a gypsy woman even offered to read my fortune. I declined, even though I was mildly curious. The heat and humidity are a force to reckon with, though. My dress clings to me, and I wish I could say the same about my hair, but it sticks in every direction.

"This city is beautiful," I exclaim as we make a pit stop to eat a quick lunch. We've been walking for hours through the city, visiting famous landmarks. So far we've been to Bourbon Street and Jackson Square. We've also been to St. Louis's Cathedral and right now, we're on Royal Street. This strip of land is every food lover's dream.

"I noticed. You barely paid attention to me all

morning."

I shrug. "You're nothing to sneeze at, but New Orleans is totally eclipsing you."

Max pinches my ass, making me bump into the next person waiting in line in front of me.

"Keep your hands to yourself, Bennett," I warn.

"I thought you liked my hands," he volleys back in a low voice. "Actually, you love them. You said it this morning. Repeatedly."

He woke me up by touching me *everywhere*, so of course I was worshipping them.

"Different circumstances," I mouth, elbowing him in the ribs.

Max and I are currently waiting in line to buy a jambalaya to go, and I'm salivating just looking at the food. The smell is intoxicating, further accentuating my hunger—and I stuffed myself with beignets a mere few hours ago.

When we're in front of the counter, the vendor asks in a knee-melting Cajun accent, "What would you like?"

I tell him my order, letting out a deep sigh. The vendor seems unfazed, but Max cocks an eyebrow.

Max's voice is clipped when he tells his order, and he watches me intently as we leave.

"What?" I ask innocently, shoving a spoon of jambalaya in my mouth. Holy hotness. My mouth is on fire. This dish is not for the fainthearted.

"So how come every time someone speaks to

you, you make puppy dog eyes?" he asks with a frown.

"I can't help it. Cajun accent is sexy." My words only further accentuate his frown. I love seeing him riled up.

"Right, if you think this is sexy we won't go to England anytime soon."

"You might want to cross off Australia too," I chime in. "Their accent is to die for as well."

"No trips to Australia, then." That last word sounded dangerously close to a growl.

"Not sure what that says about me, but I love seeing you all territorial like this."

"Is that so?"

"Yep."

He eyes my food. "Does that earn me the right to taste your jambalaya?"

Mine is with chicken, while his is with chorizo and chicken.

I sigh dramatically. "I draw a hard line at food, but because I love you so very much, you can have one spoonful."

We continue our tour in the afternoon, but my mood grows dimmer, and my entire body tenses. A knot settles between my shoulder blades, and the closer we get to six o'clock, the tighter it gets.

"We should head in the direction of the bar if we want to be there when it opens," Max says cautiously.

"Yeah. Let's do that."

He kisses my forehead before lacing an arm around my waist. We walk like this toward the bar, which is at the edge of the French Quarter. A large Open sign blinks above the door when we arrive, and it does nothing to calm my nerves.

***

"I want to go inside by myself," I tell Max. His expression instantly tightens, his jaw ticking.

"Not a good idea. What if—"

"This is something I need to do alone."

"Emilia—"

"I'm not going to change my mind."

A loaded silence follows, but I don't back off. Eventually, he points to the coffee shop across from the bar, saying, "I'll sit there and wait for you."

As he enters the coffee shop, I turn and inspect the old building that houses the bar. It has a charm of its own even among the other beautiful buildings surrounding it. I looked up the bar online as soon as Max told me the name. It has a long history, and it changed ownership about fifteen years ago. That's when it entered my father's possession. Only a mere four years after he left Grams and me. Over the years, I imagined many scenarios why my father didn't make contact. Most often, I feared he was a drunk, or homeless, and was too ashamed to show his face. Never in a million years did it cross my mind he was the owner of a successful bar in the heart of New Orleans.

Squaring my shoulders and taking a deep

breath, I push the door open. There are a few patrons inside already, sitting at the tables scattered around the dimly lit room. I fix my eyes on the counter, where two men are working. One is in his twenties, the other one is unmistakably my father. Now that I have him in front of my eyes, memories of him as a younger man flood my mind. High cheekbones, tiny black eyes, and a small stature.

All the air leaves my lungs and my throat constricts. I grasp the counter for support in a small gesture, afraid my legs might give way.

"Can I get you anything, miss?" the twentysomething asks. I shake my head, moving along until I reach the part of the bar where my father is.

He snaps his head up, opens his mouth, and then blinks without saying anything. His features contort, his eyes growing cold and wary.

"Emilia?"

My throat seems incapable of forming any words, so I just nod.

"I have an office in the back, let's go in there and talk." His voice is just as cold as his eyes, with just the tiniest hint of unease. My legs seem to have the consistency of lumber as I follow him, and nausea settles at the back of my throat.

Once we enter his office, I try to fix my eyes on something that will calm me. No such luck. I can't find anything to latch on in this tiny, strange place.

"What are you doing here?" he asks. "How did you find me?" Going straight for the punch. So this is how this will be. Okay, then.

"Why did you leave us?" I toss back.

Running his hand through his black hair peppered with white strands, he gestures for me to sit in the chair in front of his desk, which I do. He sits behind it.

"Why did you never call or write?" I continue. He joins his hands over the table, looking at me like a stranger, which I suppose is what I am.

"Emilia, your mother and I were very young when she became pregnant with you."

"That's not an excuse," I say dryly.

"I didn't ask for you to be born. I loved your mother very much, but I begged her not to have you."

Bile rises up my throat, but I keep my composure, determined not to show this asshole that his words hurt. Damn it, I don't want them to hurt.

"I couldn't change her mind. Hell, I practically had no say in her choice. When you were born, I tried to do the right thing. But you know what it's like for a high school drop out to find work?"

"Hard, I imagine."

"I loved your mother. But things got very hard, very fast. She changed from the sweet girl I fell in love with to a woman who was constantly nagging and whining. There was always some drama going on, something she needed for herself or for you. Look, I'm not proud of my past, but I did what I had to do."

"Leaving your nine-year-old daughter after her mother had just died?"

"You had Grams to take care of you. It's not like you were on your own."

"Yeah, no nine-year-old needs her father," I say sarcastically. "You didn't even ask Grams to move away with you."

At least that was what my Grams always said.

"No, I didn't. I needed to be free to start over. Hard to do that with a kid. It was too much responsibility, and I knew I was meant for more. And I was right. Look at what I did here. I became successful."

"While Grams worked herself to the bone to keep both of us afloat." The punches keep on coming. I think sometime between entering his office and sitting on his chair, I became numb, which is just as good, because otherwise I couldn't take this.

"Did it ever occur to you to reach out to us? After you built… all this?"

"I figured if you'd done well without me up to that point, there was no real need."

"You figured," I deadpan.

He shakes his head, avoiding looking at me. "It would have been hard to explain to my wife."

"You're married?"

Even through the veil of numbness, the words still hurt, like a knife being twisted around in my chest, again and again.

"Yes, I have a beautiful wife, named Tracy, and four children."

"When did that happen?"

"I married her nine years ago. The timing was right, you know... to start a family."

Max told me his detective had a lot of information about my father, but after I learned about his bar, I didn't want to know more. Now I wish I had asked. Maybe it wouldn't have hurt so much. Grams always said that Dad was a free spirit; that he didn't want to be tied down. Little did she know. He did want a family; he just didn't want us. He didn't want me.

I look at him, dumbstruck. "I see."

"You do, right? Explaining to them about you meant—"

"Having to admit what a lowlife you are."

"Please, don't tell them anything." For the first time, he looks scared.

"Don't worry. I didn't come here to expose you. I didn't even know there was anyone I could expose you to. God, I'm an idiot. I shouldn't have come."

He throws his hands up in the air. "Why did you come? What did you expect? You're past the age where you can ask for money."

What the hell? How can I be related to this person? How can Grams be related to him? There's not one mean bone in her body, while he seems to be made entirely out of poison.

"You're a fucking idiot if you think I want your money. When I started searching for you, I expected to find out you're dead, or at least had a very good reason for not showing your face for almost twenty years. I never thought I'd find this. You having a successful life, choosing not to have anything to do with me or your own mother. And I came for Grams, because she has Alzheimer's, and she wants to see you again. I flew here hoping to convince you to pay her a visit."

For the first time since I came in, a sliver of *something* crosses his face. "Mother has Alzheimer's?"

"Yes. Do you want to see her?"

He shakes his head. "No point. I told Tracy I didn't have any living family. Best if you tell Mother you didn't find me."

My stomach sinks, which only goes to show what an idiot I am. A tiny part of me still hoped the knowledge that his mother is sick would make him want to reach out to her. What kind of coldhearted bastard wouldn't want to fulfil what is essentially his mother's last wish? I rise to my feet, massaging my neck, which has grown stiff.

"That's exactly what I'll do, you bastard." My voice is high now, but I don't give a damn. I'm two seconds away from losing my shit and throwing something at him. Anger and hurt billow inside me. "I will leave now."

"I hope you understand, but it would be for the best if you didn't come again," he says, his voice neutral.

I laugh, and even to my own ears, I sound a little manic. "Don't worry. Even I'm not that big of an idiot." Walking to the door with determined strides, I come to a stop in front of the door, my hand on the handle. Then I turn to him. "You know what, I just realized something. I lived my entire life feeling as if I wasn't good enough for you. I was wrong. You're the one who wasn't good enough for me, or for Grams. We were both better off without you. Have a nice life, Father."

I walk out of the bar with my chin held high.

Max rises to his feet the second I enter the coffee shop across from the bar. Without hesitation, I walk straight into his open arms, not caring that we're attracting stares. I rest my forehead in the crook of his neck, grateful for his strong, warm presence and the care in his voice as he utters one single word.

"Emilia?"

"Let's go back home."

Chapter Twenty-Five

Emilia

Bad things usually come in a pack. A storm hits New Orleans, delaying the flight by six hours. That means it'll be early morning when we arrive, and Max will have to go to his office directly. I will barely have time to go home and check on Grams. While we wait, I relay the conversation with my father to Max almost word for word. He goes on a rant, deservedly calling that rat all the profanities that cross his mind, and then he simply kisses my forehead, holding me in his arms. He's simply being Max—solid and quiet, and I love him for it. Still, even as I lie in his arms, it still feels like my heart was cracked open. An age-old hurt and fear have resurfaced: fear of not being wanted or good enough. It's stupid and makes me weak, but I can't help it.

"I should have bought some more beignets before we boarded the plane," I say. "I don't think I'll ever want to go back to New Orleans."

"Hey, we can arrange for you to get as many beignets as you want whenever you want them," he says softly.

"That, right there, is the sweetest love declaration in the world, Max Bennett."

We spend the rest of the flight in silence, with Max working on his laptop. The meeting with the distributors in Brazil will start one hour after we land. I feel guilty for pulling him away from work for so long, but whenever I bring the subject up, he simply shrugs, saying work can wait. I try—and fail—to sleep for the second night in a row. It's a good thing I didn't tell Grams where I was going. She doesn't have to go through the same heartbreak I am. I'll have to tell her we didn't find him. I hate lying to her, but in this case, it's better than the truth.

I am in a zombie-like state when we land. Max worked until two hours ago, after which he fell into a deep sleep. He woke up in full business mode, and even changed into a new suit while on the plane.

"I'll call you after the meeting is over," he says before we part.

"Sure. I'm going home to check on Grams, and then I'll go to the clinic." I have no idea how I'll be of any use to my patients today. I can barely keep my eyes open, or form coherent thoughts.

Half an hour later, I let myself into my house as quietly as possible, not wanting to wake up Grams or Mrs. Wilson, who was kind enough to sleep here. I leave my bag at the door, kicking off my sneakers as well and tiptoeing on the hardwood floor. It appears Mrs. Wilson is up though, because the couch on which she usually sleeps when she spends the night is empty. Weird. Maybe she slept in my bedroom. Except my bed is empty too. And so is Grams's.

"Mrs. Wilson? Grams?" I call loudly. No answer. I head back to the living room, and instantly feel something is wrong. The room is eerily quiet, as is the rest of the house. Sweat breaks at the back of my neck as I make my way through the house, checking each room again. Steeling myself, I head to the back of the house, pushing open the door to the backyard. No one is in the yard. On the coffee table in front of the sofa is a half drunk cup of tea. My stomach constricts. *Where* are they? Did something happen to Grams, and they had to rush her to the hospital? In that case, why didn't Mrs. Wilson call me?

I swipe my suddenly sweaty palms on my legs before heading back inside the house, hunting for my phone. When I find it, I dial Mrs. Wilson's number with trembling hands.

"Hi, Emilia," she answers, and my stomach constricts at the tightness in her tone.

"Mrs. Wilson, where are you? Where's Grams?"

"You—you're home?" she stutters.

"Yeah, I got back just now. Where are you?"

"I'm two blocks away, with Mrs. Andersen and Mrs. Jensen. We're looking for Grams."

I grip the nearby chair for support. The two women she mentioned are our neighbors. "What do you mean, looking for her?"

"She took off." Her voice is trembling now, and my heart squeezes as I realize she's crying. "She had a rough night, barely slept and woke up at four o'clock. I made tea for both of us and we were in the backyard. Then I went inside the house to bring sugar for our tea. It wasn't in its usual place, so it took me quite a bit to find it. When I went back, your Grams was gone."

I take a deep breath, attempting to calm myself. "When was this?"

"One hour ago."

"One— Jesus!" My mind races with scenario after scenario, each more pessimistic than the one before. She could be anywhere. She could be hurt. She could be— No, I won't go there. "Why didn't you call me?"

"I didn't want you to worry."

"She's my grandmother. Of course I will worry!" My voice comes out as a shout, one I instantly regret. I know she meant well. "I'm sorry, Mrs. Wilson. Where are you exactly? I'll come right away."

She gives me the address, and I slip on into my sneakers with lightning speed, not even bothering to tie my shoelaces before leaving the house. I find the three women huddled around a bin at a crossroads, looking lost.

"Where have you searched?" I ask as I reach them. I'm shaking like a leaf—the fear and exhaustion eating away at me.

"Well, we've been up and down the main

streets, and we haven't seen her," Mrs. Andersen says.

"How about the neighbors? Did anyone see her?"

Mrs. Wilson shakes her head. "No. We asked them already. It's early morning, so not all of them are up, but...."

"Have you alerted the police?"

"Yes, they are searching already, but haven't reported anything back."

Panic coils through my veins, threatening to suffocate me as the thought sinks in, slashing and unforgiving. *Grams is lost.* Far above us, thunder breaks across the sky. Almost unwillingly, I look up. The clouds are gray and heavy.

"Let's search for her too. We have to find her before it starts raining," I say, and my voice sounds hollow to my own ears. "She can't be that far. The neighborhood is small."

I don't say what we all must be thinking. That by now, she could have left the neighborhood already. *No, she hasn't. She didn't. She couldn't.* I cling to this last hope with all my being.

"My weekly book club meeting starts in fifteen minutes," Mrs. Anderson says, her eyes lighting up.

"We can ask them to help. They all love your grandmother," Mrs. Jensen adds.

"That's a great idea," I say, relieved. "Thank you."

Within fifteen minutes, we have a party of eight, armed with umbrellas and flashlights, in addition to the two police officers already searching the area. Even though it's morning, the sky is so dark with clouds that we might need the flashlights.

"All right, listen up," I say loudly, holding up a map of the neighborhood. "We should divide and each take a street. Please look even in places you don't think a person would linger, such as behind trash cans. I also brought some pics of Grams. You can show them to passersby and ask them if they saw her."

There is a round of nodding, and then we start the search party. I go to the local bakery first, knowing how much Grams loves his bread and sweets, but the vendor hasn't seen her. I leave him my number, and he looks at me with pity as he assures me he'll call me if Grams shows up.

I go inside every shop on the main street of the neighborhood, and then I look at the back of the streets, leaving no stone unturned. But Grams is nowhere to be found.

After an hour, the rain descends upon us, pouring with a vengeance. The umbrella isn't helping much, because the wind is strong, scattering raindrops everywhere. My phone rings, and Mrs. Wilson's name appears on the screen.

"Did you find her?" I hold my breath as a desperate hope surges through me.

"No. I'm so sorry, honey. Everyone is seeking shelter from the rain. The umbrellas aren't helping."

My stomach sinks as my hopes plummet. "You stopped searching?"

"We can always continue after the rain stops."

"But she's out there in the rain." I bite my lip hard, fighting tears. Where is she? I can't let anything happen to her.

"I'll search with you, okay? Everyone else from the book club is too cold to go on. But the police officers are still searching, right?"

"Yes. I also called MedicAlert." It's an emergency service helping locate people with Alzheimer when they get lost. "They're searching too, but I feel as if I have to do something."

"I'll continue the search too."

"I—thank you, Mrs. Wilson. Call me if you have any news."

But the next time she calls me, it's not to give me any good news. "I can't go on, sweetheart. There is water in my shoes, and the rain is so strong, I can't see a damn thing."

"I know," I say through sobs. "You go home and make sure you don't catch a cold, Mrs. Wilson."

My heart constricts at the very real possibility that Grams might catch a cold, or worse, develop pneumonia. Neither the police nor the search service has reported anything good.

"You should go home too, girl. I'm sure the police will find her."

I know her words are meant to calm me down, but they just fuel my panic. "Thank you, Mrs. Wilson."

With a deep breath, I shove the phone into my pocket and then start my search again. Half an hour later, I am drenched to the bone, and the rain is so heavy I can barely see in front of me. When a gust of wind completely ruins my umbrella, I'm forced to seek shelter from the rain too, stepping inside a coffee shop. Yet the moment I'm inside, the ceiling seems to cave in on me, suffocating me. I force myself to take deep breaths, to no avail.

Grams will have sheltered herself. I know she has.

I fumble with my phone, desperate for someone to tell me it will be all right, that Grams will be fine. That's when I realize whom I need. Max. Without hesitation, I call him. He doesn't pick up the first time, but I call him again. Finally, he answers.

"Hi!" I say through sobs.

"What's wrong?"

"Grams is missing. She left the house, and we can't find her, and now it's raining, and I can't even see in front of me, and I don't know what to do. The police are still searching, but if they haven't found her until now...."

"Where are you? I'm coming where you are right now."

That's when I remember that Max has an important all-day meeting today.

"No, I'm sorry. I forgot about your meeting. I'll deal with this on my own."

"Emilia, just give me the damned address. I'll be there."

I give him the address and then buy a cup of

steaming coffee, clutching it in my hands for dear life. The rain intensifies, so all I can do is wait. And waiting kills me. I sit at a small table by the window with my forehead pressed to the glass and hugging my knees to my chest.

Max finds me in the same position when he arrives, and my entire body is numb.

"You're soaked," he says, sitting next to me.

"I know." I hate how defeated I sound.

"Let's get you home and changed."

"No," I say vehemently. "If I go home, it means I failed her."

"Emilia, I'm sure Grams is somewhere waiting for the rain to pass."

"I— Help me brainstorm."

"What?"

"Places where she might have gone. I tried to think about that while I was there, but I was too panicked—"

"Okay," Max says. He takes my hand in his, rubbing the back of my palm with his thumb. I instantly feel calmer than I've been in hours. Calm enough to think.

"What were her favorite places in the neighborhood?" Max asks.

"The bakery, but I was already there, and they hadn't seen her. The movie theater, which is closed. The gazebo in the park, the library, and the store with knitting supplies. I've been everywhere."

"How long has she been missing?"

A knot forms in my throat as I look at the

time displayed on my phone. "Five hours. The police are also looking, and also a service specialized for these cases, but…."

We exchange brief looks, and I know exactly what he's thinking.

"I don't think she left the neighborhood, she couldn't walk much without tiring," I explain. "She looks fit, but she tires quickly."

"That means she must be close," Max says with such conviction that I almost believe him too. "Is it possible for the disease to make her think she might be somewhere else?"

"What do you mean?"

"Well, she mistook you for your mother. Maybe she could think that she's in some other area where you used to live."

"Oh," I exclaim, realizing what he's getting at. Hope fills me anew as I brainstorm out loud, remembering her favorite places in the other cities we lived. "The church, the flower shop…. I know where the church is here, but I don't know if there is any flower shop. There isn't one on the main shopping street."

Max pulls out his phone, typing on it. "There are three in the area. The closest is two blocks away."

"Let's go to the church first. It's closer."

The heavy rain has dwindled to scattered raindrops, which makes things somewhat easier. Max's phone rings nonstop, but he doesn't answer.

"You should go back to the office," I insist,

hating to know I'm keeping him away.

"I'll deal with it later. Let's focus on finding Grams now."

When we arrive at the church, the priest tells us Grams hasn't been there. Bile rises in my throat, my vision blurring for a split second. At my insistence, Max and I go around the building once, making sure she's not in the vicinity, which she's not. Next we go to the first two flower shops on Max's list, but there is no sign of Grams.

"Where is she?" I say through tears. "Where?"

Max squeezes my hand reassuringly, but as we walk back toward the main square, he looks in the distance, lost in thought. I can't help notice that some of the light in his eyes has faded. Then he blinks, snapping his head to me.

"Look...."

I follow his gaze to the bakery, and then I start running as fast as I can, stepping into puddle after puddle of water, and not caring one bit. Because right in front of the bakery, looking around with wide, fearful eyes, is Grams.

When I'm in front of her, I want to hug her, and then I remember I'm soaked. Thank God she isn't.

"Grams?" I ask tentatively.

She looks up at me, smiling. "Emilia, darling. Thank God. I went out to buy bread, but forgot where the bakery was. Now I found it and want to go home, but I don't remember the way back, so I thought it would be best to wait for you. I had to hide from the rain. What took you so long?"

I laugh, relieved to hear her stern voice again. Most of all, I'm happy that she is safe.

"I got lost too," I say. "Come on, Grams, let's get you home."

Ten short minutes later, we are home. I've already announced to everyone involved in the search that I've found her. Grams grows agitated as she starts to acknowledge the events of the day, growing confused about what she was doing at the bakery and how she got there. I manage to calm her down and convince her to go to bed. Within minutes of her head hitting the pillow, she falls asleep. I wait a while, afraid she'll get up and disappear again, but eventually I leave her room on my tiptoes, texting Mrs. Wilson to thank her for watching Grams this weekend. Ms. Adams is about to arrive to start her shift. The last thing I want to do is leave Grams again today, but there is no way I can take more time off from the clinic.

***

I find Max in the small kitchen, talking on his phone. He's with his back to me, in front of the window.

"What do you mean they left? Go after them. Keep them there. Do you know how much work it was to bring them to the negotiations table?"

The person at the other end of the line is

yelling loud enough that even I can hear him. "*You shouldn't have left if you wanted to seal the deal.*"

"I can be there in half an hour, forty minutes tops. Go after them and bring them back in the meeting room," Max says, his voice growing hard.

I only hear snippets of what the other man is saying, but I catch the words *already left* and *the deal fell through. You just lost your company millions.*

"God damn it, Anthony, you think I didn't want to be there instead of dealing with all this shit? I'm done now. I'll be there as soon as possible. Go after them." He puts his phone away, turning around. His whole body stiffens as he sees me in the doorway. One million thoughts race through my mind, overwhelming me.

"Emilia... I didn't mean—"

"To say you didn't want to be here and dealing with this shit? My shit?"

"Yes. No, I mean—"

"I heard you," I assure him. Anger and pain swirl inside of me, the combination too much for me to bear at this moment. I'm emotionally and physically exhausted. "You should go, deal with your meeting."

"Forget the meeting. I'm not going anywhere leaving things like this." He runs an agitated hand through his hair, walking toward me. "I'm sorry. Look, I put my foot in my mouth, but you know I didn't mean it. I just wanted to shut up that moron and.... Jesus, Emilia. You know I want to be here for you, no matter what. Tell me you know that."

He reaches his hand out to me, but I pull away. "It will wear you down eventually," I say softly.

"What?"

"All my problems." I fiddle with the hem of my shirt, unable to look him in the eye. "Your life is beautiful and easy, and mine is not. You'll resent me one day. I don't want that."

Max sets his jaw, training his eyes on me. "Because of what happened today? You can't be serious. I'm sorry for what I said, but I want to be next to you."

"For now." My voice is weak, undependable, and I hate it. "But if it happens again and again, it will eventually wear you down, and you'll want someone with no cares."

He looks at me stunned. "I'm not your father, or that asshole ex-fiancé of yours. You're projecting your fears on me, and it's not fair."

"Maybe I am," I admit, "but the possibility of them becoming true is high, so it's just better if—"

"That's the stupidest thing I've ever heard."

"Don't raise your voice. You'll wake up Grams," I say angrily. "And don't call me stupid."

"I'm not," he says, now equally angry. "You can't expect me to stand here in front of you and take all of this with a shrug. We have a good thing—"

"Stop it, Max, please. Don't make this hard."

"I sure as hell don't plan to make this easy." He paces around the kitchen, fuming.

Biting the inside of my cheek, I ball my hands

into fists, digging my nails deep into my palm. "Please go, Max. You being here already cost you millions of dollars." Men have walked away from my life for much less.

Max stops pacing, snapping his head to me. "You heard that?"

"That Anthony guy wasn't exactly quiet."

"Fuck Anthony and the millions. I don't care about that. I care about you. There will be enough deals. There is just one of you."

"Stop, Max," I say stubbornly. "Please go."

"You know what? I will go. I'm sorry for putting my foot in my mouth, but you're not being rational. Call me when you calm down, and we'll talk again. And I swear to God, if you don't call, I'll drive here and knock down your front door."

Chapter Twenty-Six

Emilia

The second Max leaves the house, a deep sense of loss takes up residence in my stomach. I almost run after him, but stop myself. Cold shivers overtake my body and tears stream down my cheeks.

I need a warm shower, and then everything will be better. But the dreadful feeling of having made a huge mistake doesn't leave me even after I finish the shower. The hot water did nothing to calm down my shivers, which have now turned into tremors. Was Max right? Was I really projecting my fears? I must have. My father left me in Grams's care after Mom died. Paul ditched me when Grandma became sick. There was a time when I believed every man I cared about would eventually leave.

Except Max. My sweet, loving Max, who drops everything to be by my side when I need him, but hearing him say he didn't want to *deal with all this shit* hurt. I know his heart is in the right place, even if his mouth isn't, but I'm still pissed. Still… pushing him away the way I did….

When I spent that first night with him, I made him and myself the promise to put my fears aside, which I did. But seeing my father opened that age-old wound, made me bleed insecurities and fears, left me vulnerable. Turned me into an idiot.

I hurry out of the shower, searching for my phone. It has no battery, of course. My heart leaps to my throat in the time it takes the phone to jolt to life after I plug it in. With trembling fingers, I pull up Max's number and call him. No answer. Drawing in deep breaths, I tell myself that he must be in his meeting by now, trying to salvage it.

Emilia: I need to talk to you. Please call when you have time.

Max doesn't call though. I try not to panic on my way to the clinic. He's probably still in the meeting after all. But by the time two hours have passed, the skin on my entire body feels as if I have needles stuck in every hair follicle. I check my phone obsessively the entire day, even calling Max three more times in between patients, but he doesn't answer, or write back. I chew the inside of my cheek until I can taste blood in an effort to withhold tears. What if he's changed his mind? He must have, why the radio silence otherwise?

"What's wrong with you today, sweetness?" Mrs. Deveraux asks while we're doing water exercises. She's my last patient for the day, and I have zero energy left.

"I've had some rough few days," I admit.

"Tell me," she encourages.

I hesitate, fearing I might honestly burst out crying if I recount everything, but I can't keep it all in any longer. Gripping the edge of the pool tightly with one hand, through sobs and tears, I recount the trip to New Orleans, losing and finding Grams, and pushing Max away. Mrs. Deveraux listens intently, not interrupting me once.

"Honey, listen to me. There are good men in this world, and bad ones. Unfortunately the bad ones tend to be in the majority, and they have the unfortunate tendency to spread their seed as widely as possible. Your man is one of the few good ones."

"I know."

"And any good man knows that every woman who has faced hardships has baggage. It's our prerogative. I think you should go home now and rest. You've been through too much emotional turmoil to work or make any decisions."

Sniffling, I shake my head, removing my hand from the edge of the pool. Damn it, I've grasped it so tightly it left a mark in my palm. "This is my last session. I can't clock out before finishing it."

"I'm your patient, and I can always say I wasn't feeling well enough to go through with the session. No one will question me."

I laugh out loud for the first time today, because that is completely true. Mrs. Deveraux is a force to be reckoned with.

"I don't want to sleep," I admit. "I want to talk to Max."

"Then go get your man."

Watching the bottom of the pool, I ask, "What if he doesn't want that?"

"I don't think so. It is a possibility, true. Men are known to change their minds, especially when it comes to women. But I don't think your man is that type. Even if he wanted distance, he would have the decency to talk to you about it."

"Then why isn't he picking up?"

Mrs. Deveraux leans on her back, floating on the water. "A million reasons."

"I hope you're right," I say, itching now to get out of the water and check my phone again.

"Come on, girl, let's you and I get out of this pool."

My phone still has no incoming messages or missed calls, and I dial up Max twice to no avail. Mrs. Deveraux's words ring in my ears as I get dressed, and fear creeps up in my veins. What could have possibly happened? She's right. He's not the type to disappear off the face of the earth. At least not without a good reason. As I walk out the front door of the clinic, I'm giving serious thought to calling Alice and asking if anything happened, but then I notice Alice herself sitting on one of the benches in front of the clinic. That's when I know something must be wrong.

"Alice? Is anything wrong?" I ask with my heart in my throat, approaching her.

She rises to her feet as she sees me, pushing

her curtain of dark hair out of her face. "Now, now, don't panic."

"Max?"

"He was in an accident."

Blood rushes in my ears the moment she utters those words, panic sweeping across every cell of my being. I begin to shiver. "When? What happened? Is he all right?"

Alice nods once, and the shivers subside somewhat. "He was rushing to the office, and a car crashed into his."

"Oh my God."

"He injured his left knee—again, but he'll be fine. They did some tests, but except for a lot of bruises and his knee, there's no damage. He'll probably need some more physical therapy."

My eyes sting with unshed tears as I shake my head.

"Half the family is at the hospital," Alice informs me. "But I have a feeling Max wants you there too."

"Did he say anything?"

"He was mumbling something about not understanding women, but I didn't manage to get anything more from him. Have a hunch it's got to do with you."

I stare at my hands, unable to look her in the eyes. "Are you mad at me?"

"Do you love my brother?"

"Yes," I say without hesitation.

"Then I'm not mad at you." A grin lights up

her face. "Let's go."

***

Max

"Mother, I'm fine," I say for the hundredth time, not that it helps. I'm in the hospital bed, and she's been hovering around me for the past fifteen minutes.

"You'll be more comfortable if I move this pillow," she explains. I stop protesting and just let her do her thing, because it seems to bring her some peace of mind.

"Thank you. Is everyone else still outside?" I was given a room to rest in between scans and tests, and when they brought me in here, most of the family was camping inside already. Alice made them all go back out into the hallway and they took turns coming in to see me.

"No. Just Christopher. I sent everyone else home. And Alice went to Emilia's clinic to let her know what happened."

"Okay." I attempt to keep a neutral expression, because otherwise, I'll practically serve myself on a platter for Mom to question me, but she sees right through me.

"Did anything happen with Emilia?"

For a split second, I actually consider placating her with a nonanswer such as *Nothing*, but if there is one person I can't fool, that's my mother. So instead, I tell her in detail what happened since we went to New Orleans. Mom listens quietly, nodding and cursing Emilia's bastard of a father, her eyes tearing up when I mention our search for her grandmother.

"Poor Emilia. That's a lot to go through in twenty-four hours," she says. Then I fess up about putting my foot in my mouth. Mother's expression instantly changes, becoming more severe.

"You need to apologize for that. It was the last thing that poor girl needed."

"I know, Mom. And I did apologize. I just don't think she heard me. Still, she didn't have to push me away."

"My dear boy," she says gently, sitting at the edge of the bed. "Fear can make us irrational. It's an emotion, and it can cripple anyone. When your father had that accident last year, I was a mess."

I remember that night crystal clear. My mother, who always keeps her cool and encourages everyone else, was almost catatonic with fear as we were waiting for Dad to come out of surgery. It was the first time I saw Mom in that vulnerable state, and it scared the shit out of me. Even now, talking about it makes her teary-eyed. Right, time to cheer her up.

"You mean you weren't a mess when you heard about my accident? I'm offended."

"Keep upsetting me, and I'll give you something to be offended about, young man." Mom smacks my good leg with the back of her palm. "You know, I always hoped you and Emilia would end up together."

"What do you mean?" I ask quickly.

"You've been in love with her since you were nine years old. It was puppy love, but still love."

"Not true. We were best friends."

Mom rolls her eyes, shaking her head. "Then why did you scare off all the boys around her?"

"Because they weren't good enough. One had made a bet with his friends that he'd be Emilia's first kiss. I heard him. He was lucky all I did was scare him off."

She offers me that patented smile of hers that says, *You know nothing, son of mine.*

"Is that what the Johnson boy did too? You scared off that poor boy too, and Emilia was heartbroken because she couldn't participate in the dance competition."

"He did want to kiss her, and he was also a lousy dancer. Why would you offer to take a girl to a dance competition if you can't dance? He would've embarrassed her."

"Why didn't *you* offer to take her to the dance?"

"Because I was afraid she'd say no."

She claps her hands once, smiling triumphantly. *Well, hell. Looks like I know nothing, indeed.* This is a skill that only Mom possesses—making me feel smarter and dumber at the same time.

I open my mouth and close it again, but I'm saved from answering by Christopher, who just burst through the door, holding bags with take-out food.

"Found Chinese food two blocks away," he

informs me, pointing to the tray of hospital food the nurse left next to my bed a while ago. I took one spoonful of that stuff and almost gagged.

"Give it here. I'm starving."

"I'll leave you two boys, then," Mom says, rising from my bed. "Max, should I call the nurse? Do you need anything?"

"Nah, I'm all right."

She gives me a knowing look before leaving the room.

"Did you buy that for you or for me?" I ask Christopher, who's helping himself to my take-out box.

"Just doing some quality control," he says through a mouthful, handing me the box. "By the way, you have the look of someone who got Mom slammed."

"Shut up. I can kick you out of the room even with a fucked-up leg."

Chapter Twenty-Seven

Emilia

My stomach is in knots all the way to the hospital and on the elevator ride to Max's floor. When we reach the door to the room he's in, I'm surprised to only see Mrs. Bennett and Christopher standing in front of it.

"Mom kicked out everyone else earlier," Alice informs me. "It was getting too crowded."

Mrs. Bennett smiles warmly, and something in her expression tells me she's up-to-date with everything that happened between Max and me.

"How is Max?" I ask the two of them.

"He's had better days," Mrs. Bennett says, "but he's all right."

"I think you'll finally agree with me that I'm the better looking one," Christopher says with a wink. Alice elbows him in the ribs, giving him the stink eye.

"He's not sleeping, is he?" Suddenly I'm apprehensive to see him, the space between my shoulder blades tightening almost painfully.

"No," Mrs. Bennett answers.

Taking a deep breath, I clasp my fingers around the handle to his door, pushing it open. My heart stills when I see him lying in bed, the side of his face purple with bruises and one leg bandaged. Oh God, he must be in so much pain. Closing the door behind me, I stand at the foot of the bed, unsure what to say, where to begin.

"Christopher's right. He is the better looking one of the two of you today," I blurt out.

"Bad ice breaker, Jonesie." Max lifts up the corner of his lips on the unbruised side of his face. Right, if he can smirk, then he's definitely not in too much pain.

"What were you expecting?" I ask, pacing the room. I'm in a dilemma. Part of me is still pissed for what he said, and the other part wants to climb in the bed next to him and kiss the living daylights out of him.

"Something along the lines of making me apologize for talking shit, and then you apologizing for pushing me away, and promising you'll never do it again. I'll start. I'm sorry for what I said. I really didn't mean it."

My throat stings as I whisper, "Max, I'm sorry too, for pushing you away."

"Say that again, and add the *I'll never do it again* part." He cocks an eyebrow. "That's very important."

"You're bossy."

"I've earned that right." He points at his foot with one hand, and at the bruised side of his face with the other hand.

"You did," I admit, chewing on my lip. "I promise not to push you away again."

"You mean it, Emilia?" he asks, and now his expression is dead serious. I nod, yearning to touch him, to feel closer to him, to soak in his warmth and all the good things that come with Max. "Part of it was my fault. What I said—"

"I think part of me knew you didn't mean it. I was just trying to read into things. By the way, was the deal with Brazil rescued?"

"No, but it doesn't matter. We'll find new partners. Come here." He pats the side of the bed on his unhurt side. I almost fly to him, climbing on the bed with lightning speed.

"Wow. I've never had such an enthusiastic response when inviting a girl in bed."

"The bruised face and bandaged leg really do it for you," I assure him. "Alice said you might need a physical therapist again."

"Lucky I know a sexy one who wants to make things up to me, so she has to do everything I ask. You'd better get me in shape for Logan and Nadine's wedding." He's inches away from me. Unable to hold back any longer, I touch the side of his face with my fingers, nestling the side of my body closer to him.

"If you're gonna climb me, you'd better do it properly."

"Or what?" I challenge, but I slip under his cover. Since he must lie on his back, I climb with half my body over his uninjured half.

"I'm sure I can think of a way to make you

pay," he says devilishly.

"If I kiss you, will you hurt?" I ask, inspecting the bruise.

"Eating wasn't a walk in the park, so I think kissing my mouth is out of the question. But there are plenty of other body parts that need your attention—all uninjured." Putting his mouth to my ear, he whispers in a low, seductive voice, "Especially the Emilia sensor."

"You're so full of shit," I say with a grin, enjoying this immensely. "Not even an accident or lying in a hospital bed can get your mind out of the gutter."

"I want you to make me some promises, Emilia." He speaks the words against my temple, and my body instantly tightens. Sucking in a deep breath, I nod. "I love you more than I thought possible. Actually, today I had a revelation. I've been in love with you since we were kids."

I snuggle tighter against him, my heart soaring. "Yeah?"

"Yep. And no, you're not allowed to make fun of me for not realizing it earlier. It took you a while too."

"Mmmm...." I roam with my forefinger at the base of his neck, a suspicion gnawing at me. "So you realized it all on your own?"

"Mom might have said a few things that... helped."

I grin so wide my face almost hurts, and I bury my face in his neck. "I'm going to give you so much shit for it. Just wait until you can walk on both legs."

"That's gonna be something if I need both legs for it."

"What were those promises you wanted me to make?" I pepper his shoulder with kisses, waiting for his answer with my heart in my throat.

"First, that you'll do that," he points to my lips, "as often as possible. You're also welcome to put that mouth anywhere else you want."

"I think I can do that," I tease. "What else?"

"That you'll cater to my every need until I'm one hundred percent healthy again."

I twist one of his nipples lightly, making him yelp. "You're going to milk this accident thing for all its worth, aren't you?"

"You can bet on it. I also want us to move in together. We can find an apartment or a house big enough for the two of us, and Grams plus her caretaker."

"You thought everything through, didn't you?" I whisper.

"I might have already made a list with potential properties last week. What do you say?"

"Hell, yes. I love you."

"I love you too, Emilia," Max says simply. He breathes in deeply, and I have a hunch things are about to veer on the serious side. "I want you to promise me that you'll talk to me when something is wrong."

"I promise. I shouldn't have let what

happened in New Orleans affect me so much. It brought up all my insecurities and pushed me into a black hole, and I only realized it after you left my house. But I promise I won't freak out and pull away again."

"Also promise that you'll be patient with me even when I put my foot in my mouth."

"That's part of your charm, Max. You've been doing that since the first time I met you."

"What are you talking about? I was a perfect nine-year-old gentleman that day."

I press my lips together, smiling. "Correction. I can tell even when you're mentally putting your foot in your mouth. First time we met, you thought my boots were ugly as hell, didn't you?"

"Yeah. Damn, and I was so proud I didn't say that out loud."

"That was my lucky day. I was afraid of the thunder and you made me feel welcome and happy, which I hadn't been in a long time. You had me the moment you said, *I'll be your friend.*" I lift my head, kissing the corner of his mouth.

Max cups my cheeks with his hands, looking me straight in the eyes. "Good, because I've loved you since I was nine, and I want to love you until I'm ninety-nine, and I won't accept anything less than all of you."

"Max... you have all of me. You do. You always have, and always will."

"Always?"

"Always."

Epilogue

Emilia

Four months later

Nadine and Logan Bennett's wedding takes place on a bright September day at the old Bennett ranch, which is now turned into a B&B. We're all sitting outside on rows of chairs separated by a red carpet in the center, waiting for the bride and groom to arrive. The Bennett men all wear tuxes, and I've made up my mind. Bennett men in casual clothing are charming. In suits, they are delicious. But Bennett men in tuxes are irresistible. Max sits next to me, his hand resting on my upper thigh as he talks to Blake, who is sitting on his other side. The second the "Wedding March" starts, I squeeze Max's hand, turning in my seat.

Nadine is possibly the most beautiful bride I have ever seen. She wears a princess-style, white dress, and her hair is styled in waist-long curls the color of chocolate. Mr. Bennett is walking her down the aisle. Logan is waiting for his bride at the end of the aisle.

I hang on every word during the vows, and do a good job at withholding my tears, until Logan turns his head slightly to Nadine and I catch the shimmer in his eyes. That look right there should be in the dictionary next to the word *love*. It reminds me of my patient Mrs. Henderson, and the loving look on her husband's face every time he picks her up from the clinic. With a jolt, I realize the ache I felt whenever I saw the Hendersons is now gone. Max kisses my temple, catching one of my tears with his thumb.

"Don't cry," he whispers in my ear. "Don't forget, I'll always have your ass. I'm too fond of it to ever let it go."

I chuckle at the reminder of our word play on *I'll always have your back*, and place a chaste kiss on his cheek. After the ceremony is over, we all move inside the wedding tent, which is elegant and huge, given that it can comfortably house the two hundred guests and allow for a generous dance floor. Grams and her new caretaker are sitting at the table closest to the door. Max and I debated whether bringing her would be a good idea. I feared that seeing so many strangers might set her off, but Max convinced me to try, saying that she and the caretaker can always just head inside the house if the wedding becomes too much. So far, so good. I never told Grams about the meeting with my father. Instead, I told her we couldn't find him at all, which hurt her, but not nearly as much as the truth would have.

"I think Mom and Dad should seriously

consider moving into the wedding business," Alice comments, walking in step with Max and me.

"That wouldn't be a bad idea," Max replies. Abruptly he snaps his head to his sister, narrowing his eyes. "Is *he* here?"

"Who?" I ask, but judging by Alice's grin, she knows whom Max is talking about.

"Apparently Alice has been carrying a torch for a childhood friend," Max informs me. "She won't tell me who he is."

"Smart girl." I wink at her.

"But I'll tell you when he'll be back in the country. Pinky promise."

Max winces. "My masculinity just took a hit at that word."

"Your masculinity will recover." She kisses his cheek before turning on her heels and chatting up some of the other guests.

"Do you want to take a walk outside?" Max asks.

"I'd love to."

This is the first time I'm at the ranch, and I've been dying to look around. A lot is different since I last saw it fifteen years ago, and I didn't have time to catalogue every change when we arrived. Stepping out of the tent, I take in the facade. It has been completely redone, as was the roof. I had expected them to have added a wing since they turned it to a B&B, but the size and shape of the house is intact. I can still tell where everyone's bedroom was.

What I did notice right from the get-go is that the color of the gate is the exact same shade of vivid green it was when I first stepped through it when I was nine. We've almost reached the gate when we see Eric and Pippa in the far corner of the yard, each carrying a twin.

"Those girls are so beautiful," I comment with a sigh. They are dressed with identical miniature white dresses. The only difference between them is that they wear headbands of a different color.

Max's eyes light up at this. "Can't wait until we have a few of our own."

It takes a few seconds for the meaning of his words to become clear to me, and a few seconds more to form a witty response. "You're getting ahead of yourself. You didn't even put a ring on this." I tap my ring finger playfully.

His lips twitch. "Planning on doing it soon, but I already lived up to my non-romantic reputation by blurting I love you in the middle of the street. I'll do this by the book. It'll be a nice, grand gesture."

"Will it involve Christopher distracting me while you prepare it?" I bat my eyelashes playfully. "Might give him the chance to finally kiss your girl, get back at you."

Max growls. "I'll never live that down. But no, Christopher won't be involved in the proposal."

Butterflies spring in my stomach, my heart beating at lightning speed. "Only you can do a preproposal and not even realize it." Lacing my arms around his neck, I add, "Six months ago, you were claiming that kids and marriage weren't on your radar, and here you are. What happened to you?"

"You did." He cups the side of my cheeks, kissing the tip of my nose. "I'm so happy you walked through this gate twenty years ago."

"Good thing I lost my key." Even to this day I remember how scared I was, and how warmly the Bennetts welcomed me. One thing became clear to me after seeing my father again. Grams said blood is blood, but blood isn't necessarily family. Family is love and support, and Grams and I have found our family with this loud and meddling clan.

"You did it again," he murmurs, tilting my chin up.

"What?"

"Had an entire conversation in your head without including me. Care to share?"

"I was just thinking how lucky Grams and I are for having all of you. And how much I love you."

"Damn, and I thought you were making plans to get rid of my tux."

"My mind isn't as dirty as yours," I reply, even as my body heats up from his nearness, the way he rubs my lower lip with the pad of his thumb doing unspeakable things to my senses.

"I love you, Emilia, and I won't tire of telling you this every day. In fact, it'll be a privilege to tell you this every day, and to take care of you and future mini Emilias."

"Or mini Maxes."

This moment here in front of the gates is so

perfect, I want to store it in my memory forever. It's pure and beautiful, and ours.

Until someone interrupts.

"Lovebirds," Pippa calls to us. "I need your help."

"I bet Pippa can't tell her girls apart if they didn't have the headbands," he whispers to me as we head to Pippa.

"She's their mother. Of course she can tell the difference."

"We need you to hold the girls for a few minutes until we do some pictures," Pippa says.

"Sure."

As Pippa places one girl in Max's arms and Eric places the other in mine, I ask, "Which one is which?"

"Mia wears the pink headband, and Elena the red one."

Max gives me a triumphant look, but doesn't say anything. After Pippa and Eric are out of earshot, Max says, "Quick, let's exchange the girls and change their headbands."

"You've got to be joking."

He's not. In the span of two minutes, we do the exchange. I take Mia from his arms, giving him Elena, and then pry the pink headband from Mia's tiny head, replacing it with Elena's red one. Max expertly places the pink one on Elena's head, then kisses her forehead gently. Oh, God, I just found my kryptonite. Max in a tux carrying a baby. I'd do anything he asks right now, which apparently includes pranking his sister.

When Eric and Pippa return, she extends her hands to Max, taking Elena from his arms. "Sweet Mia. Did you miss me?"

"Bingo," Max exclaims, making Pippa, Eric and myself jump. "That's Elena. We exchanged their headbands. I was sure you couldn't tell them apart without the headbands."

Eric chuckles, taking Mia out of my arms, while Pippa breaks into giggles. "I can't believe you. Now you're using my daughters to prank me?"

"Of course, someone has to carry the pranking legacy," Max says seriously.

"I'm sorry I played a part in this," I tell her, "but I can't tell your brother no when he wears a tux and carries a baby."

Max winks at me. "Good to know."

"You've gotten even cockier than usual since you met Emilia again," Pippa remarks, resting Elena's head on her shoulder. Mia starts crying, so Eric quickly walks away to calm her down. Pippa confessed to me a while ago that the girls seem to cry in tandem, so it's best to separate them when one of them starts crying.

"Are you jealous that none of your matchmaking skills were needed in our case?" Max asks.

Pippa doesn't answer, merely smiles. The silence stretches to several seconds, and her smile turns from kind to wicked.

"Who gave you the number of the clinic?"

Pippa asks Max.

"My assistant... who said you gave it to her," Max says in a defeated voice.

"Wait, what?" I ask.

"After my dearest brother told me he needed a therapist I started researching the best clinics. Found your name eventually, and I thought... well, you never know what happens when old friends meet again."

With that enigmatic end of the sentence, Pippa enters the tent.

I elbow Max, who seems stuck in some kind of stupor. "Safe to say your sister hasn't lost her touch."

"You don't say."

"Let's go back to the wedding."

As we enter the tent, Max asks, "So which one of the singles in my family do you think will be next in line?"

I open my mouth to say I have no idea, but then I see Christopher, who is currently at the bar, looking at the bride and the groom. I wonder if he feels he's missing something when he sees all the couples around here.

"I'll give you a hint. He looks a lot like you."

THE END

Other Books by Layla Hagen

The Bennett Family Series

Book 1: Your Irresistible Love

Sebastian Bennett is a determined man. It's the secret behind the business empire he built from scratch. Under his rule, Bennett Enterprises dominates the jewelry industry. Despite being ruthless in his work, family comes first for him, and he'd do anything for his parents and eight siblings—even if they drive him crazy sometimes. . . like when they keep nagging him to get married already.

Sebastian doesn't believe in love, until he brings in external marketing consultant Ava to oversee the next collection launch. She's beautiful, funny, and just as stubborn as he is. Not only is he obsessed with her delicious curves, but he also finds himself willing to do anything to make her smile. He's determined to have Ava, even if she's completely off limits.

Ava Lindt has one job to do at Bennett Enterprises: make the next collection launch unforgettable. Daydreaming about the hot CEO is definitely not on her to-do list. Neither is doing said CEO. The consultancy she works for has a strict policy—no fraternizing with clients. She won't risk her job. Besides, Ava knows better than to trust men with her heart.

But their sizzling chemistry spirals into a deep connection that takes both of them by surprise. Sebastian blows through her defenses one sweet kiss and sinful touch at a time. When Ava's time as a consultant in his company comes to an end, will Sebastian fight for the woman he loves or will he end up losing her?

AVAILABLE ON ALL RETAILERS.

Book 2: Your Captivating Love

Logan Bennett knows his priorities. He is loyal to his family and his company. He has no time for love, and no desire for it. Not after a disastrous engagement left him brokenhearted. When Nadine enters his life, she turns everything upside down.

She's sexy, funny, and utterly captivating. She's also more stubborn than anyone he's met…including himself.

Nadine Hawthorne is finally pursuing her dream: opening her own clothing shop. After working so hard to get here, she needs to concentrate on her new business, and can't afford distractions. Not even if they come in the form of Logan Bennett.

He's handsome, charming, and doesn't take no for an answer. After bitter disappointments, Nadine doesn't believe in love. But being around Logan is addicting. It doesn't help that Logan's family is scheming to bring them together at every turn.

Their attraction is sizzling, their connection undeniable. Slowly, Logan wins her over. What starts out as a fling, soon spirals into much more than they are prepared for.

When a mistake threatens to tear them apart, will they have the strength to hold on to each other?

AVAILABLE ON ALL RETAILERS.

Book 3: Your Forever Love

Eric Callahan is a powerful man, and his sharp business sense has earned him the nickname 'the shark.' Yet under the strict façade is a man who loves his daughter and would do anything for her. When he and his daughter move to San Francisco for three months, he has one thing in mind: expanding his business on the West Coast. As a widower, Eric is not looking for love. He focuses on his company, and his daughter.

Until he meets Pippa Bennett. She captivates him from the moment he sets eyes on her, and what starts as unintentional flirting soon spirals into something neither of them can control.

Pippa Bennett knows she should stay away from Eric Callahan. After going through a rough divorce, she doesn't trust men anymore. But something about Eric just draws her in. He has a body made for sin and a sense of humor that matches hers. Not to mention that seeing how adorable he is with his daughter melts Pippa's walls one by one.

The chemistry between them is undeniable, but the connection that grows deeper every day that has both of them wondering if love might be within their reach.

When it's time for Eric and his daughter to head back home, will he give up on the woman who has captured his heart, or will he do everything in his power to remain by her side?

AVAILABLE ON ALL RETAILERS.

The Lost Series

***

Lost in Us: The story of James and Serena
There are three reasons tequila is my new favorite drink.
• One: my ex-boyfriend hates it.
• Two: downing a shot looks way sexier than sipping my usual Sprite.
• Three: it might give me the courage to do something my ex-boyfriend would hate even more than tequila—getting myself a rebound

The night I swap my usual Sprite with tequila, I meet James Cohen. The encounter is breathtaking. Electrifying.

And best not repeated.

James is a rich entrepreneur. He likes risks and adrenaline and is used to living the high life. He's everything I'm not.

But opposites attract. Some say opposites destroy each other. Some say opposites are perfect for each other. I don't know what will James and I do to each other, but I can't stay away from him. Even though I should.

AVAILABLE ON ALL RETAILERS.

***
Found in Us: The story of Jessica and Parker

Jessica Haydn wants to leave her past behind. Hurt by one too many heartbreaks, she vows not to fall in love again. Especially not with a man like Parker, whose electrifying pull and smile bruised her ego once before. But his sexy British accent makes her crave his touch, and his blue eyes strip Jessica of all her defenses.

Parker Blakesley has no place for love in his life. He learned the hard way not to trust. He built his business empire by avoiding distractions, and using sheer determination and control. But something about Jessica makes him question everything. Not only has she a body made for sin, but her laughter fills a void inside of him.

The desire igniting between them spirals into an unstoppable passion, and so much more. Soon, neither can fight their growing emotional connection. But can two scarred souls learn to trust again? And when a mistake threatens to tear them apart, will their love be strong enough?

AVAILABLE ON ALL RETAILERS.
***
Caught in Us: The story of Dani and Damon

Damon Cooper has all the markings of a bad boy:
- A tattoo
- A bike
- An attitude to go with point one and two

In the beginning I hated him, but now I'm falling in love

with him. My parents forbid us to be together, but Damon's not one to obey rules. And since I met him, neither am I.

AVAILABLE ON ALL RETAILERS.
***

Standalone USA TODAY BESTSELLER
Withering Hope

Aimee's wedding is supposed to turn out perfect. Her dress, her fiancé and the location—the idyllic holiday ranch in Brazil—are perfect.

But all Aimee's plans come crashing down when the private jet that's taking her from the U.S. to the ranch—where her fiancé awaits her—defects mid-flight and the pilot is forced to perform an emergency landing in the heart of the Amazon rainforest.

With no way to reach civilization, being rescued is Aimee and Tristan's—the pilot—only hope. A slim one that slowly withers away, desperation taking its place. Because death wanders in the jungle under many forms: starvation, diseases. Beasts.

As Aimee and Tristan fight to find ways to survive, they grow closer. Together they discover that facing old, inner agonies carved by painful pasts takes just as much courage, if not even more, than facing the rainforest.

Despite her devotion to her fiancé, Aimee can't hide her feelings for Tristan—the man for whom she's slowly becoming everything. You can hide many things in the rainforest. But not lies. Or love.

Withering Hope is the story of a man who desperately needs forgiveness and the woman who brings him hope. It is a story in which hope births wings and blooms into a

love that is as beautiful and intense as it is forbidden.
AVAILABLE ON ALL RETAILERS.

***

Your Inescapable Love
Copyright © 2016 Layla Hagen
Published by Layla Hagen

All rights reserved. No part of this book may be reproduced or transmitted in any form, including electronic or mechanical, without written permission from the publisher, except in the case of brief quotations embodied in critical articles or reviews.

This is a work of fiction. Names, characters, businesses, places, events, and incidents are either the products of the author's imagination or used in a fictitious manner. Any resemblance to actual persons, living or dead, or actual events is purely coincidental.

This book is licensed for your personal enjoyment only. This book may not be re-sold or given away to other people. If you would like to share this book with another person, please purchase an additional copy for each person you share it with. If you are reading this book and did not purchase it, or it was not purchased for your use only, then you should return it to the seller and purchase your own copy. Thank you for respecting the author's work.

Published: Layla Hagen 2016
Cover: http://designs.romanticbookaffairs.com/

***
Acknowledgements

There are so many people who helped me fulfil the dream of publishing, that I am utterly terrified I will forget to thank someone. If I do, please forgive me. Here it goes.

First, I'd like to thank my beta readers, Jessica, Dee, Andrea, Carrie, Jill, Kolleen and Rebecca. You made this story so much better!!

I want to thank every blogger and reader who took a chance with me as a new author and helped me spread the word. You have my most heartfelt gratitude. To my street team. . .you rock !!!

Last but not least, I would like to thank my family. I would never be here if not for their love and support. Mom, you taught me that books are important, and for that I will always be grateful. Dad, thank you for always being convinced that I should reach for the stars.

To my sister, whose numerous ahem. . .legendary replies will serve as an inspiration for many books to come, I say thank you for your support and I love you, kid.

To my husband, who always, no matter what, believed in me and supported me through all this whether by happily taking on every chore I overlooked or accepting being ignored for hours at a time, and most importantly encouraged me whenever I needed it: I love you and I could not have done this without you.

<<<<>>>>

YOUR INESCAPABLE LOVE

YOUR INESCAPABLE LOVE

Printed in Great Britain
by Amazon